NO LOOSE ENDS

A PETER BLACK THRILLER

DAVID ARCHER

VINCE VOGEL

RIGHTHOUSE

PRAISE FOR THE PETER BLACK SERIES

PETER BLACK THRILLERS
Burden of the Assassin (Book 1)
The Man Without A Face (Book 2)
Unpunished Deeds (Book 3)
Hunter Killer (Book 4)
Silent Shadows (Book 5)
The Last Run (Book 6)
Dark Corners (Book 7)
Ghost Operative (Book 8)
A Fire Burning (Book 9)
Dawnlight (Book 10)
Dead Ice (Book 11)
No Loose Ends (Book 12)

UNLOCK AN EXCLUSIVE ORIGIN STORY

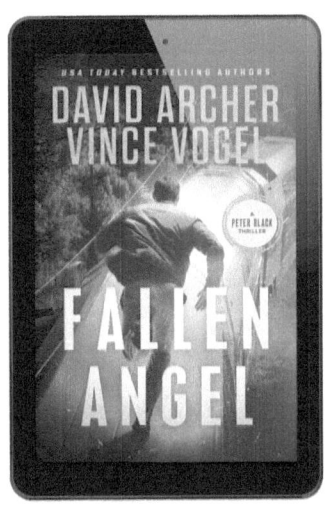

Get the **exclusive Peter Black origin story, *FALLEN ANGEL***—a full-length prequel **not sold and not available anywhere else**. Plus *MUCH* more.

Scan the QR code, or visit:

vip.righthouse.com/peter-black

(Easy to unsubscribe. No spam. Ever.)

ONE

DUST billows around the armored SUV as Olivia Wren speeds toward the meeting point on the outskirts of Tijuana. Heat shimmers in waves off the cracked, arid ground, vultures gliding lazily in wide, ominous circles overhead.

In the back, two DEA SWAT operators sit rigidly upright, faces taut, eyes scanning their surroundings. Each grips an M4A1 carbine, body armor cinched tight across their chests. The mission is an inter-agency affair, DEA muscle paired with CIA oversight —a delicate, uneasy partnership that rarely works cleanly across borders.

Olivia adjusts the strap of the pistol holstered against her thigh, but her other hand fidgets at her lap, nervously working over a small set of rosary beads, the polished wood clacking softly between her fingers. She forces herself to stop fiddling, tightening her grip on the wheel, eyes fixed on the road ahead.

To the east, the edge of the city emerges through the dusty haze—a cluster of low buildings and shacks, poverty etched into every sagging roof and sun-bleached wall. Beyond them lies the open patch of barren land designated as the rendezvous point. The Mexican military is already there, arranged in a stark, disciplined formation. At least a dozen soldiers stand motionless, fully outfitted in body armor and combat helmets, weapons held at the ready. Behind them sit two rugged Hummers and an armored personnel carrier, machine guns mounted and trained forward, ready to unleash at a moment's notice.

The SUV slows to a halt, gravel crunching beneath its tires. For a moment, there's absolute stillness. Olivia exhales steadily.

"You ready for this?" she asks the men in the back.

They both nod in unison.

"Then let's go."

Opening her door, Olivia steps out confidently onto the parched earth. Immediately, her two escorts exit the vehicle, flanking her protectively, their weapons pointed downward but fingers tense near the triggers.

Olivia meets the gaze of the lead Mexican officer, a man with hard eyes, a bald head, and an expression devoid of warmth. His uniform is immaculate, the insignia of the Sonora Federales catching the sun. Guilherme Hermoné—head of the task force in the state—regards her with the faint disdain of a man who's spent too long knee deep in the trenches of a drug war.

She advances deliberately, boots kicking up dust, her pulse quickening slightly despite her practiced composure.

"Good morning," she says firmly.

Hermoné glances skeptically at the two DEA escorts, noting the thin protection. "Is this all you've brought? Two men?"

Olivia glances briefly behind her, then locks eyes with him again. "Less is more," she replies curtly.

Hermoné shrugs, expression dismissive. "Bueno, estúpidos gringos. Váyanse a morir. A ver si me importa," he mutters.

OK, stupid Americans. Go get yourselves killed. See if I care.

Olivia raises an eyebrow calmly. "Puedo hablar español, ¿sabes?"

I can speak Spanish, you know?

He smirks slightly, unembarrassed. "Well, I told your superiors to ensure you came with at least a six-man team. Instead, you brought two."

"The border's only four miles away. What's the bother?" Olivia responds confidently.

Hermoné gestures toward the low buildings to the east. "You see the city?"

She turns, eyes narrowing. "Yes."

"The Sinaloa cartel own that entire territory. Inside those buildings are Sinaloa soldiers, armed and trained as well as we are. I come with my entire squad because this land belongs to the enemy."

Using a hand to shield her eyes from the sun, Olivia assesses the buildings carefully, aware they'll have to pass them to reach safety. She reassures herself silently; the route is well-planned, avoiding built-up areas. It should take only six minutes to reach the safer zone of the US border beyond cartel reach.

"Where's the perp?" she asks sharply, straightening her posture.

Hermoné whistles shrilly. One of his men disappears momentarily into the armored carrier, re-emerging seconds later, escorting a handcuffed Eduardo 'El Toro' Sanchez.

Olivia observes him carefully.

Eduardo lives up to his nickname—a powerful, broad-shouldered man, muscular and thick-necked, with eyes that burn with defiance. But Olivia and her DEA partners are not interested in his intimidating frame. What matters is that Eduardo is the reckless, hot-headed younger brother of Miguel 'El Lobo' Sanchez, leader of Mexico's largest cartel, the Sinaloas.

As the agents move to take him, Eduardo sneers, voice rough in Spanish. "¿Esto es todo lo que tienen?"

Is this all they have?

Hermoné answers flatly, "Es todo."

It is.

Eduardo grunts a short, humorless laugh, shaking his head as they drag him toward the waiting SUV.

As the DEA men secure him into the back of it, Olivia turns back to Hermoné.

"Gracias," she says briskly.

He nods curtly, expression unreadable. Olivia swiftly climbs back into the SUV, the DEA special agents following suit, taking seats on either side of Eduardo.

As they pull away, Olivia silently reassures herself again. Six minutes until the border.

The outskirts close in fast, dust giving way to low, sun-baked buildings and tight streets—the city district Guilherme Hermoné pointed to moments ago.

She grabs the radio. "Bryant, Kline, this is Wren. ETA no longer than six minutes."

Static crackles. "Copy that," Agent Bryant's voice replies.

Six minutes. She repeats it in her head like a mantra. Six minutes to the border. Six minutes to safety. Her fingers fumble at the rosary beads looped around her wrist, the cool shapes clicking softly together before she clenches them tightly in her fist.

The first narrow streets force them to slow. Traffic thickens, crawling between dented cars, buses wheezing smoke into the air. Olivia's eyes scan the rooftops. Figures linger—too still, too focused.

Five minutes.

Her gut tightens as she scans the thick crowds lining the streets. Were those rifles? Or just pipes? She can't be sure. Her escorts shift in their seats, scanning with sharp, trained eyes.

Four minutes.

A faint buzz pricks her ears. She spots it—a quadcopter drone hovering above the street, camera angled down. It's not the only one. Another glints in the distance, drifting lazily but deliberately.

Then the crowds along the sidewalks begin to melt away. Groups slip into doorways, vanishing behind rusted shutters. In seconds, the bustling street becomes eerily empty.

Three minutes.

They round a corner—and slam the brakes. A truck burns in the middle of the road, flames licking the sky, black smoke twisting upward.

Olivia throws the SUV into reverse. Gravel sprays as they back up fast—until another truck rolls in from behind, blocking their retreat.

Two minutes.

The edges of the rooftops come alive with movement. Dozens of men step into view, rifles catching the sun. The kill box is sealed. Olivia's hand instinctively closes around the rosary beads again, knuckles whitening, as the first barrels dip toward them.

Her eyes flick to Eduardo. There's a faint curl at the corner of his mouth—a smile he can't quite hide.

From somewhere above, a voice bellows in Spanish: "¡Suelten a Eduardo!"

Release Eduardo!

"Okay," Olivia says, her voice calm and clipped. "Looks like we're going to have to do this the hard way."

She draws her pistol, her gaze roving over the street, looking for angles, cover. A dingy bar catches her eye—a plywood door with a rusted padlock hanging from the outside. Possible entry, if they can get there alive.

"You two flank me," she tells the special agents. "I'll take the perp."

"How did they know our route?" one of the DEA men mutters.

"Or what vehicle we'd be in?" adds the other agent.

"Doesn't matter," Olivia snaps. "We'll figure it out later. For now, we need to get out of here."

She climbs into the back, shoves open the SUV door, and yanks Eduardo with her. A moment later, they're out on the street —Eduardo in front as a human shield, Olivia at his back, the two special agents moving in close on either side, rifles up and steady.

The rooftops are now crowded with figures in military-grade body armor, weapons gleaming under the sun. They move like trained soldiers—disciplined, precise. Not street thugs. Not amateurs.

For a moment, the world hangs suspended in heat and dust.

Somewhere far off, the faint, jaunty strains of a mariachi band drift lazily through the air, absurd in the stifling silence of the standoff.

One minute thirty seconds.

Shouts keep coming from above. "¡Suelten a Eduardo!" Voices echo off the walls, growing sharper, more insistent.

Olivia's eyes never stop moving—tracking the rooftops, the narrow street, the thin plywood door of the bar. She flicks her gaze sideways to one of the special agents. A single nod.

The man reacts instantly, yanking a smoke grenade from his vest and popping the pin. It lands with a clink, billowing thick white cover into the street.

"Move!" Olivia barks.

They sprint through the haze. The DEA special agents hammer bursts from their M4A1s, forcing rooftop shooters to duck back behind cover. Eduardo stumbles forward, coughing, dragged by Olivia's grip on his arm.

One minute fifteen seconds.

The bar door looms. Olivia raises her pistol, sights lining up on the padlock. One clean shot—*crack!*—and the lock explodes. She drives her boot into the plywood, the door giving way with a splintering snap.

Inside, it's dim and stale. Dust motes drift through weak sunlight slanting in from grimy windows. Tables are overturned, glasses scattered on the floor like forgotten debris from another life.

They dive in just as rounds tear through the flimsy doorway, splintering wood and spraying dust into the air.

One minute.

The street erupts—gunfire hammering the bar's front in a deafening, splintering storm. Plaster dust clouds the dim interior as rounds rip through tables and smash bottles. The DEA men return fire, but the rooftop angles keep the kill zone pinned.

A mechanical whine cuts through the chaos. Olivia's head snaps toward the open side window just in time to see a drone sweep past, its underside bristling with a crude bundle of explosives. She shoves Eduardo down hard.

The blast outside shakes the walls and sends glass raining down. Shouts rise from both ends of the bar. Heavy boots pound against the floorboards—front entry forced. One special agent yanks a flashbang from his vest and lobs it toward the advancing shadows. The room is drowned in light and sound; in that moment, Olivia surges forward.

They smash out the rear door into a narrow alley. Gunfire pours down from upper windows, bullets spitting sparks from the walls. Olivia drags Eduardo behind the skeletal remains of a dumpster while the special agents lay down short, sharp bursts.

Forty-five seconds.

They bolt across the alley into the yawning entrance of a crumbling apartment block. The stairwell door slams behind them. One special agent shoves a warped dresser across it. Outside, the cartel slams into the barricade, shouting threats and curses.

Through peeling hallways, tenants peer out—wide-eyed, murmuring in Spanish. The pounding at the stairwell grows louder. Then—boom—the whole door shudders, an explosion flaring in the hall. Screams ripple through the building.

"Move!" Olivia barks, forcing Eduardo onward. Doors slam shut up and down the corridor.

Thirty seconds.

They push deeper into the building, turning a corner into a section stripped to bare concrete and timber. Scaffolding leans against unfinished walls, loose wiring hangs from the ceiling, and the air smells faintly of plaster dust. Buckets of paint and stacks of tile line the hallway—a worksite caught mid-job.

Shouts echo closer now, boots pounding. The cartel is gaining, their rifles clattering in bursts that snap against the walls. One special agent swings his carbine toward the sound, sending a line of suppressive fire down the corridor. Gunmen duck into alcoves and doorways, shouting orders back and forth.

Moving backward, Olivia keeps Eduardo in front of her, using his bulk as a shield as they reach—

A dead end.

Twenty seconds.

A sledgehammer leans against the wall, left by the workers. Without hesitation, one of the special agents grabs it and swings hard, smashing through the thin plaster. Dust explodes into the air, revealing the dim interior of the next apartment, the scent of fresh paint and new wood sharp in their nostrils.

The other special agent holds the line, rifle barking in short, controlled bursts. The hammer smashes again—then again—until a jagged hole opens wide enough to climb through. They spill into the room, boots crunching over debris.

From there, it's a desperate warren-run: wall by wall, room by room, the sledgehammer battering new openings while muzzle flashes light the gloom behind them. Occupied apartments blur past—frightened tenants crouching in corners, eyes wide with terror—as the covering escort fires through each breach, keeping the pursuers just far enough back for Olivia to haul Eduardo through.

Still, the voices are getting closer. More boots. More gunmetal clatter. The building shakes under the violence coming for them.

Ten seconds.

They burst into the building's far corner, lungs burning, boots pounding. Olivia throws her shoulder against the wall and risks a glance through a window.

Below, the street is a kill zone—half a dozen men in full body armor stand in formation, their movements sharp and disciplined. Sunlight flashes off the tubes of the RPGs slung across their shoulders, one already being leveled upward. She catches the faint hiss of shouted orders, the metallic clink of a round being loaded.

Zero. Time's up.

Her gut twists. "Get down!" she shouts.

A flash. The roar of the rocket fills the air. Then impact—everything convulses in a rush of fire, smoke, and flying debris.

Olivia barely has time to pull Eduardo down. The blast tears through the apartment in a bone-shaking roar—walls erupting inward, a fireball swallowing the far corner.

One special agent vanishes in the explosion, a blur of flame and debris.

The other, coughing and blinded by dust, turns to cover Olivia but is cut down instantly, automatic fire shredding him as the cartel surges through the breach.

Her ears ring. The world is muffled chaos—shouts warped and distant, like she's underwater. Dust turns everything into a choking fog. Olivia blinks, finds her pistol, and moves.

A shadow looms in the haze. She raises the weapon—two shots. A man drops. Another silhouette staggers into the room— three more rounds, center mass.

Eduardo is on the floor, blood streaking his temple, dazed but alive. She yanks him up, shoving him forward, forcing her own balance as the floor groans under them.

They stagger into the next apartment, ducking low. Behind them, the shattered corner gives way with a deafening crack. Concrete and rebar peel away and plunge into the street below.

It scatters the soldiers.

Olivia doesn't stop to look. She slams her boot into the emergency exit door on the far wall. It bursts open with a shriek of metal. She drags Eduardo through, into the open air, away from the collapsing ruin and the gunmen inside.

As well as separating them from the cartel soldiers, the falling building has bought Olivia time.

Time she doesn't intend to waste.

They move fast, weaving through backstreets and service alleys, keeping away from main roads. Olivia's mind races, eyes sweeping every shadow.

Halfway through a narrow lane, Eduardo makes his move, throwing his considerable bulk sideways and slamming his shoulder into her. Even with his hands bound, he's strong enough to knock her off-balance. He tries to pivot, to run.

Olivia recovers instantly. She's smaller, faster, and far more dangerous than Eduardo thinks. One step, a twist of her body, and she sweeps his legs away and slams him into the ground, her pistol pressed hard into the back of his head.

"You done?" she hisses.

Eduardo breathes hard, eyes narrowed but silent. She hauls him up, shoving him forward again.

The sun dips low, painting the horizon in gold and blood-red. In the distance, she sees it—the border. A long, crawling line of traffic waiting for clearance.

"What you gonna do now, little girl?" Eduardo asks, his tone mocking.

Olivia doesn't answer right away. The rendezvous is out—someone tipped the cartel. It could have been through the Mexican side... or her own. She's not about to hand Eduardo over until she knows who she can trust.

She guides him toward the line of vehicles, eyes scanning for opportunity. Then she sees it: a white camper van, parked and empty. The cab and the living space are separate, a sliding door between them—that's good for what Olivia needs it for. The owners are nowhere in sight—probably in the diner across the lot, a neon *OPEN* flickering in its window.

Moving quickly, Olivia picks the lock and yanks the side door open. The interior smells faintly of coffee and cheap air freshener. She pushes Eduardo inside, hustling him toward the tiny bathroom compartment at the rear.

He resists just enough to earn himself a quick, hard blow from the butt of her pistol. His knees buckle, and he collapses inside. Olivia drags him into the cramped space, shuts the door, and wedges it closed.

It's best he remains unconscious, anyway. She can't risk him trying to signal the customs agents when they reach the border.

She steps back, heart pounding, listening to the hum of traffic in the distance. No official channels. No help. Just her and a high-value cartel prisoner, hidden in a stranger's camper.

Footsteps crunch on the gravel outside. Through the small, tinted window, she sees a couple walking toward the van from the diner, laughing, oblivious. They climb into the cab, start the engine, and roll forward—joining the slow-moving line toward the border.

In the dark, rocking interior, Olivia keeps her pistol in her lap and her eyes on the thin curtain to the cab, counting the seconds until they hit the border—and whatever waits beyond it.

TWO

PETER BLACK MOVES EASILY around the kitchen of his Virginia home, sleeves rolled up, the warm scent of simmering Wagyu beef filling the air. On the counter beside him, a tablet stands propped up, its screen showing Michael's grinning face and Mayu leaning into frame.

"Careful, Dad," Michael says, his voice crackling through the speaker. "If you keep that on the heat, it's going to get tough."

Mayu, her tone gentle but firm, adds, "And remember, gyudon is about balance—don't stir too much, or the meat will break apart."

Peter smirks, adjusting the pan. "I've survived war zones, Mayu. I think I can handle a bowl of beef and onions."

"You've never had my gyudon before," she replies, mock-serious. "Now add the mirin. Slowly."

Between seasoning tips, Michael starts talking about their work volunteering at the southern border. His voice shifts, losing some of its earlier levity. "It's rough down here. There's so much desperation. People will risk anything. And the cartels—" He trails off, pressing his lips together. "Put it this way, it's dangerous, even for us."

The conversation drifts back to the kitchen. Mayu coaches

Peter through the next step—layering thinly sliced onions over the beef—when Michael leans closer to the camera. "So... the proposal? You still going through with it?"

Peter hesitates, glancing at the small velvet box sitting at the edge of the counter. "Yeah. I think so. I'm just nervous. Lena's been in Uganda for three months. Three whole months without seeing each other. Feels like forever."

Mayu smiles faintly. "Then maybe it's time."

Peter chuckles, though there's a flicker of nervousness in his eyes as he places a lid over the gyudon, ready to be reheated later.

He exhales. "Yeah... maybe."

Two hours later, Peter stands in the departure lounge of Dulles International Airport, a bunch of flowers in one hand as he scans the crowd. His other hand rests in his pocket, fingers brushing the small box hidden there.

He exhales slowly, eyes fixed on the stream of arriving passengers, waiting.

Lena appears at last, stepping through the glass doors with the slow weariness of someone who's been in the air too long. The flowers in Peter's hand feel heavier as he takes her in—hair slightly mussed from travel, eyes shadowed, her smile faint.

They close the distance, and for a heartbeat he's back there—on Svalbard, the frozen wind in his face, the white endlessness all around them. Lena in her insulated parka, hunched over a microscope in the research station as she worked toward a cure for the virus he'd wrestled from the hands of a megalomaniac. They had fallen in love in the middle of chaos, their bond forged under tension, then tempered during six months in isolation on that icy island.

But here and now, the reunion feels awkward. Her hug is brief, her eyes not quite meeting his.

He puts it down to the long flight. Jet lag.

The drive back to his place is silent, streetlights strobing across the windshield. She hasn't even commented on the flowers resting in her lap.

Dinner is quiet, the table lit by the soft glow of candles, the smell of gyudon lingering faintly in the air. Outside, the wind sighs against the windows, a low hum beneath the clink of cutlery.

Peter feels the weight of the velvet box in his pocket, fingers brushing it as he searches for the moment. He leans forward, ready to speak, but Lena beats him to it.

"Peter, listen—there's something I need to say first," she says gently, eyes filled with a regret he hasn't seen before.

He stills, closing his hand discreetly around the ring. "All right," he says quietly.

She takes a breath, her gaze dropping to the plate before lifting to his. "Our relationship... it thrived because of what we went through. The danger, the intensity—it kept us close. But now... months apart, living in different worlds... it's not the same."

Peter sits back, the words landing heavily. "We knew it wouldn't be easy," he says. "We've done long distances before."

"This isn't the same," Lena replies softly. "In Uganda, I felt like I was part of something important. You're doing your work... and I'm doing mine. And somewhere in between, we stopped being us."

He swallows the tightness in his throat and nods once. "I understand."

They eat a little more, the conversation turning to neutral ground—safe topics like the weather in Uganda, the trip back, the research she's leaving behind. But the warmth is gone, replaced by something resigned.

After the plates are cleared, Lena reaches for her phone. "I should get going. I've called an Uber."

Minutes later, Peter stands on the doorstep with her, the chill of the night air between them. She steps into his arms for a brief hug and whispers, "Sorry" before pulling away.

Tonight wasn't meant to be like this.

He watches as she walks down the path, climbs into the

waiting car, and closes the door. The Uber pulls away, taillights fading into the dark.

Peter sighs and walks back inside.

That's when the phone in his pocket vibrates. He pulls it out, encrypted number flashing on the screen.

"Hello?" he says, answering as Lena's Uber disappears around the corner.

"Peter..." Olivia's voice is ragged, like she's been running.

"Olivia, long time—"

"No time for pleasantries," she cuts in sharply. "I've been compromised. I'm not sure, but I think there's a mole inside the agency. You're the only one I trust. Meet me."

Peter's tone hardens. "Understood."

There's a pause, then she adds, "Remember that little Italian place we went to after Manila?"

Peter thinks a beat. "The one by the harbor?"

"Yes. It was the twelfth of April. Same side of the street as the bakery." Her voice is calm but deliberate, and he knows she's not talking about a restaurant.

"I'll bring the good bottle," he says, slipping into the code they've used before. "The red label. Should be there around... breakfast time."

"That works," she replies. "The door will be unlocked."

They both know the "Italian place" is a safehouse in San Diego. 124 Harbor Street—near the waterfront but away from tourist eyes. The "red label" means he's coming alone and armed.

"Hold tight," Peter assures her once they're finished. "I'll be there by morning."

The line goes dead. Peter stays there a moment, staring at the encrypted number fading from his phone screen.

If he wanted something to take his mind off tonight, this is it.

THREE

THE CAMPER VAN had crossed the border without incident. Ten minutes later, the couple pulled into a roadside motel lot. As soon as she was sure they were gone, Olivia slipped out the side door, keeping low between the parked vehicles, dragging Eduardo with her.

She'd spotted a sedan two rows over—keys dangling from the ignition, courtesy of a careless owner fetching ice from the motel lobby.

An hour later, Olivia eases the stolen sedan into the narrow garage of the safehouse, engine ticking as she kills it. She stays in the driver's seat for a moment, eyes flicking to the side mirrors, scanning the quiet street as the garage door rattles shut behind her with a hollow clang, sealing her in. Her hand drifts automatically to the rosary beads looped at her wrist, the smooth shapes clicking together in the silence before she forces herself to let go.

She pops the trunk. Eduardo "El Toro" Sanchez lies inside, wrists bound behind his back, eyes glittering with contempt.

"Out," she orders.

He climbs stiffly onto the concrete, and she marches him through a side door into a basement stripped bare of comfort—no windows, just exposed cinderblock walls and a single radiator bolted to the floor. She shoves him down and clips his cuff chain to the metal.

Removing his gag, she steps back.

He speaks immediately.

"They already know where you are," he says, the smirk curling his lip.

"Your mole in the CIA?" she fires back.

El Toro's smile widens, slow and deliberate. "No. Not them."

"Then what? Someone in the DEA?"

He shakes his head slowly. "Not them," he repeats mockingly. "The spirits. El Brujo's demons. They are the ones that see you."

"Spirits?" Olivia scoffs, though her voice has an edge.

"Spirits protecting us, seeing you by your fear. El Brujo and his demons will come for you. They'll tear your soul from your body."

Her jaw tightens. "And who is El Brujo?"

Eduardo leans forward, the bare bulb overhead catching in his eyes until they seem to burn. "A sorcerer," he says. "One who speaks with the dead. And the dead see you. They see right where you are, and they're telling El Brujo right now. Telling him so my brother can send his people."

"Shut up," she snaps, a tremor in her voice she can't quite hide.

Eduardo laughs softly. "Your fear gives them strength. It's what they feed on. It's what they see."

Olivia's fingers twitch toward the beads again, almost against her will, brushing them like a lifeline.

FOUR

THE DEPARTURE LOUNGE at Dulles hums with the usual low chaos—boarding calls, rolling luggage, the hiss of espresso machines. Peter Black moves steadily through the crowd, his carry-on slung over one shoulder, phone pressed to his ear.

He doesn't even register that he was here only two hours ago for very different reasons.

"Officially, Olivia's missing," Mark Deacon says without preamble, his voice carrying a low urgency beneath the static of the call. "Let me help."

Peter glances toward the gate, eyes sweeping over the passengers milling around. "Not yet, Mark," he says evenly. "Trust is thin right now."

Deacon exhales hard. "Peter, I've worked with her for years. If something's happened—"

Peter cuts him off, lowering his voice. "I said not yet. I need to know who's clean before I bring anyone in. That includes you."

He moves toward the boarding line, eyes scanning the terminal glass, the gate signage, the mirrored surface of a vending machine—checking angles without looking like he's checking.

"Fine," Deacon says finally, his tone tight. "Just... keep me in the loop."

"We'll talk when I'm on the ground," Peter says, ending the call before Deacon can argue.

He steps into the boarding line, fingers tightening around the strap of his bag. His nerves are drawn taut, his mind shifting into mission readiness. Whatever waits in San Diego, he's already fully primed for it.

However, thirty feet away, a man sits at a café table with a coffee he hasn't touched, phone in hand, eyes locked on Peter. He speaks quietly into the microphone.

"He's boarding for San Diego. Flight number UAL755."

The reply comes crisp and cold through his earpiece: "Good. We'll have someone waiting."

The call ends, and the man lowers his gaze, pretending to read the news on his phone, but his eyes keep flicking up to track Peter as the boarding line moves forward.

Peter hands over his ticket and steps onto the jet bridge. The phone call is still echoing in his head, but it's the feeling between his shoulder blades—the prickling certainty of eyes on him—that sticks.

FIVE

THE DESERT NIGHT presses close over the San Diego border facility. Banks of harsh fluorescent lights cast stark white over the steel enclosures, throwing long shadows across the cracked concrete floor. Beyond the tented roof, the horizon is a black expanse pricked with the glow of distant sodium streetlamps.

Inside, rows of cages hold clusters of weary faces, the metallic tang of chain-link mixing with the sour scent of sweat and unwashed clothes. The hum of the lights merges with the low murmur of Spanish, broken by the occasional wail of a child or the rattling clink of someone shaking the bars.

Michael moves between the cages with a crate of bottled water, boots scuffing softly. Mayu kneels beside a young woman with blistered feet, carefully wrapping them in clean gauze. The cool air carries the faint scent of bleach from a nearby cleaning station, unable to mask the deeper smells of exhaustion and road-dust.

A woman steps forward to the mesh, her hair plastered to her temples, eyes red-rimmed. "Por favor... mi hija," she whispers. "Cinco años." *My daughter. Five years old.* "Se la llevaron cuando me arrestaron." *They took her when I was arrested.*

Mayu meets her gaze and nods, voice soft but steady. "I'll find out," she promises, pressing her hand to the woman's through the cold steel.

Farther down, a man sits alone in another enclosure, his right hand bound in a filthy strip of shirt, dark blood seeping through. His eyes, black and unblinking, follow Michael and Mayu like a predator tracking prey.

Mayu turns to an ICE agent. "Can you open it? That wound will infect if someone doesn't clean it."

The agent shakes his head. "He's flagged—suspected coyote. Possible cartel."

The man tilts his head slightly, lips curling in a humorless smile, his gaze like a caged wolf assessing its keepers.

They move on.

Somewhere near the intake area, two agents speak in hushed tones about Tijuana—about something violent that erupted earlier tonight. "Sounded like a war zone," one mutters. But here, the war is quieter, fought against fatigue, injury, and the grinding uncertainty of what tomorrow holds.

A burst of static cuts the air. An agent's radio crackles—words fuzzy under the hiss.

"Copy—got a group of stragglers about four miles out in the flats. They won't last long if someone don't get out to them."

Michael and Mayu exchange a quick glance, and within moments they're in the back of an ICE transport truck, the diesel engine rumbling as it lurches into the desert darkness.

The landscape ahead is swallowed by shadows, the moon a thin blade of silver above. Headlights sweep across pale dust and twisted shrubs until, at last, shapes emerge—bent silhouettes moving slowly against the empty night.

The truck slows to a crawl, tires crunching over loose gravel. Out of the wavering silhouettes ahead, a woman suddenly breaks from the group, stumbling toward the headlights. Her face is streaked with dirt and dried tears, hair matted to her cheeks, her breath spilling white in the chill night air as she repeats: "Ella está enferma." In her arms, a small child hangs limp, head lolling against her shoulder.

"¡Al suelo! Get on the ground! Now!" an ICE agent bellows, stepping forward with his hand already resting on the grip of his holstered sidearm.

"Wait—she's saying—wait!" Michael blurts, moving in quickly. "She's saying the little girl's sick!"

Mayu is already there, easing the child from the woman's desperate grip. She lays her on the truck's cold steel tailgate, the metal biting against her knees as she leans over. Her hands work fast, lifting the grimy shirt to reveal a small, distended belly. Her fingers press gently against the skin, her expression shifting from concern to alarm.

"Michael," she whispers, her tone clipped and urgent, "she's a mule. I think the package burst."

The words hit him like ice water. "We have to get her to the hospital now," he says, already reaching to lift the girl.

"She stays," the ICE agent cuts in, voice flat, motioning sharply to the woman. "Orders."

"Please," the woman begs, tears spilling anew. Her voice cracks on every word. "Por favor, ayuden a mi hija." *Please help my daughter.*

Michael meets her gaze—a pleading, desperate stare—and nods once, solid. "We'll help your daughter," he promises, his voice taut with urgency.

He and Mayu lift the child carefully into the cab, Mayu cradling her against her chest as if shielding her from the night itself. Behind them, the agents order the woman to her knees in the dust.

As the truck lurches forward, Michael turns in his seat for one last look. In the sweep of the retreating headlights, he sees her—a small, still figure in the darkness, hands behind her head, eyes locked on the vehicle carrying her daughter away.

Then she vanishes into blackness.

SIX

OLIVIA MOVES through the narrow rooms of the safehouse like a shadow, pistol in hand, the weight of it grounding her as her mind ticks through possible threats. Her free hand brushes the rosary beads at her wrist now and again, the cool edges reassuring her, though she hates that she needs the comfort.

She's already checked the deadbolts twice, but she goes again —touching each lock, each window latch, giving the frames a subtle shake. The street outside the front window is still and suburban: parked cars, a faint wind in the hedges. Ordinary.

Too ordinary.

The monitors for the security cameras hum in the living room, their grainy feeds showing four angles of the property: the front porch, the driveway, the garage, the narrow strip of yard behind the house. Nothing moves—until it does.

The security light bursts on. A shadow. There for a heartbeat in the top right camera. Gone before she can register it.

She leans closer, scanning. The feed flickers faintly, static edging the corners of the screen. She tells herself it's a loose wire.

From the basement, Eduardo's voice drifts upward—low, murmuring, rhythmic. The sound of it sends a chill crawling up her spine. Her fingers tighten on the rosary again, beads biting into her palm, before she forces her hand back to the pistol grip.

She descends halfway down the steps and finds him where she left him: cuffed to the radiator, eyes half-closed, lips moving in a quiet chant.

"Nzambi, beba la sangre que doy...
Ndoki, devorar la carne que ofrezco...
Espíritus de Kiamina, huelan el miedo de esta mujer...
Koma, Koma, rompe las paredes de esta casa...
Abre el camino para El Brujo...
Trae la sombra, trae el filo, trae la muerte...
Mi corazón por su corazón, mi sangre por su vida...
Mbanza! Mbanza! Mbanza!"

Nzambi, drink the blood I give...
Sorcerer, devour the flesh I offer...
Spirits of Kiamina, smell the fear of this woman...
Strike, strike, break the walls of this house...
Open the way for El Brujo...
Bring the shadow, bring the blade, bring death...
My heart for his heart, my blood for her life...
Mbanza! Mbanza! Mbanza!

Olivia steps in front of him.

"Prayers?" she asks, voice flat.

He opens one eye, slowly and deliberately, the smirk forming lazily. "Not prayers. Invitations."

"To who?"

He tilts his head as though listening to something only he can hear. "Friends."

"Friends?"

"Yes."

"Your friends aren't coming," she snaps back, irritated by his smugness. "But my friend *is* coming."

The smirk grows across his face. "He'll be too late."

"Why?"

"Because mine are already here."

She goes to retort something, but a faint scratch interrupts her —a sound from somewhere along the siding outside, like fingernails dragged lightly over wood.

Olivia freezes. Her hand slips to the beads again, clutching them hard, as though their familiarity can drown out the sound.

She hurries upstairs and makes another round of the windows. The sound follows her—on the east wall, then the north, then gone.

Back in the living room, she notices something on the porch feed: movement at the very edge of the light. The suggestion of a figure, just beyond the camera's reach.

Eduardo's voice rises from below, his words faster now, more insistent. "They see you, Olivia... they see your fear."

"Shut up," she snaps, more sharply than she means to.

Then—black. Every bulb, every screen, the hum of the fridge —all snuffed out in an instant. The safehouse plunges into a suffocating dark.

They've cut the power.

Her heart slams against her ribs as her eyes adjust. Outside, in the thick quiet, something whispers—faint but distinct, curling through the night air and into the bones of the house:

"Te vemos, Olivia..."

We see you, Olivia.

SEVEN

MICHAEL BURSTS through the sliding glass doors of the ER, the cold fluorescent light hitting him like a slap. Mayu is right behind him, the small girl limp in her arms, her skin clammy and ashen.

"Need a trauma bay—now!" Mayu shouts. Heads turn—nurses, an orderly pushing a wheelchair, a security guard.

A triage nurse leaps from her desk, already snapping on gloves. "What's wrong with her?"

"Possible internal drug rupture," Mayu fires back, shifting the child onto a gurney that materializes from somewhere behind them. "Cocaine or heroin—we don't know which. She's tachy, breathing shallow. No radial pulse."

"Bay Three!" the nurse barks to a pair of med techs who take off at a run, pushing the gurney ahead. Michael and Mayu jog alongside as it hurtles down a hallway lined with curtained bays, the air thick with disinfectant and adrenaline.

Inside the trauma room, the atmosphere becomes controlled chaos. A doctor—mid-forties, wiry, his ID reading *Dr. Gordon*—snaps on a mask. "IV wide open, two large-bore. Get tox screens running."

A respiratory tech fits an oxygen mask over the child's tiny face while another nurse pulls up her shirt to place EKG leads. The monitor chirps to life, showing erratic numbers that make Mayu's stomach knot.

"She's crashing," one of the nurses warns.

"Prep for emergency laparotomy," Dr. Gordon orders without looking up. "If it's ruptured, we don't have time to play detective."

Two orderlies move in, unlocking the bed's wheels and steering it toward the double doors to the OR. Mayu steps forward instinctively, but Michael catches her arm. "They've got her now," he says quietly.

Mayu stays rooted beside him as the gurney disappears through the swinging doors. They slam shut, leaving them in the sudden stillness of the corridor, the smell of antiseptic and the faint echo of hurried footsteps lingering in the air.

An hour later, the ER waiting room is a pocket of fluorescent-lit purgatory—too bright, too cold. Michael paces a narrow path between rows of plastic chairs, his hands buried in his pockets. Mayu sits hunched forward, elbows on her knees, eyes fixed on the floor.

After a moment, she rises and crosses to him without a word, pressing her forehead against his chest. He wraps his arms around her, feeling the tension still thrumming through her muscles.

The swinging doors finally open, and a medic steps out, pulling off a disposable cap. The man's eyes are tired, his voice low but clear.

"She's alive," he says. "Luckily it was only a small leak. We removed the packages in time. She'll need monitoring, but she's stable."

Michael exhales, his relief leaving him momentarily weak. "Has this happened before?" he asks, his voice rasping from the strain.

The medic's jaw tightens. "It's becoming routine. The cartels don't care who they use or hurt. Kids, parents, anyone vulnerable.

She's not the first... and sadly won't be the last. They treat life like it's disposable."

Michael glances down at Mayu. She's already looking back at him, the weight of the medic's words settling between them like a shadow. Neither of them says it aloud, but both know: They've just brushed against something much larger, and darker, than they imagined.

EIGHT

THE SAFEHOUSE BREATHES in the dark. Olivia moves quietly from window to window, triple-checking the locks, every step echoing on bare floorboards. Her fingers continue to stray down to the rosary beads looped at her wrist, the smooth shapes rolling anxiously between her thumb and forefinger before she forces her hand away again.

In the basement, Eduardo "El Toro" Sanchez hums a slow, guttural chant. "Kimbanda, Kadiempembe, nkita..." The syllables grind against her nerves, each one dragged from somewhere deep and old.

"Shut up," she mutters from the top of the basement stairs.

He smiles through the dim. "They're inside the house already. You just can't see them yet."

A faint sound drifts through the house—a floorboard whispering under weight. Not hers. She holds still, counting her own breaths. Somewhere, glass ticks faintly, like a window being tapped by a long fingernail.

She moves along the hallway, SIG drawn, her other hand trailing the wall. Her beads click once more in her grip before she shoves them back into her sleeve, cursing herself for even reaching for them. Shadows seem to pulse in the corners. Twice she turns, sure she's seen movement, but finds only the shifting dark.

From outside comes a scrape—metal on metal. Then another, from the opposite side of the house. Whoever's out there, there's more than one.

Olivia steadies her weapon at the kitchen doorway. A shape slides briefly across the window—tall, slow, deliberate.

She edges forward, boots silent on the worn linoleum, senses narrowing. Somewhere behind her, floorboards sigh.

She spins, firing into the dark hallway. Three sharp cracks that shatter the silence. The muzzle flash burns a brief image of empty air.

Then arms like steel bands wrap around her from behind. She twists, slamming an elbow back, but the grip is unyielding, iron-tight. A breath grazes her ear.

"Te vemos, Olivia," a voice whispers, low and cold.

We see you, Olivia.

The gun is wrenched from her hand. The dark closes in.

NINE

THE FIRST OPERATIVE stands alone near the terminal's glass doors, a paper cup of coffee cooling in his hand. The sliding doors sigh open, spilling a rush of travelers into the humid evening air. Among them, Peter Black emerges—tall, broad-shouldered, a small travel bag slung at his side.

The operative's fingers tighten around the cup as he murmurs into the mic clipped to his collar. "Target in sight. Exiting now."

A quiet voice crackles back in his ear. "I've got you. Look left."

A dark sedan glides into view at the curb, slowing just enough for the rear door to swing open. The operative steps inside without breaking stride.

The driver—the second operative—keeps his gaze forward.

They watch as Peter raises a hand, hailing a San Diego yellow cab. It slides to the curb, brakes sighing. Without hesitation, he gets in, door shutting with a muted thump.

"He's moving," the first man says.

The sedan eases into the flow of cars leaving the terminal. They hang back two car lengths, letting other vehicles drift between them and the cab.

"He's heading west," the spotter reports, eyes locked on the taxi's taillights. "Looks like downtown."

"Then we hold distance," the driver says evenly. "He's trained. If he makes us, it's over."

Barely fifteen minutes later, the taxi eases to a stop in front of an aging apartment block on the frayed edge of downtown—stucco walls stained with rust, balconies sagging under chipped railings. A single flickering light buzzes over the entrance, throwing long shadows onto the cracked sidewalk.

From their car half a block away, the two men sit in still, watchful silence. Through the dust-streaked windshield, they track Peter Black's reflection in the stairwell windows as he climbs. First floor—light snaps on. Second. Third. Each landing flares briefly with sterile brightness before going dark again, his shadow moving steadily upward.

Seventh floor. The glow lingers, then shifts as Peter steps into a corner apartment. Warm rectangles of light spill from the windows as he flicks the lights on, only to vanish as he reaches up and pulls the blinds shut.

"You see Wren?" the first man asks, eyes narrowing.

The driver shakes his head. "No."

"Me neither."

They exchange a glance, an unspoken decision made. Both men slip from the car, shutting the doors softly. The air is damp and cool, the street quiet except for the faint hiss of a passing bus. They keep to the edge of the sidewalk, moving like ghosts toward the building.

A quick scan of the entrance shows no security cameras they can see, no curious neighbors. The second man produces a small lock pick set from his jacket, kneeling briefly at the stairwell door. The faint click of tumblers is the only sound before the latch yields and the door eases open.

Inside, the stairwell smells faintly of mildew and overused detergent. The walls are stained with old leaks, the overhead bulb casting a sickly yellow glow. They ascend slowly, boots whispering on worn concrete, the echo of each step swallowed by the oppressive stillness.

At the seventh floor landing, they pause just short of the apartment door. The first man tilts his head close to it, listening.

"You hear them?" the second man whispers.

The first man presses his ear against the door, his breath slow and measured. After a moment, he straightens and shakes his head. No sound.

Without another word, he slides the picks into the lock. With a muted snick, the door gives.

Weapons raised, they push inside, sweeping the small space in tight, practiced arcs.

The apartment is bare—sparse furniture under a fine layer of dust. No pictures, ornaments, or personal effects. Just emptiness.

A couch draped in a dusty sheet. A single coffee table. A sagging mattress in the corner. No voices, no movement. Only the creak of the floor beneath their boots and the faint hum of the city outside.

They sweep through the small space, clearing corners in smooth, practiced arcs. Even the air smells stale, like it hasn't been disturbed for weeks.

Then the first man freezes, nostrils flaring. "You feel that?"

A faint draft brushes past them, whispering against the hairs on their necks. They trace it to the far side of the apartment, where a narrow door stands ajar in a corner bedroom. The second man nudges it wider with the muzzle of his pistol.

The cool night air spills in through an emergency exit. The rusted metal steps of a fire escape lead down to an alleyway.

"Son of a—" the first man mutters, breaking off as both rush to the blinded windows. They yank them open in unison, shoving aside the blinds.

Far below, bathed in the amber glow of the streetlights, Peter Black crouches at the rear wheel of their sedan, blade in hand. A quick, deliberate slash, and the tire deflates with a hiss. All four are now rapidly collapsing beneath the car.

He straightens, glancing up at them. Not hurried, not rattled —just a cool, deliberate glance that lands on them like a slap. His expression is unreadable, save for the faintest edge of disdain. He slips the knife away, turns, and walks toward a nondescript sedan parked a few spaces down.

From his pocket, he produces a set of keys. Unlocks the door. Slides into the driver's seat. The engine turns over, smooth and confident. Just like him.

"Son of a bitch," the second man mutters, bitterness dripping from every word. "He knew we were tailing him from the goddamn start."

They can only watch helplessly as Peter pulls away, taillights dwindling into the night, leaving them stranded, outplayed, and humiliated.

TEN

TWENTY MINUTES LATER, Peter arrives at the safehouse. He kills the engine and sits for a moment, the hum of the cooling motor fading into the stillness of the street.

Something is wrong.

He can already feel it—the kind of wrong that settles deep in the gut, silent but certain.

Not once since he arrived in San Diego has Olivia picked up her phone.

The safehouse sits quiet in the glow of a single streetlamp, the air thick with the hush of late night. But the front door... it hangs a few inches open, pale light spilling from the narrow gap.

The power is back on.

His hand tightens around the grip of his pistol as he opens his door onto the street. The metallic click of it shutting behind him is unnaturally loud. Each step toward the house feels heavier, his senses tuned to the smallest detail: the faint crunch of gravel underfoot, the muted hum of electricity in the streetlights, the way the light flutters faintly across the threshold.

He slips inside. The air smells of dust and copper—blood— and under it, a sharp tang of spent cartridges. The living room is a mess: an overturned chair, papers scattered like windblown leaves, a table leg splintered clean through.

On the wall, a single dark hole blooms in the plaster at chest height. A shot fired but not the kill shot. He imagines her here, Olivia, steady hands aiming as the fear creeps over her.

There's blood—near the entryway, smeared along the edge of the couch. Not hers, he hopes. But the rest tells the story. She fought hard. Fought until they overpowered her.

Peter moves room to room, each step slow, deliberate. A shattered lamp lies across the hallway. The bathroom door is cracked, the mirror inside spiderwebbed from impact. He keeps moving, reading the violence in every detail.

A faint scuff across the linoleum draws his eyes to the basement door, ajar in the dim light. The hinges groan softly as he pushes it wider.

He starts down the steps, each creak of wood sinking him deeper into the quiet, into whatever waits below.

The basement air is colder—damp stone and the sour bite of mildew—but there's something else layered beneath it. Something heavier. Metallic. Burned.

Halfway down, Peter catches the flicker of light from a bare bulb swinging slowly overhead, casting long, restless shadows over the floor. His boots stick faintly on the boards as he takes the final steps.

Then he sees her.

Olivia lies at the center of the concrete floor, her body arranged with deliberate, obscene precision. Her arms are spread wide, palms up, as if offering herself to something unseen. Her face is pale, framed by dark hair matted to her skin. But it's her eyes—gone—that freeze Peter in place.

Where her eyes should be are twin, clean cavities, ringed in the faint, bruised red of torn tissue. The lids have been neatly trimmed away, leaving raw, dark hollows that seem to stare back at him with an emptiness far worse than sight.

His gaze moves higher, and his stomach knots. The top of her skull is missing entirely, the bone cut with surgical perfection, as if lifted away like the lid of a box. Inside, there is only darkness and the faint glisten of drying blood. The brain is gone, taken as neatly as the eyes.

Lower still, her chest bears the same methodical violence. Her sternum has been split, ribs forced apart to expose a gaping void where her heart once beat. The edges of the wound are too clean, too exact, like the work of someone who knew precisely where to cut.

Someone who has done this many times before.

Around her, the blood has been used to scrawl looping, jagged symbols across the walls—sacred marks of Palo Mayombe, each one meant to bind and command spirits. Circles within circles, locked with sharp, knotted lines that twist into shapes resembling both eyes and mouths, as if the walls themselves are watching. Crude depictions of nkisi cauldrons, horned silhouettes, and the forked cross of Zarabanda drip darkly in the flicker of the bare bulb.

The symbols seem to press inward on the scene, their placement deliberate—designed to trap the soul of the sacrifice within the space, feeding it to the spirits called by the ritual.

Peter's stomach turns as he takes them in, the blood appearing to throb and shift in the trembling light, as though the drawings are alive... breathing... waiting.

There's no sign of Eduardo. Only her.

For a long moment, Peter just stands there, the pistol slack in his hand. A part of him refuses to move closer, afraid the finality will settle in.

"Oh, Olivia..." His voice cracks, a whisper barely audible in the oppressive stillness. "What did they do to you?"

Grief claws at him—raw and immediate—but under it, a slow, steady heat begins to build. Not shock. Not even rage yet. Something deeper. The iron certainty that someone will pay for this.

He forces himself to step forward, kneeling beside her. His

shadow swallows her face as he closes his eyes briefly, forcing down the tremor in his breath. He takes in every detail, imprinting it—every mark, every drop of blood, every obscene curve of the symbols—so he will never forget.

When he stands, his face is set. Whatever killed her, whatever took her eyes, her heart, her mind—he will find it. And he will burn it to the ground.

ELEVEN

THE SAFEHOUSE IS a swarm of controlled chaos. Police tape flutters in the night breeze, pulsing red and blue from the cruiser lights parked at the curb. CSU techs in Tyvek suits move in and out of the doorway like pale, silent ghosts, carrying evidence trays and cameras. The coppery tang of blood lingers faintly in Peter's nostrils, setting a fire beneath his bubbling rage.

He stands just beyond the yellow tape, the coastal chill seeping into his bones. One detective, tall and broad in a creased blazer, flips open a battered notepad. His partner, younger, sharper, keeps his gaze fixed on Peter like he's reading a suspect.

"You said you knew the victim?" the older one asks.

Peter keeps his voice even. "We worked together. Professionally."

"Professionally meaning what, exactly?" the younger presses.

"We work for the government."

"What type of work?" the younger one asks.

Peter turns to him. "Sensitive work."

The older detective's brow creases. "You walked in before calling us?"

"I saw the door ajar. The lights were on. I went in to check. Found her in the basement... already gone."

"You touch anything?"

"No," Peter says, shaking his head. "I didn't even check for a pulse. It was clear nothing could be done."

They scribble notes in silence, the muted clicks of their pens blending with the hum of CSU equipment inside. A tech emerges, cradling a plastic evidence tray. The older detective's eyes flick toward it, then back to Peter.

"Anyone you can name who might've wanted her dead?"

"In our line of work, there's plenty." He glances toward the open doorway, catching a glimpse of red scrawled across the wall before a tech moves to block it. "But no... No specific names come to mind."

A sharp honk breaks the rhythm of the scene. A dark, late-model sedan rolls up to the curb, parking under a streetlight. Two men step out—plain suits, calm movements, the kind of confidence that doesn't need to be loud.

Peter recognizes them instantly. The same two who followed him from the airport. The car is new.

They flash badges to the nearest uniform, who nods and gestures them forward.

The younger detective mutters, "Looks like friends of yours."

Peter doesn't reply. His eyes track the men as they cross the tape without hesitation, their steps deliberate. One addresses the detectives in a low, even voice.

"DEA. We'll need a moment with Mr. Black."

The detectives exchange a glance before stepping aside.

"Peter Black?" the taller one asks, voice steady. "A word in private."

Peter's jaw tightens, but he nods, falling in step as they lead him toward their car. Behind him, the safehouse—and what it now represents—recedes into the night.

Peter slides into the back seat of the dark sedan, the door shutting with a heavy thunk that muffles the noise from the crime scene. The smell of stale coffee and cigarettes fills the close air. Both men turn slightly in their seats, their eyes level on him—

calm, professional, the kind of gaze that measures every flicker of expression. It's something they teach them at Quantico.

"I'm Special Agent Moorling," the first man says, voice low and steady. "This is Special Agent Patrick."

Peter gives a short nod. "You already know who I am."

Moorling's mouth twitches in the faintest hint of a smile. "We do."

"After all," Peter adds, "you've been shadowing me since Dulles."

Patrick gives a small shrug. "We prefer 'observing.' And we'll admit, you're one hard man to observe. That empty apartment routine? Cute. And the tires"—he lets out a dry chuckle—"messy. Made the boys back at the field office laugh their asses off."

Peter doesn't flinch. "So why have you been following me?"

The two agents exchange a glance before Moorling answers, voice steady. "Olivia Wren. We were supposed to meet her here in San Diego. To question someone she was holding. A man named Eduardo Sanchez."

Patrick's eyes stay on Peter. "You know the name?"

Peter gently shakes his head. "No."

"She never mentioned him?"

"No. Just that she was in trouble."

"She tell you what type of trouble?"

"No. She gave me her location, and I got on the next plane. I was hoping she'd explain once I got here."

"Well, your friend was picking up Eduardo in Mexico when she was ambushed in Tijuana, close to the border crossing at San Ysidro. She was with two of our special agents. Both are believed to have died in the firefight. Olivia managed to make it out with Eduardo. After that, she went dark. Hours later, she pings us— short, no details. Says she's across the border, been compromised, doesn't know who to trust, and is heading to a safehouse. Wouldn't say where. But she mentions calling a friend for help."

"And you figure friend means me," Peter says flatly.

"Correct," Moorling replies. "We figure 'friend' means

someone from the agency. Someone she'd trust under fire." Moorling's eyes narrow slightly, watching Peter for any tell. "So we pull travel records. Look at every active CIA operative who happens to be booking last-minute transport to San Diego."

Patrick gives a small, humorless smile. "And guess who pops up the second he buys a ticket online? You were flagged before you'd even parked your car in the airport lot."

Peter lets out a slow breath. "And that's how you found me."

"Correct," Patrick confirms. "Our agent at Dulles watched you board, confirmed the ID. We've been on you ever since."

Peter's gaze slides sideways.

Outside the tinted glass, the crime scene lights paint the street in harsh red-blue pulses, each flash washing over the street like a slow heartbeat. Inside the car, the air is heavy—three professionals, each knowing the other is holding back more than they're saying.

Peter turns his eyes back to the DEA agents, his voice level but edged.

"What did you want with Olivia?"

Moorling's gaze doesn't waver. "The man she picked up in Tijuana. Eduardo Sanchez, this man"—he holds out his phone, the screen glowing with a still image of Eduardo "El Toro" Sanchez—"is a man we want for questioning."

Peter studies it briefly. "And what exactly do the CIA and DEA want to question him about?"

"A lot," Moorling replies, his tone clipped. "What your friend Olivia and the Agency wanted him for? We can't say for certain. Probably tied to the fact that his brother runs Mexico's largest cartel—the type of guy US intelligence might want to speak with regarding the safety of their southern border."

Peter shifts his attention to Patrick. "Then what did *you* want him for?"

Patrick's voice takes on a harder edge. "We're investigating the disappearance of a US senator's son last year." He taps his phone again, bringing up grainy CCTV footage.

"This was taken just over the border," Moorling adds.

The video is washed in the neon glow of Tijuana's party district, bars and clubs spilling light onto a crowded street. Groups of laughing tourists weave past the camera's frame, clutching plastic cups, draped in beads and party hats.

Peter watches as the camera tracks a young man—early twenties, neatly dressed—walking alone along the edge of the chaos. Moorling narrates quietly: "You're looking at Felix Carmichael. He was partying with friends. They'd been bar-hopping most of the night when he got separated from the group."

A black Cadillac glides up to the curb beside Felix, the vehicle's glossy paint catching the shifting colors of nearby neon. A slender female hand emerges from the rear window, her fingers brushing lightly along the young man's chin. He grins, leaning in to exchange a few words. Then, without hesitation, he opens the door and climbs into the back seat.

The Cadillac pulls smoothly away, swallowed by the movement of the street, leaving only a momentary gap in the crowd where he had stood seconds before.

"He was never seen again," Patrick says grimly. "And he's just the highest-profile case. In the past few years, American disappearances south of the border—especially young partygoers—have spiked nearly a thousand percent. No ransoms. No contact. People simply vanish."

"Isn't this usually something the FBI handles? What's the DEA's angle?"

Patrick answers. "Once the Bureau tied it to cartel activity, they brought us in. We've been running point ever since."

"So you think this Eduardo Sanchez and his brother are part of it?" Peter asks quietly.

Moorling leans in, lowering his voice. "We think his brother's cartel is behind it..." He pauses, his expression darkening.

"But you said there's no contact—no ransom demands."

"We did."

"Then why do you think it's them?"

"The FBI traced the Cadillac. It came back to a man named Javier Acosta."

"And who's that?"

Agent Moorling slides the phone across his lap toward Peter. The screen crackles to life with a grainy, side-profile photograph: the man's features blurred, face softened by poor lighting. Yet his eyes—unnaturally dark, deep pits—burn through the image.

"This is Javier Acosta," Moorling says quietly. "Born in Havana in 1975. His mother was a Cuban high priestess in Palo Mayombe—one of the most feared in her circle. You know Palo Mayombe?"

Peter nods. "Yeah. Voodoo."

"That's right," Moorling goes on. "From the time he could walk, Acosta was surrounded by ritual altars, animal blood, and whispered incantations. He learned to slit a goat's throat before he could read. He grew up with narcotics on the kitchen table and skulls in the closet."

Peter leans forward, his eyes narrowing.

Patrick picks up the thread, his voice quiet and steady. "When he was twelve, his mother was gunned down in what was officially called a 'drug dispute.' After that, Acosta drifted—first into petty hustles on the streets of Miami, then across the Gulf into Mexico City. That's where he began selling himself as a tarot reader, a healer, a spiritual cleanser. He claimed to see futures, remove curses, speak with the dead. But his real gift wasn't magic—it was charm. Traffickers, bent cops, and bored socialites all started lining up for his services."

Moorling's tone hardens. "By the time he was twenty-five, he was being paid in bricks of cocaine and envelopes of cash by men who ran cartels. He'd convinced them that his rituals—Palo Mayombe—could protect their shipments from law enforcement and curse their enemies. That's when he met a wealthy heiress from Monterrey named Maria Andrade. Now she's called La Bruja. Witch. She became his high priestess, his partner, and some say the real architect behind what came next. It's also probably her hand that sticks out of that Cadillac and strokes the chin of our senator's son."

Patrick nods grimly. "Together they formed Los Narcosatánicos. Their sacrifices started small—chickens, goats, snakes. Then came zebras smuggled from private zoos. Lion cubs. And eventually..."

Peter's voice cuts in, quiet and dark. "People."

"Exactly," Moorling says. "We believe whoever killed Olivia Wren was one of Acosta's followers—hence the ritualistic manner. And if that's true, this isn't just a cartel problem—it's a cult problem. And those are harder to kill."

Peter presses the edge of the screen. "And how do Eduardo Sanchez and his brother fit into this?"

Moorling flicks through a series of photos—grainy surveillance stills, telephoto shots of a sprawling hacienda ringed with guards. "Miguel 'El Lobo' Sanchez—Eduardo's older brother—was one of Acosta's earliest adherents, drawn in by the promise of occult power. Four years ago, he was a nobody—just a low-level enforcer for the Sinaloa cartel, running collections and doing wet work when told."

Patrick leans in, voice taking on a darker weight. "Now? He's running the whole operation. Not just Sinaloa—he's swallowed two rival cartels in the past three years. Took their leaders out, seized their territories, folded their surviving soldiers into his own ranks. His territory stretches from Sonora to the Gulf. He's feared from Juárez to Veracruz like he was the devil himself."

Moorling's tone hardens. "Every rival who's tried to challenge him has ended up dead, disappeared, or—according to whispers —offered in sacrifice. Sanchez's power isn't just fear of the gun anymore. It's fear of what walks in the dark with him."

Patrick nods grimly. "And as long as Acosta and La Bruja are under Sanchez's protection, his power base stays supernatural in the eyes of his men. They fight harder, kill without hesitation, because they believe they've got the devil on their side."

Peter studies the image for a long beat before saying quietly,

"Sounds like they believe it because no one's proved them wrong."

He hands the phone back. The cold glow from the screen fades as Moorling pockets it.

Peter reaches for the door handle.

"What are you going to do?" Patrick asks, his tone deceptively casual.

Peter pauses just long enough to look back at him. "Go home," he says, voice flat.

Then he's out of the car, the door shutting behind him with a dull, final thud. He walks away without looking back, disappearing into the pulsing red-blue haze down the street.

But Peter Black isn't going home.

Not tonight.

Not for a long time.

Not until he's crossed the border into Mexico—right into the heart of the darkness that killed Olivia Wren.

TWELVE

THE HILLS of Sonora sleep under a bruised velvet sky, their slopes thick with the scent of wet earth and orange blossoms. Moonlight threads the clouds in silver ribbons, catching on the tiled roof of Miguel "El Lobo" Sanchez's sprawling estate—a colonial masterpiece turned fortress. White stucco walls glow faintly in the dark, their edges swallowed by manicured gardens that roll out like a green sea toward the black silhouette of distant mountains.

Beyond the hedges, pastures stretch toward the horizon where massive, snorting bulls pace under the eye of night watchmen. The low rumble of their hooves drifts toward the villa, mixing with the occasional creak of wrought-iron gates swinging open for a patrol. Every few minutes, a flashlight beam slices the dark, sweeping along stone walls crowned with razor wire, pausing on the slow glide of a shadow.

The private bullring sits silent now, its sand pale under the cold light. But even in stillness, it radiates a strange energy—like a Roman arena waiting for blood.

At the main gate, armed guards stand in formation, rifles slung across their chests, eyes sharp beneath brims of black caps.

From the south road, a convoy approaches—three black

SUVs, their headlights dimmed, engines a deep growl that carries across the fields. Dust lifts in their wake, hanging in the cool air.

The lead vehicle halts at the gate. A guard peers inside, then steps quickly back. The gate yawns open without further word, and the convoy rolls inside like ink spilling across parchment.

When the first SUV stops in the courtyard, the driver's door opens, and a giant steps out. They call him "El Monstruo." He is a man built like a siege engine—seven feet if he's an inch, his shoulders broad enough to block the doorway behind him. His skin is a lattice of black Aztec tattoos, curling over muscles like carved stone. The designs climb his neck, framing a thick jaw and mouth fixed in a permanent half-snarl. Black hair falls in tangled ropes to his shoulders, gleaming like oil in the courtyard lights. His eyes are dark pits—expressionless but heavy with an animal threat. Even the guards avoid his gaze.

Behind him, the rear doors open. Two men in black windbreakers step out carrying a reinforced medical case, its chrome edges glinting under the lanterns hung from the arches. They handle it with care, their grips steady and their steps unhurried.

From the second vehicle, Eduardo Sanchez emerges, his squat frame dwarfed by the men flanking him. His face is pale but defiant, eyes flicking up toward the looming villa. El Monstruo jerks his chin in a gesture to follow, and the group falls into step.

Marble steps gleam beneath their boots as they ascend toward the heavy oak doors. Somewhere deep inside, a dog barks once, sharp and guttural, before going silent again. The doors swing inward, spilling golden light across the courtyard and swallowing Eduardo into the opulence of his brother's world.

The air is heavy with the mingled scents of sandalwood incense, cigar smoke, and the musk of animals. Beyond the marble foyer, a live tiger prowls lazily inside a gilded cage, its golden eyes following them with predatory patience. Peacocks strut freely across the polished stone floors, their tails fanning briefly in the light before folding like living tapestries. Trails of droppings dot the marble behind them.

The walls are hung with oil paintings—bullfights, colonial saints, and shadowy figures draped in ritual garb—between the art, glass cases display knives, machetes, and tarnished relics whose uses are better left unspoken.

They pass beneath a high arch into a massive chamber. At its far end, Miguel "El Lobo" Sanchez sits on a high-backed throne carved from dark wood, the arms adorned with snarling wolf heads. The wall behind him is an armory—pistols, rifles, and shotguns plated in gold, gleaming under spotlights. Between the weapons hang ritual objects from Palo Mayombe: iron cauldrons, carved sticks bound with feathers and bones, and bundles of dried herbs tied with red thread.

El Lobo's eyes, hard and unreadable, lock onto Eduardo as he's brought forward. His voice is calm, but it cuts like a razor.

"Welcome home, brother."

Eduardo swallows, his gaze fixed on the marble floor. "Miguel... I apologize for my carelessness."

El Lobo waits.

"It was that woman," Eduardo mutters. "She came to my club, said she was looking for work. Gorgeous. Smiled like she actually cared. I let her... I let her trick me."

His hands knot together, damp with sweat. He glances up, searching his brother's face.

"Yes, you did," El Lobo says evenly. "My friends in the government tell me she worked you for four weeks. Convinced you she loved you."

Eduardo's jaw tightens. "She knew how to play me. Drinks after work... other places..."

El Lobo's mouth curls—not quite a smile. "They say she sent you pictures. The night she drew you out."

Eduardo says nothing.

"In a latex nurse's outfit," El Lobo adds, mockery curling through the chamber. He sweeps a glance across the room; a few men chuckle. Eduardo's eyes drop to his hands.

"I didn't think," he says quietly. "I just went."

"And the place was crawling with federales," El Lobo snaps, rising from his chair. "You walked straight into the oldest trap in the book. Do you know how many men I lost trying to get you back in Tijuana? Then risking it all by sending my best people into US territory. How much money? And more than that—respect. You are my blood. What you do reflects on me, Eduardo. How many times do I have to tell you that?"

The air between them thickens with incense and unspoken judgment.

"But I'm home now," Eduardo says, almost pleading.

"Yes," El Lobo replies, his voice going flat. He turns to the hulking figure beside Eduardo. "We should go to the temple now."

El Monstruo nods once, a slow, heavy gesture.

Eduardo glances nervously between them. "We're... going to the temple?"

"Yes," El Lobo replies. "You must be blessed before you can return fully to my house. Now come, brother. El Demonio and La Bruja are waiting for us."

The massive chamber seems to close in, the gold-plated guns and ritual charms gleaming like watchful eyes as El Monstruo begins leading them toward the far doors.

The congregation spills out of the villa into the warm night air, their footsteps muted against the flagstone path. Above them, the hills rise like dark sentinels, the wind carrying a mingled scent of earth, candle wax, and something metallic—and rotten.

El Monstruo walks at the head of the column, the medical case dangling from his huge hand as if it weighs nothing.

They move in a loose but watchful formation, El Lobo close behind, Eduardo to one side, ringed in by armed men. Others follow at a respectful distance, their expressions wary, as if proximity to what lies ahead carries a price.

At the edge of the estate, the ground falls away to a clearing where the temple looms. It is not a church but a structure that feels older than the soil it stands on. Its walls are black stone, patched with moss and age-darkened mortar. The roofline is crowned with carved effigies—wolves, horned figures, and human faces frozen in silent screams. A pair of heavy iron doors bear the sigils of Palo Mayombe, daubed in crimson and ocher, their images shifting in the flicker of torchlight as though the entire structure were alive.

Inside, the air is thick, humid and suffocating, laced with the tang of burning herbs, rotting offerings, and dried blood. Shadows swim across the stone walls, painted in looping and jagged glyphs. The flicker of dozens of candles turns the markings into living things, shapes that seem to lean forward, whispering in a language older than the Catholic empire that tried to bury these ancient beliefs.

Eduardo's pulse hammers in his ears. Every breath feels heavy, as though the temple itself is breathing with him, competing for the air. Somewhere in the darkness, unseen things shift and stir—bones clink softly, and the faint hiss of sand sliding over stone echoes in the rafters.

At the altar, Javier "El Demonio" Acosta waits. He wears a long, blood-dark robe embroidered with gold thread. His eyes are black hollows under the cowl. Beside him stands La Bruja—tall, veiled, her hands folded loosely before her, fingertips glinting with gold rings shaped like talons.

El Monstruo steps forward, lowering the case onto the central table with surprising care. The metallic clasps click open. Acosta's hands move slowly, reverently, as he draws forth the contents one by one. Olivia Wren's heart, red-black and gleaming in the dim light. Her eyes, resting in small ritual bowls, clouded yet disturbingly alive in the candlelight. The brain, pale and ridged like an alien fruit.

In the center of the room squats the nganga—a black iron cauldron banded with rust and studded with nails. Its interior churns with a foul mixture of earth, bone fragments, feathers, dried blood, animal skulls, and the warped shapes of offerings too far gone to name. The smell rising from it is a thick, cloying blend of decay and musk, undercut by the acrid bite of burned herbs.

Acosta places each organ into the cauldron with care, his lips moving in a low chant. La Bruja steps in beside him, her voice higher, weaving around his in hypnotic counterpoint. The room's occupants lower themselves to their knees in unison, heads bowed.

The fire beneath the nganga snaps to life without warning, as though fed by an unseen breath. Flames lick upward, painting the room in red and gold. Smoke billows thick and greasy, coiling around the kneeling forms, clinging to skin and hair, pressing into the lungs like a weight. Eduardo fights the urge to cough, his stomach twisting as the stench of burning flesh and herbs fills him.

The chants grow louder, faster, a rolling tide of syllables that seem to bypass language and crawl directly into the spine. Shadows stretch and contort on the walls, the carved effigies leering down from the high beams.

Then silence, sharp and absolute. Acosta raises his hands. "Come forward, Miguel Sanchez."

El Lobo steps from the kneeling crowd. Acosta and La Bruja place their hands on his head, their voices resuming in deep, resonant tones. The flames gutter and flare, casting the three of them in stark relief—wolf, witch, and priest—bound together under the black roof of the temple.

Acosta's dark gaze then shifts to Eduardo. It's like a curtain falling—whatever light there was in those eyes is gone, replaced by something cold and inevitable. Two cultists move instantly, their hands clamping onto Eduardo's arms with bone-crushing force.

"Hey—what the hell is going on?" Eduardo's voice cracks, panic shredding his bravado. He twists violently, but their grip doesn't budge. "Miguel! Brother! What is this?"

El Lobo doesn't move from where he stands, his shadow stretching long in the candlelight. "Little brother," he begins, voice as steady as it is merciless, "you have been a thorn in my side since our days at the orphanage. Your impulsiveness has weakened us. Your recklessness has cost lives. You've taken much from me... from all of us." His tone dips lower, almost ceremonial. "It is time, at last, for you to give something back."

Eduardo's breath comes fast and shallow. "Miguel—please—"

But the plea dies as El Monstruo's vast hand clamps down on his shoulder, forcing him to his knees. Acosta steps forward, blade glinting in the shifting firelight. His movements are swift and merciless—there's a flash of steel, a wet sound, and Eduardo's scream rips through the cathedral like a living thing.

The chanting rises again.

With the precision of a surgeon, Acosta extracts the first offering—one of Eduardo's eyes—and lays it gently into the bubbling nganga. Then the second. His screams falter into broken, shuddering sobs. Blinded. Pathetic. The blade sinks again, this time into his chest. He doesn't fight it.

Some cutting and pulling and the heart emerges slick and steaming, lifted high for all to see before it joins the rest in the cauldron's roiling depths.

The flames surge, devouring the offerings, the smoke thickening until it clings to skin and tongue. The air reeks of burned flesh, bitter herbs, and something sweet and rotten beneath it all.

Acosta and La Bruja face the kneeling congregation, their voices rising in unison, blessing El Lobo and his men in the name of blood, fire, and darkness. Around them, hardened killers bow their heads, crossing themselves not in the sign of the cross but in something far older and far more dangerous.

The pact is sealed.

THIRTEEN

THE DINER IS HALF-ASLEEP at this hour, all humming refrigerators and the faint hiss of a lone cook at the grill. Outside its rain-specked window, the first edge of the sun pushes over the low hills, casting a pale gold over the sprawl of the San Diego–Tijuana border. From where Peter sits alone in the last booth, black coffee cooling between his hands, he can see the long steel fence snaking across the horizon, the haze rising from the detention camps on the US side. The razor wire glints like frost.

He watches it in silence. That thin line between two countries is worth billions in product and blood. A corridor for narcotics, weapons, and flesh—every inch contested by men who'll kill over a street corner, a crossing point, a smuggler's debt. The war to control it leaves bodies in the dirt and families in the wind. And yet here it is, basking in the morning light like it's just another day.

The bell over the door gives a tired jingle. Mark Deacon walks in, scanning the diner with the casual precision of someone who's made a life out of knowing where all the exits are. He slides into the seat opposite Peter without a word, placing a folder on the table between them.

"You look like hell," Deacon says finally.

Peter takes a sip of his coffee, eyes still on the fence. "Been a long night."

Deacon nods, letting the silence hang for a moment before flipping open the folder. Inside are satellite images, police reports, and—most damning—a USB drive he slots into a tablet. He turns the screen toward Peter. Doorbell-cam footage fills the display: an empty suburban street, until it's not. A huge man strides past, massive frame—a giant. Long black hair flows from his head like a mane, thick tattoos snake around his neck. But that isn't what catches Peter's attention. Something dangles from his fist. Olivia's rosary beads catch the streetlight with each swing.

Peter's jaw tightens. His hand curls around the coffee cup until the porcelain creaks.

"Local PD picked it up in their initial sweep of the neighborhood," Deacon says. "Didn't know what they had. I made sure we got a copy before it disappeared into evidence limbo."

Switching the tablet off, he continues, "Olivia was deep into some cross border mess. Human trafficking. Large groups of migrants from across Latin America—Honduras, Guatemala, El Salvador—have been going missing."

He taps a page in the folder—grainy satellite images of trucks on a desert road. "They're loaded onto transport convoys, promised safe passage north. But somewhere between Chiapas and Sonora, they vanish. No calls to their families, no bodies found. Just gone."

Peter finally turns to face him.

Deacon continues. "Olivia stumbled onto it while embedded with a joint task force. She was working a narcotics pipeline op—following the money from meth labs in Michoacán through middlemen in Texas. The deeper she dug, the more she saw the same names coming up in both dope shipments and missing-persons reports. That overlap led her off the drug trail and straight into the trafficking networks."

Deacon's voice lowers. "Her investigation led her to Miguel Sanchez. She was tracking a migrant convoy that disappeared two months ago—nearly seventy people, including children. We believe the convoy was intercepted by Sinaloa gunmen during a turf consolidation. Word is, the victims were split between cartel work camps and... other purposes." He doesn't elaborate, but his eyes say enough.

Deacon flips another page. "Another thing I found out was the route Olivia took through Tijuana. It was organized by State Police. They even offered to give her an armed escort, but Olivia turned it down."

Peter leans in, frowning. "So State Police knew the route?"

"They did."

"Then it's something to look into."

Deacon's silence is answer enough. They leave it there.

Peter takes a slow breath, then says, "The DEA agents— Moorling and Patrick—they told me about someone else. Javier Acosta. Cuban-born, Palo Mayombe priest. He's supposed to have the ear of the Sinaloa leadership... and the power to keep them bulletproof."

Deacon's frown is instant, deepening as he leans back in the booth. "That's not in the report." He drums his fingers once against the folder. "But it wouldn't be the first time a cartel's dabbled in that kind of thing. The whole Latin narcotics scene is full of weird rituals and saints you've never heard of. Superstition's currency down there."

Peter says nothing, letting him go on.

Deacon's gaze drifts toward the dust-streaked window. "You ever hear of Jesús Malverde?"

"Who?"

"Jesús Malverde. Patron saint of drug dealers. Folk hero. Bandit who robbed the rich to give to the poor, or so the story goes. Now his image is all over shrines from Sinaloa to LA— candles, medallions, statues in tinted glass cases. Traffickers pray to him before a run, leave offerings when they get home alive. It's a whole culture."

He looks back at Peter, his expression sharpening. "But it's all bullshit. Palo Mayombe, Malverde, Santa Muerte—doesn't matter which mask they use. It's nothing more than superstition to put the shits up the low-level dealers. Makes them think twice before skimming product or crossing the boss if they believe there are spirits watching them all the time." Deacon shrugs once drily. "Cheaper than CCTV, I guess."

He then closes the folder. "Anyway, long and short of it all is that you're officially reinstated."

"The agency is backing me?"

"They are. But this mission stays between you and me. If Olivia thought someone inside the agency had compromised her, we take that seriously. We work on the assumption she was right."

Peter leans back, studying him. "Management's good with that?"

"We've got their say-so. But they don't want this turning into a public mess. The border's a political swamp—one they're not eager to wade into."

Deacon leans in slightly. "And one more thing—we need to steer clear of the local CIA man. Jonny Hernandez. He's got his own games running down there."

Peter huffs a humorless breath. "I know him. Did a couple of wet jobs with him back in the Azrael days. South America."

"Then you know how he works. He's territorial as hell. We start stomping around his AO, we'll be stepping on toes. Best to keep our distance. That said..." Deacon's mouth twitches faintly. "Management is curious to see what the one-man army of Azrael can do. So we've got a budget."

Peter raises an eyebrow. "A budget?"

"Nothing fancy. Enough to get us kitted out, get us across the border, get us the tools we'll need to dig. We'll have to keep a low profile—no air strikes, no burning cities down. Not yet."

Peter's gaze hardens. "Then it's final. We go in. Find out who killed Olivia. Everyone who had a hand in it, everyone connected to it."

His voice is low, absolute.

"Then?" Deacon asks.

Peter's eyes drop to the folder, then lift again—cold and certain. "Then we burn them all. No loose ends."

FOURTEEN

THE MOTEL ROOM smells faintly of body odor and cheap coffee. It's 6:00 a.m. when Michael's alarm slices through the heavy quiet.

He silences it and pushes himself upright. Four hours' sleep hasn't lightened the weight in his bones. Across the bed, Mayu is already sitting up, hair tied back, eyes still glassy with fatigue.

They left the hospital in the small hours, the image of the little girl still fresh in their minds. Now another day at the border waits for them.

Outside, the sun is barely up, the sky washed in a pale, tired blue. The drive toward the detention camp is quiet, the road running straight and flat toward the looming fences. The first tents rise on the horizon—vast khaki structures anchored in neat rows. These are the processing areas, the first stop for anyone caught crossing.

Then come the detention zones—high chain-link cages topped with spirals of razor wire. Inside, clusters of men, women, and children sit slumped on the ground, wrapped in metallic emergency blankets. Some stare blankly through the fencing; others turn away from the passing vehicle as if retreating into themselves. Floodlights, still burning from the night, give the scene a sterile, unnatural glare, like an operating room without walls.

Michael turns off the highway and into the gravel lot, the early sun throwing long shadows across the chain-link perimeter. Beyond the fence, a row of white tents flaps lazily in the morning breeze.

At the main gate, an officer waves them through and rattles off the morning briefing. Another twenty-five people were brought in overnight—pulled from small boats drifting just off the coast. Most had been at sea for days, the officer tells them, battered by storms and surviving on brackish water and stubborn will. Full medical checks come first before processing.

As they walk toward the medical tent, Mayu keeps her eyes on the officer.

"Will we be able to see the little girl today?" she asks. "The one at the hospital."

"You can go once the new arrivals are processed," the officer replies without looking up from his clipboard.

Mayu nods, splitting off toward the detention area. Inside, the air is close and sour, the sound of shuffling feet and murmured voices carrying over the clink of the fencing. As she passes one section, a hand shoots out from between the wires—thin fingers, callused from hard work.

It's the woman from last night. The one carrying the girl. Her voice trembles. "How is she? My little girl?"

Mayu steps closer, lowering her voice. "She's okay. We're going to visit her soon. I'll let you know how she's doing afterward."

Relief floods the woman's face, softening the hard lines of her cheeks. Mayu hesitates, then asks gently, "What's her name?"

The woman's eyes flicker with something—confusion? She hesitates before finally answering. "Rosa."

It's a beat too long, and Mayu notices it. But the moment passes. She nods, offers a small smile, and moves on toward the medical tent where the newcomers wait, pale and shivering after their days at sea.

Michael kneels beside a man slumped on a folding chair, listening to the sluggish beat of his heart through a stethoscope. Nearby, Mayu gently pries a tin cup from a young boy's hand, replacing it with a bottle of electrolyte solution.

The new arrivals are in worse shape than most—skin salt-burned, lips cracked, eyes hollow from days of staring at open water. Mayu is helping a nurse apply ointment to a man's sunburn when the flap of the tent stirs and a uniformed ICE officer steps in, scanning the line of volunteers before fixing on them.

"You two," he says, jerking his chin. "Boss wants a word."

Michael exchanges a quick look with Mayu. "Now?"

"Now," he replies flatly.

The officer's name is Gary Stanton. They follow him out into the glare, past rows of fenced enclosures and the ever-present hum of generators. Gary leads them toward a prefabricated office set just back from the main camp. The place has the look of a command post—antennas sprouting from its roof, satellite dishes aimed skyward.

Inside, the air is cold and smells faintly of leather polish. Behind a broad government-issue desk sits Charles P. MacCready, ICE field office director. He could have stepped straight out of a '60s prison flick. His hair is slicked straight back, silver glinting at the temples. Mirrored aviators hide his eyes, but Michael and Mayu can see their own reflections in them—small, contained, and under his control. Black leather gloves rest neatly on the desk, fingers together, as though they've been arranged with a ruler.

MacCready doesn't stand, doesn't offer a chair. Instead, his gaze tracks them slowly and deliberately, the way a hawk might study field mice from a fencepost.

"You two were with the group that intercepted that little girl yesterday," he says at last. His voice is smooth, but every word carries weight, like gravel rolling in an oil drum.

Michael nods. "We were."

MacCready finally shifts his eyes to Gary Stanton. "That'll be all, Gary. Shut the door on your way out."

"Yes, sir," Stanton says, pulling the door closed behind him.

MacCready leans back just enough for the leather of his gloves to creak. "You know they didn't come over land?"

Michael and Mayu shrug.

"Didn't come through any of the usual rat trails or coyote holes. No, these folks came from something else... something we've been chasing for almost a year."

Mayu shifts her weight. "What's that?"

"A tunnel." The word drops flat between them. "Not some smuggler's hole you crawl through on your belly, either. This one's built right. Reinforced. Lit. Big enough to run a little rail car through. Somebody put serious money into it. Somebody who knows how to make people vanish without leaving a footprint."

Michael frowns. "And you think this group came through it?"

"I don't think," MacCready says evenly. "I know. And when that little girl got sick, they became a liability. You can't move sick cargo. They dumped 'em somewhere they'd be found. Easier to lose a shipment than risk the whole line getting burned."

Mayu's jaw tightens. "The parents aren't talking, I take it?"

MacCready's mirrored lenses tilt toward him. "They never do." His tone doesn't change, but the air in the room seems to thin. "They fear the cartels more than they fear God, and a hell of a lot more than they fear us. But the girl..." The reflection of Mayu in his shades tilts slightly. "...the girl might talk. Kids don't know when to keep secrets yet. And if she's seen something—a steel door, a set of tracks, the smell of diesel in the dark—we can use that."

Michael glances at Mayu, then back to MacCready. "And you want us to—what—interrogate her?"

"Not interrogate." His lips curl, almost a smile but not quite. "Talk. You've been there since she came in. She trusts you. If she's gonna give anything up, it'll be to you, not to me or one of my badge-toting friends here."

Mayu's voice is cool. "If she's able, we'll try."

MacCready nods once—approval or dismissal, it's hard to tell. "Good. You'll go with two of my men. You'll have as long as you need. And if you find that tunnel..." He lets the pause stretch, the hum of the AC filling the gap. "...you let me know before anybody else. Understand?"

Michael nods. "Understood."

Gary Stanton and one other ICE agent appear in the doorway, both armed, both wearing the wary, watchful expressions of men who expect trouble in every shadow. MacCready doesn't look at them when he says, "They'll take you."

Michael and Mayu turn to follow, and as the door swings shut behind them, MacCready's mirrored shades catch the light, sending a flash across the room like a signal no one wants to receive.

FIFTEEN

TWENTY MINUTES LATER, the ICE Tahoe crunches to a halt in the hospital's staff parking lot, tires hissing over damp asphalt. Morning light falls cold and thin between the gray clouds, the kind that makes everything feel sharper. Michael and Mayu move quickly across the lot, the agents close behind.

Inside, the corridors are hushed except for the distant whine of a floor polisher and the muted shuffle of nurses starting their shift. They move past reception, heading for the pediatric wing.

The closer they get to the girl's room, the more Mayu's pace quickens. But when they round the corner, they stop.

The chair beside the door sits empty. Inside, the bed is too— sheets rumpled, still warm. The IV stand tilts at an awkward angle, its line hanging loose.

The girl is missing.

"Where's the agent?" one of the ICE men snaps, scanning the hallway. "There was supposed to be someone posted here all night."

"She wouldn't have left her," Gary Stanton, the senior agent, murmurs, as he glances around.

He pulls out his phone and dials.

They stand in a tense cluster, the air thick with stale disinfectant and something faintly metallic.

A tinny ringtone cuts through the quiet.

At first, it seems distant, maybe somewhere down the hall, but then the sound sharpens, bouncing off the walls in a way that makes it feel closer. Much closer.

Gary lowers his phone, frowning. He trades quick glances with his partner. The ringtone keeps chiming, tinny and insistent, and now there's no mistaking it: It's not coming from another room at all.

It's right here with them.

Somewhere to their left.

Their eyes track the sound until they land on a scuffed, narrow door with a metal handle. A supply cupboard.

The agents draw their sidearms and close in. Gary wraps his gloved hand around the knob and pulls.

The door swings open.

The ICE officer is there—folded, crumpled against the shelves like a discarded rag doll. Her eyes are open, bulging from their sockets. Her throat is marked by deep bruising. She's been dead for hours.

The phone still chirps in her pocket.

Mayu steps back, her breath hitching. Michael's hands clench into fists. The fluorescent lights above hum with static in the silence.

"Where's the girl?" the other agent barks at a passing nurse.

The nurse's eyes go wide. "Girl? No... I haven't—"

"Check every hallway," Gary Stanton orders.

While Gary stays behind with the body, the rest move fast, weaving through the sterile maze of corridors toward the security station.

Somewhere in the back of Michael's mind, a cold thought takes root. Whatever happened here didn't start at this hospital. Someone planned this. And if they planned this... they were already three steps ahead.

They move—fast. Mayu and Michael push past startled nurses, flashing urgent questions. Heads shake, eyes widen. No one has seen her. No one noticed her go.

They hit the security hub. Inside, a heavyset man in a rumpled polo leans back in his chair, three cups of cold coffee littering his desk. The wall of monitors hums, cycling through different wings of the hospital.

The ICE agent with them slaps a badge onto the desk hard enough to rattle one of the coffee cups.

"We need the last hour's footage from pediatrics. All of it."

The guard grumbles as he rolls his chair forward. "You picked a bad day. Cameras have been glitchy as hell since this morning."

His fingers tap the keyboard, pulling up a wall of miniature feeds—parking lot, lobby, corridors, elevators.

The images spool backward in jagged bursts, jumping in time. They stop on the pediatric wing—just an empty hallway, time-stamp flickering in the corner.

"Go back further," Michael says.

The guard scrubs the timeline in reverse. The feeds stutter and rewind: the parking lot in grainy black and white, a few cars gleaming under sodium lamps; the lobby with its neat row of plastic chairs. But just before the time stamp they want, each camera freezes—then the picture dissolves into fizzing static.

"Hold it there," Michael says. "Back up two seconds."

The guard does, and there it is again—perfectly clear until a lone figure moves into frame. The moment they step inside the camera's view, the image shivers, blurs, and washes out to snow.

The guard leans closer. "Every time he walks past it messes with the cameras. It's like the guy's a ghost."

Michael's tone is flat. "Not a ghost. He's wearing an RF jammer."

The guard squints at him. "A what?"

"Your cameras transmit their feed via Wi-Fi? 2.4 or 5 giga-hertz?" Michael's voice has a sharp edge now.

The guard shrugs. "Think so."

"Then every time he comes near one, he kills its signal with a frequency jammer."

They keep scrubbing forward, following the trail of distortion. The fuzz jumps from parking lot to lobby cam, from lobby to corridor, each time swallowing a few more seconds of footage before spitting out the feed again, just in time to catch the empty space where the figure had been.

By the time the signal jumps to the pediatrics corridor, everyone is leaning in. The static blooms over the agent sitting outside the girl's doorway, lingers for nearly two minutes, then vanishes onto the hall cam outside.

The blur moves steadily toward the east exit—but not to the parking lot.

"He's going toward the incinerator," the guard mutters, narrowing his eyes at the tiny screen.

The timestamps show another two minutes passing while the figure is there, the camera on the incinerator door locked in a haze of interference. When the picture clears, the blur is gone—until another feed picks it up, crossing the lot toward a waiting car. The angle is bad, the plate unreadable, the make and model swallowed by glare.

"I'll get someone to check the road cameras," the ICE agent says.

"Don't bother," the guard replies. "That street dumps right onto the freeway. Rush hour. You won't spot him in that mess. Not if you don't know his face or his car."

Mayu's eyes stay fixed on the frozen image of the incinerator's corner, shadowed and still. Her voice is quiet, almost to herself.

"I'd like to know what he was doing behind the incinerator."

The three of them step out into the cool morning air. They cross the parking lot and head behind the hospital. The hum of the incinerator is a low, constant growl in the corner of the yard. The sky is the color of wet concrete, and the smell—hot metal and something acrid—hangs thick.

A row of oversized, wheeled medical waste bins sits along the wall, lids sealed, red biohazard symbols peeling from their sides. Steam curls from the vents in the incinerator's flank.

The ICE agent flips open the first lid. Inside is crumpled surgical drapes, soiled gauze, used tubing coiled like dead snakes. He slams it shut and moves to the next.

Michael feels his jaw tighten. He knows what they're about to find—feels it in the hollow pit of his chest before it happens.

The third bin's lid creaks open. For a moment, all they see is more of the same—plastic, cloth, stained latex gloves. Then Mayu's hand freezes mid-reach.

Nestled in the refuse is the small shape of the girl, her dark hair matted against a pale cheek. The folds of a hospital gown are bunched around her, tangled in the debris as if she'd been thrown there without a thought.

Mayu's breath breaks. She leans in, lifting the child with trembling arms. The body is light, limp. When she lays her gently on the asphalt, the harsh daylight reveals it all: the stitched line running down her chest and belly, the ugly crook of her neck.

Someone has broken it.

Mayu's eyes brim over, tears spilling unchecked down her face. "How could someone do this to a child?"

The question hangs in the morning air, unanswered, as the low growl of the incinerator seems to swell behind them.

SIXTEEN

THE MAN IS tall and lean in a wiry way that hides his strength. Black hair slicked back from a lined forehead, a thick moustache framing a mouth set in perpetual stillness. His clothes are all black—creased slacks, a crisp shirt, leather shoes that carry no sound on the cracked San Diego sidewalk.

He lowers himself onto a bench beside the road, the wood splintered and sun-bleached, a satellite phone resting heavy in his hand. The plastic is warm against his palm as he powers it on. A low hum, a faint hiss of connection, and then the call goes through.

"Hello?"

"It is me," he says in Spanish, his voice quiet, measured.

"Ah. El Gusano. How did it go?"

"It is done."

"Good. A terrible business, but one which had to be done. You will receive payment the usual way. Goodbye, old friend."

The line clicks dead. El Gusano lowers the satellite phone slowly to his lap, letting out a long breath through his nose. His face is stone—no satisfaction, no regret. Just another job.

A light tapping breaks his stillness. He turns. At the edge of the bench, a little girl with curly black hair stands on the curb, small hands clasped in front of her, head tilted.

He rises to his feet.

"Grandpapa!" She beams.

The ice in his eyes melts in an instant. He bends, scooping her up into his arms with a smile that erases the killer from his face entirely. Deep lines crease warmly at the corners of his eyes.

"I thought I told you to stay in the car," he says, his voice suddenly rich with affection.

"I couldn't wait. Are we finally now going for hamburgers?"

"Sí. But any more shenanigans and we won't be having ice cream."

"Ohh, I promise to be good. I'll stay in the car next time. I swear on my life." She crosses herself with quick, solemn little fingers.

It makes him laugh softly, a true laugh.

Still holding her, he walks back to the curb. The black sedan waits with its engine ticking softly. He settles her into the back seat, buckles her in, and slides behind the wheel.

The car pulls away, merging into the traffic, leaving behind nothing but the faint swing of the pay phone door in the morning breeze.

SEVENTEEN

MICHAEL AND MAYU push through the main gate of the detention center, the hot border sun already burning the dust into the air. The metallic tang of the chain-link and razor wire mixes with the faint hum of the generator powering the flood-lights that still blaze over the yard.

MacCready is waiting just past the checkpoint, leaning against a government SUV. His mirrored shades reflect the glare back at them. No chance of reading what's behind them.

"Have you spoken to the mother?" Mayu asks before he can open his mouth.

"Yes," MacCready says evenly. "I've had people in there with her for the past hour. She ain't talking."

Mayu's jaw tightens. "Then I'll talk to her."

She starts forward, but two ICE agents step into her path, broad shoulders filling the gap in the gate corridor.

"What are you doing?" MacCready calls after her, voice still calm but weighted with warning.

"Her daughter is dead," Mayu snaps, turning her head just enough for her words to cut through the dry air. "I want to ask her who is responsible."

"And I told you," MacCready says, pushing off the SUV. "She won't talk."

Mayu turns back and keeps walking.

Michael moves to follow, but MacCready's gloved hand clamps around his arm, stopping him mid-step.

"You need to control her," MacCready says, low and deliberate. "Otherwise I can just as easily get the IRC to move you twos somewhere else."

Michael meets the mirrored lenses for a long moment, his own reflection warped and ghostlike in them. He says nothing, just pulls free and continues after Mayu. The sound of MacCready's leather gloves creaking as he cracks his knuckles lingers behind him like an unspoken threat.

The detention center's corridors hum faintly with the electric buzz of fluorescent lights. Mayu's boots scuff against the linoleum as she strides toward the interrogation wing, jaw tight.

She pushes through the door to a small cinderblock room. An ICE agent in a khaki shirt is sitting across from the mother, dark hair tangled, wrists shackled to a thick steel loop in the bolted table.

"I'd like to talk to her," Mayu says.

The agent shrugs. "Be my guest."

"Alone."

The man frowns. "I'm not sure about that."

"She's shackled," Mayu points out, nodding at the heavy cuffs. "She's not going anywhere."

He hesitates, then shifts in his chair. "Yeah, but I can't just leave you with her."

"Please." The word is clipped, but her eyes don't leave his.

After a beat, he exhales sharply through his nose. "Fine. Your call." He pushes back his chair and slips out, the door clicking shut behind him.

Mayu pulls the seat forward and sits opposite the woman. "¿Podemos hablar?"

The woman nods faintly.

Mayu studies her, noting the way her gaze drops to the table. "She wasn't your daughter, was she?" she says in Spanish.

The woman's eyes flick up sharply, then away again. Silence.

"It doesn't mean you didn't care for her," Mayu adds softly.

The woman's lips tremble. "No... no, I did. She reminded me of my own. I have two niños back in Honduras. I know what it is to be a mother."

Mayu nods slowly. "What happened?"

"She got sick," the woman whispers. "On the way. I begged them to get us above ground."

Mayu's brow furrows. "Above ground?"

The woman freezes, eyes darting up.

"So there is a tunnel."

Her face drains of color.

"You know how to get there?"

The question lands like a blow. The woman crosses herself quickly, her chains clinking against the table. "They will kill me."

"Not in here."

"I have already received messages."

Mayu leans in. "From who?"

"I cannot say. But they tell me... my life is in danger. That I should never have let you take the child away."

"Who spoke to you?"

She shakes her head rapidly. "Please... I can't. They will find my children. Kill them. They see everything. Know everything."

"Who are they?"

The woman's eyes glisten with tears as she meets Mayu's gaze. Her voice is a trembling whisper. "You want to know who they are?"

"Yes," Mayu says.

The woman hesitates, then slowly works the top button of her blouse. Her fingers tremble as she tugs the fabric aside, pulling the neck of her T-shirt down to expose her collarbone. There, burned deep into the flesh, is a crude scar—a brand.

It is the outline of a goat's skull within a spiked circle, the eyes hollow pits, curling horns forming the shape of a crescent moon. The edges are jagged from the iron's uneven heat, the skin around it puckered and waxy.

"Los Narcosatánicos," she hisses, her voice breaking.

The name hangs between them, thick with dread.

EIGHTEEN

THE MORNING AIR is cool and sharp, carrying the dry tang of hay and the musk of restless animals. Miguel "El Lobo" Sanchez stands at the edge of the corral, one hand resting on the sun-warmed rail, the other turning a gold ring slowly on his finger. In the pen below, his prize bull paces in slow, deliberate arcs.

The beast's hide gleams satin-black over slabs of rippling muscle, its shoulders twitching with every shift of weight. The massive head dips, horns catching the morning light like polished ivory blades. Each breath steams in the air, curling into pale smoke before fading. It moves the way Miguel does when anger builds beneath the surface—controlled, patient, never rushing but promising sudden, devastating violence the instant it is needed.

As he watches, his thumb continues to trace the engraved symbol on the ring: a goat's skull enclosed in a jagged spiked circle, the curling horns forming a crescent moon.

A shadow falls across the dust behind him.

"They're here," a guard murmurs.

Miguel doesn't turn right away. He watches his bull complete another slow circuit of the pen, hooves grinding into the dirt, tail flicking with irritation. Then he looks up.

Two men approach with one of Miguel's main smugglers, Carlos Aguirre, between them. The smuggler's Stetson is pulled low, but Miguel sees the tightness in his jaw and the sheen of sweat despite the cool air. Carlos has worked for him for years, moving product, keeping schedules. But even old dogs get put down when they piss on the wrong rug.

Miguel's voice is quiet, almost lazy, but it carries the weight of a tethered predator.

"Recently, we had a situation."

Carlos swallows. "Boss, I can explain—"

Miguel lifts a hand. "Let me speak."

Carlos's eyes drop to the dirt.

"You allowed people to leave the tunnel and go off on their own," Miguel says, each word measured. "You allowed product to leave the assembly line. What do you say to this?"

Carlos looks up for permission. Miguel gives the faintest nod.

"The girl was sick."

Miguel's lips tighten. "So fucking what? She wouldn't be the first to die. She won't be the last."

"But that woman—the one with the children—she wouldn't let it go. I thought she might run. So I let them off at a ventilation shaft. No one saw."

Miguel's gaze stays steady, unblinking, like the bull watching a matador's smallest movement. "But the little girl... She was separated from the rest. The narcotics were found. They were going to ask her where she'd come from."

"It was dark—she wouldn't have known."

"You should never have taken the risk," Miguel says flatly. He steps closer, his voice dropping to a predator's whisper. "Because it has meant that I have had to take my own risks. I have had to silence the situation."

"The girl is dead?"

"Yes. But she should have died in the tunnel. Your letting them go saved no one. Instead, it has condemned *you*."

Hands clamp on to Carlos's arms. His hat hits the dirt, rolling to the edge of the corral. He thrashes hard, boots grinding and slipping in the gravel, scraping for purchase as if he could claw himself free through sheer desperation.

"Boss, please!" he chokes out, his voice cracking. "I've served you my whole life—don't do this!"

The guards wrench him backward, dragging him in jerks across the dirt, his heels leaving furrows as he kicks and stumbles, eyes darting wildly to Miguel for mercy.

But Miguel does not move. He only watches, his expression carved from stone, as Carlos is hauled away into the shadows.

Miguel makes his way toward the sunken arena at the far end of the property, two of his men falling in behind him. The pit lies carved into the earth, ringed by a low concrete wall. Down below, its dirt floor is packed hard by hooves, gouged and scarred, stained darker in places where blood has seeped into the ground.

The snort of the bull echoes from beyond one of the gates that line the edge of the pit, deep and resonant, as if the animal itself were anointed—an executioner dressed in flesh and fury.

From behind the far gate comes Carlos's voice—high and desperate.

The gate swings open. Carlos stumbles in. He immediately runs for the closing door, pounding on it with both fists as it slams in his face. "Boss! Please! I've never done anything but serve you!"

Miguel looks down at him from the wall, the gold ring glinting as he turns it.

Carlos catches sight of him. "Boss, please!"

"I'm sorry, Carlos. But your failure could have led to the discovery of the tunnel."

Miguel turns to one his men. Nods.

The other gate bursts wide, and the bull thunders out—a black blur of muscle and bone.

Carlos dodges once, twice. The third charge catches him in the gut, a horn punching through with a sound like tearing cloth. The bull lifts him high and slams him into the wall. There is a sound like cracking twigs. Something in Carlos's back snaps loudly enough to echo.

He slides down, spilling into the dirt, still alive, one hand reaching out.

The bull is relentless. It tramples him, hooves breaking his hip, then lowers its head to gore again, shoving him across the arena floor like a rag doll until all motion ceases. Still, it stomps and tosses, eyes rolling white with rage.

Miguel watches without a flicker. The bull, like him, has no pity—only the satisfaction of removing a problem.

When it is done, Miguel turns and walks away.

"Give the organs to El Demonio," he says to one of his men, bored, his thumb absently stroking the ring's symbol.

NINETEEN

LATE NIGHT off the western coast of Mexico.

The ocean is black glass, unbroken until the slow rise of the submarine's conning tower punches through. Water sluices down its flanks as the beast emerges from the deep. The hatch swings open, and Peter climbs out into the night, the salt wind sharp in his lungs. Deacon follows, hauling up a drybag and the folded dinghy.

They work in silence. The inflatable hisses softly as it fills. Peter steadies it while Deacon secures the pump. Minutes later, the two men lower it carefully into the Pacific, climbing down after it with the ease of men long used to carrying their lives in silence.

The submarine recedes into the dark as they paddle toward shore, its hulking shape vanishing beneath the waves like some leviathan returning to the deep. Ahead, the Mexican coastline glimmers faintly—moonlight on rock, the yellow smear of distant sodium lamps.

They make landfall in a narrow cove hemmed in by jagged cliffs. Peter runs the bow up onto wet sand, then pulls a knife and cuts the dinghy open in one clean slice. The hiss of air fades into the night. Together, they drag the husk into the scrub, burying it beneath sea grass and driftwood.

On the shore, they strip off their wetsuits, pulling on dark clothes. The duffel is laid out between them: weapons wrapped in oiled cloth, stacks of pesos and dollars, forged IDs, clean bank cards, and a laptop sealed in waterproof casing. The tools of men stepping off the map.

Peter checks a pistol, slapping the magazine home. Deacon zips the bag shut. Neither speaks.

Above the cove, the lights of a small town blink faintly against the horizon—cheap bars, shuttered tiendas, and the narrow veins of roads leading deeper inland. Toward Miguel Sanchez. Toward Los Narcosatánicos.

Peter swings the bag over his shoulder. Deacon pulls his cap low.

"Ready?" Deacon asks.

Peter glances at him, eyes hard. "I was ready the second they killed her."

Deacon's mouth twitches—half a smile, half something darker. "Then let's make them regret it."

Without another word, they start walking.

TWENTY

BY LATE AFTERNOON, the caravan stretches for blocks, a river of sunburned faces and plastic jugs moving north through a small Sonoran town near the Californian Gulf. Salt is on the air, and shrimp boats speck the horizon like low clouds.

The road they walk is lined with cinderblock houses and rusting chain-link fences. Stray dogs sleep beneath bougainvillea, and the locals watch from shaded doorways.

They do not wave.

The caravan has come a long way to get here. Guatemala feels like a lifetime behind them now—feet black with river mud from the Suchiate crossing, legs cramping from days on low-riding buses and backs of pickups, nights on cardboard in church court-yards and roadside chapels.

In Chiapas, they learned to keep their heads down. In Oaxaca, they learned which police accepted bribes and which they had to flee. In Sinaloa, they learned not to ask questions about the men with the radios.

Rosa from Honduras walks with her daughter Alma asleep on her shoulder, the child's cheek pasted to Rosa's sun-roasted neck. Alma's shoes are tied to Rosa's pack to cool the blisters ballooning on her heels; every few blocks, Rosa shifts the girl to the other shoulder and keeps moving.

A Salvadoran teenager in a fake Barcelona jersey limps beside them on taped sandals. On the other side of them, a Guatemalan mason named Edgar carries a five-gallon blue water jug and a folded photo of the house slab he poured for a man in Guatemala City last year, proof he can work, that he has come for work and not for trouble.

Ahead, the caravan rounds a corner, and the sea opens full, resembling flattened pewter under the falling sun. The municipal park sits one block back from the beach—a rectangle of soccer dirt, a run of palm trees throwing skinny shadows, a low pavilion with a peeling mural of fishermen towing nets fat with silver sardines. A municipal cop leans on the hood of his truck outside the park entrance and watches the mass approach with a look that fixes on nothing.

Two white pickups with magnetic logos on their doors wait by the pavilion. BORDER AID INTERNATIONAL. In the cabs sit American volunteers. In the backs are boxes of water, packets of oral rehydration salts, foil blankets, and a pharmacy's worth of painkillers and antibiotics stamped with Spanish labels.

They wear reflective vests and ball caps against the sun, moving with the well-practiced hurry of people who know there will never be enough of anything.

"Let's triage in the shade," says Lauren, the team lead and a nurse from Flagstaff, her hair braided tightly under a faded cap. "Darius, set up an ORS station by the palm line. Keisha, blisters and wound care under the pavilion. Martin, hand out blankets only to families with infants. We've got sixty. That's it."

"Copy," Darius says, shouldering a tote.

They wade into the bodies, speaking in broken Spanish and kindness. Water first, then salts. Keisha—an EMT who's done three seasons on wildfire crews—sits cross-legged on a tarp, slicing tape with a penknife, draining blisters with a gloved hand, and teaching a thirteen-year-old how to lace his broken boot so it won't saw at his tendon. A baby with heat rash mewls against a mother's breast. A man shivers through the onset of a fever despite the heat. An old woman coughs pink into a napkin and folds it like a secret.

"¿Qué tan lejos ahora?" someone asks.

How far now?

"Unos días," Lauren says gently.

A few days.

The light slants orange and then bleeds down to copper. Women unroll blankets, men stack packs into makeshift pillows, kids chase a soccer ball with the last of the sun. The Americans take inventory and find the same bad news they always find: not enough antiseptic, not enough diapers, not enough everything. They speak in low voices at the tailgate.

"We should head back before dark," Darius says, checking his phone. No signal.

Lauren scans the road that leads out to the highway, the park perimeter, the lazy rotation of the municipal cop's gaze. "Ten more minutes."

They begin to wind down—empties into trash bags, the last ORS packets distributed, a quick sweep for anyone in obvious medical distress. The caravan settles into the quiet of people getting ready for sleep: murmurs, rustling, the soft slap of a mother patting a child's back.

The sheep are settling down for the evening.

But the wolves aren't far.

On the horizon, beyond the park's chain-link and the line of palms, something moves against the last smear of light. At first it's only shadows where there shouldn't be, a tremor in the dust that doesn't belong to the sea breeze. Then Lauren hears it: engines running low.

She looks to the municipal cop. He straightens without quite standing, eyes narrowed toward the highway. He says nothing. Doesn't even lift the radio from his shoulder.

"Load up," Lauren tells her team, voice pitched flat and calm.

Darius starts for the driver's door. Keisha reaches for the med tote. Martin freezes, eyes on the road.

The vehicles come in without headlights, dark shapes coagulating into detail: two pickups with cages welded over the beds, men standing inside with rifles; behind them, four old-school buses, primer-gray, windows painted over. They roll to the park entrance and stop as one. The municipal cop steps back from his truck and looks away.

For a heartbeat, the park holds its breath. Then the men spill from the pickups—ball caps and balaclavas, jeans, tactical vests, radios hissing, assault rifles.

The quiet ruptures.

"¡Al suelo!"

Down!

"¡Manos arriba!"

Hands up!

A shot cracks the evening, fired over heads to harvest panic. People surge to their feet, tripping on blankets as they try to run for the far gate. A woman screams the same name three times.

Carlos!

Carlos!

CARLOS!!

The men fire into the air again, then into the ground near fleeing feet, then into backs when the herd doesn't turn fast enough. The teenager in the Barcelona jersey goes down clutching the meat of his thigh, eyes wide, mouth working without sound. Someone stumbles over him and keeps going. Someone else drags him by his armpits, leaving a dark smear in the dust.

"Lauren!" Keisha shouts.

"Stay with me," Lauren says, raising both hands, stepping between the nearest gunman and a cluster of children. "Somos voluntarios. Somos médicos."

We're volunteers. We're medics.

The man flicks his gaze over her vest, her open hands, the logo on the truck. He doesn't lower his rifle. He jerks his chin toward the buses.

"¡Arriba! ¡Rápido!"

Men with pistols and radios move like cattle dogs along the edges, clubbing those who hesitate, dragging families toward the bus doors. Mothers try to keep hold of children and have their hands pried away. Rosa clamps Alma to her chest and whispers the Lord's Prayer into the child's hair. A man grabs her elbow and yanks; Rosa's grip holds. He hits her in the temple with the muzzle of his rifle and she goes to a knee still holding the girl. Another man tears Alma away and shoves her toward the nearest bus.

"Please!" Lauren shouts, stepping forward, palms still up. "Please, the children—"

A different gunman clubs her across the forearm with his rifle stock. Pain detonates like a flashbang. She falls and rolls, sucking dust, trying to keep the weight of the man's boot off her ribs. Martin lunges to pull her back and catches a punch that splits his lip. Darius reaches for the tote by reflex, and a rifle barks at the dirt between his legs.

"¡Los gringos también!" one of the men says.

The gringos too.

"Take our trucks," Lauren gasps. "Take everything. Leave—"

Hands close on the back of her vest and drag her to her feet. She throws one glance at Keisha—chin up, jaw set, fury in her eyes—and then their hands are zip-tied behind them, and they are propelled toward the last bus in the row.

The buses are already half full, people packed three to a seat, bodies pressed into the aisle. Babies wail, the thin keening sound of animals that know they're being moved. The painted windows make the interior a red-brown dusk. A man with a ledger takes count by tapping his pen against the metal seatback. Another man in a reflective vest stands at the door and nods each time the pen ticks. The system is built for efficiency.

"¡Más rápido!"

Faster.

A boy in a Spider-Man T-shirt tries to slip sideways between seats toward the back door, and a hand grabs the neck of his shirt, hauling him up like a kitten. The boy cries without tears. The man puts him in the nearest lap.

The bus engine coughs alive. Diesel fumes lick the night.

In the park, the ones who made it to the far fence cluster at the chain-link and shake. A shot rips the top of the fence, and they fall back. A man lies face-down near the goalposts, a dark pool growing under his chest. Edgar, the mason, presses both hands to the wound and looks up for someone to tell him what to do.

But there is no one.

Rosa sits on the bus holding Alma. The girl stares with the flat animal focus of a child beyond fear. Rosa looks back over the shoulder of the man behind her, searching for someone to witness, to promise, to tell her where they're going. A gun barrel nudges her ribs, and she turns around.

At the pavilion, the municipal cop climbs into his truck and closes the door. He doesn't turn the key. Just watches through the dusty windshield as the buses begin to drive away.

The last of the volunteers are pushed up the final bus steps. Keisha's eyes find Lauren's across the aisle as the doors hiss shut, a look that says *hold on*, a look that says *don't give them more than they take*.

"¡Vámonos!"

The buses roll, one after the other, out of the park and onto the road that runs along the dark line of sea. The pickups fall in front and behind, lights off until they clear the town, then headlights flare hard as they hit the highway and the world narrows to two pale tunnels of dust and asphalt. Behind them, the park breathes out—empty blankets, a dropped shoe, the thin metallic smell of blood going brown in the heat that never really leaves.

By the time the municipal cop starts his truck, they are long gone.

TWENTY-ONE

THE ROAD north cuts through scrub desert, a ribbon of asphalt laid over cracked earth and salt flats. Peter drives the battered sedan they stole in the small fishing village of Puerto Libertad, its upholstery reeking of sweat and old fish, its plates borrowed from a junkyard car in Hermosillo. Even the pistols they brought with them are old Balkan surplus, serials filed off, grips slick with other men's histories. Nothing that can be traced back to Langley. Nothing that says United States.

Beside him, Deacon stares out the window at the twin cities sprawling to the east. Nogales, Arizona and Nogales, Sonora—two halves of a mismatched mirror. "You know the history here?" Deacon asks.

Peter shakes his head.

"This town used to be one before they split it after the Gadsden Purchase in 1853. Families lived across the line, crossed back and forth for groceries, school, Sunday mass. Then the wall came in 1918. Now it's razor wire and checkpoints, and half the economy runs on smuggling. Drugs north. Guns south. Everything else through the cracks."

Peter doesn't answer. His eyes stay on the road, jaw locked.

They avoid Nogales itself and push into the desert beyond it, the stretch of badland that clings to the city's Mexican edge like a scar.

On the horizon, the desert swells into the outline of a fortress. Whitewashed walls. Guard towers stitched with floodlights. Razor wire coiled like metal snakes along the perimeter. At the gate, a column of armored pickups idles while dogs circle, handlers checking undercarriages with mirrors. Beyond the walls, steel roofs glint in the fading light.

"That," Deacon says as they approach the compound, "is Charles Rush's little kingdom."

Deacon had already briefed Peter on the man they were about to meet, Charles Rush.

Rush built his empire out of the collapse of others. A former Marine officer turned privateer, he sold his services wherever the money flowed: Nigerian oil fields, Balkan border wars, Afghan convoys. When Washington cut him loose, he went freelance full-time. Mexico gave him what he always wanted—chaos, clients with money, and no oversight. His company protects mining magnates, ex-governors, cartel defectors, anyone who can pay. He calls it a PMC. Most call it mercenary work.

"Rush protects the rich," Deacon mutters as they slow at the gate. "The police protect the cartels. And the poor are left to protect themselves any way they can."

When they stop, dogs circle the sedan, noses pressed to the steel. Guards with masks and carbines motion Peter and Deacon out. They pat them down thoroughly, rifling through wallets, fake IDs, even the seams of their boots. Their documents get passed inside, checked against lists neither man sees. Finally, a curt nod. Weapons are returned, muzzles still pointed their way.

They climb back in. The gate slides open.

Inside, the compound feels like another country. Asphalt drives, manicured gravel, prefab barracks lined neat as dominoes. Armed men on catwalks. Camera domes in every corner. Even the air smells different—cut grass, diesel, gun oil.

"Watch yourself," Deacon says as they step from the car. "Everyone here's trigger-happy."

They don't wait long. Charles Rush emerges from one of the buildings with the confidence of a man who has bought his own world. Tall, broad through the shoulders, hair silvered but cropped regulation short. He wears desert camo pants and a white dress shirt unbuttoned at the collar, sleeves rolled to the elbow. A gold watch winks at his wrist. His eyes are blue glass marred by a network of burst veins, the drinker's giveaway. His handshake is bone-crushing, his grin all salesman.

"Well, well. Mark Deacon. The prodigal son returns."

"Charlie." Deacon's tone is flat. "Didn't think you'd still be out here."

"Where else would I go? Washington doesn't know what to do with me. Down here I'm indispensable." Rush's gaze slides to Peter, sizing him up. "And you must be the partner. I've heard of you. Black, right?"

Peter doesn't reply.

Rush chuckles. "Strong, silent type. My favorite kind."

They walk through the compound. Everywhere, men pause to glance at them—hard-eyed, multinational. Colombians with faded FARC tattoos. Serbs with prison ink crawling over their arms. American vets too mean or too broken to go home. Ghosts from half a dozen wars, carrying rifles like extensions of their bodies.

"They're loyal because I give them something no one else does," Rush says as he leads them through his place. "A paycheck, a target, and revenge if they want it. Cartel took your family? I'll give you a gun to shoot cartel. Military tossed you aside? March under my flag. Simple arrangement."

Inside the main warehouse, tables groan under neat rows of hardware. Body armor. Helmets. Assault rifles with Mexican provenance. Satphones, laptops hardened against hacking. Ruggedized surveillance drones, each folded into its case like some predatory insect.

Peter runs a hand over one of the laptops. "Satellite uplink?"

"Encrypted, piggybacks off commercial birds," Rush says. "Untraceable if you know what you're doing. Range won't get you Langley-clear, but you'll see what you need to see."

Deacon checks the rifles. "All non-US issue?"

Rush smirks. "Come on, Mark. You know me better than that. Bulgarian Makarovs, Czech Scorpions, South African Vectors."

"Good," Deacon says. "We'll take two rifles, four pistols, uplink kit, and one drone. And the armored vehicle."

Rush whistles low. "Planning something heavy?"

Deacon ignores the bait. "Wire transfer okay? Offshore account."

Rush gestures to an assistant. The man disappears with a nod. "Okay with me."

They load the gear into a battered Chevrolet P30 step van parked in the shadows of the hangar. Once a delivery truck, its white paint has been resprayed matte black, its logos scraped away. The outside looks tired, rust speckling the wheel arches, but inside it's been gutted and reborn: armor-plated doors, bullet-proof glass, reinforced suspension, a superior diesel engine under the hood, and a hidden comms and surveillance array wired into the dash. A war machine disguised as a delivery truck.

Rush claps Deacon on the back as crates thud into the rear. "So what is this, Mark? You and your friend come to Mexico to start a war with the cartels?"

"You know I can't tell you that."

"Yeah, you can't tell me. That's the same as yes." Rush's grin sharpens. "Where you headed next?"

Deacon shakes his head. "Can't tell you that either."

Rush eyes them for a beat, then chuckles. "Juárez, then."

Deacon arches a brow. "Why would you guess that?"

Rush's grin fades to something leaner. "Because if you've come to hell, my guess is you're on your way to see the devil."

TWENTY-TWO

BACK ON THE US SIDE, Mayu won't let it go. The dead girl haunts her.

She and Michael push through the crowd outside the detention center gates. Volunteers cluster along the fence line, whispers running through them like static down a wire. Through the chain link, two paramedics wheel a stretcher toward an ambulance. A black body bag is strapped down tightly.

Mayu stops cold. "What happened?"

A young volunteer, pale and hollow-eyed, answers without looking at her. "The mother. The one whose daughter was found in the hospital dumpster. They say she hung herself. Custody cell, last night."

The words hit Mayu like a slap. She grips the fence until the chain bites her hands, then tears away, storming inside.

She bursts through MacCready's office door.

He doesn't even look up from his paperwork. "Don't you knock?"

"What happened to her?" Mayu snaps.

MacCready leans back, sighing like she's an irritation rather than a human being. "She killed herself. I was in the middle of disciplining the officers who allowed it to happen."

"How?"

"She hung herself."

"Hung herself?" Mayu spits the words. "That's convenient."

MacCready lets a smirk creep into his expression. "Perhaps you pushed her too far during your... interrogation. People break in different ways."

Mayu's face flushes with fury. "I didn't break her. You did. This place did."

He shrugs, spreading his hands. "Believe what you like. Either way, she's dead." His voice hardens. "And you two are finished here. I've already spoken with your NGO. Your passes are revoked."

Michael steps forward. "On what grounds?"

"On the grounds that I said so." MacCready stands, looming now, his badge catching the light. "I was going to have you escorted off the facility at lunch. But since you're already here..."

He gestures. The office door opens, and two ICE agents enter, broad-shouldered and stone-faced. Their sidearms gleam under the fluorescent lights.

MacCready smirks again. "No time like the present."

The agents step forward, flanking Michael and Mayu. Cold hands close on their arms.

TWENTY-THREE

THE ROAD into Juárez feels like a slow descent into hell. The Chevrolet step van rattles across cracked asphalt, suspension growling under the weight of its armor, desert wind scraping grit across the windshield.

The city skyline rises in jagged shapes—half-built towers beside crumbling concrete husks, billboards peeling under the sun, neon beer signs flickering even in daylight. Smoke coils from a trash fire burning away on the hard shoulder.

Grim history rides shotgun. Juárez—the city that became shorthand for murder. In the nineties, it was maquila girls found dead in the desert. Later, cartel wars turned the streets into battlefields, soldiers against sicarios, the morgues overflowing. It was called the most dangerous city in the world. The government swore it was cleaned up. But everyone who drives these roads knows better.

They don't get far inside the coiling roads of Juárez before the first reminder. A crowd of uniforms swarms a sidewalk cordoned with yellow tape. Behind it, bodies lie dumped like garbage bags, hands bound behind their backs, each with a single bullet hole in the head. A chalk-white police truck idles, lights pulsing, officers standing around smoking, their indifference louder than sirens.

Deacon watches through the passenger window. "Welcome to Juárez," he mutters.

Peter says nothing.

The van grinds on, the radio crackling in the silence. A local anchor reports in flat tones: a convoy of migrants gone missing in Sonora. Several Americans among them. No trace found.

Peter's hands tighten on the wheel.

The streets narrow, twisting deeper into the city's guts. Bars with iron grates, shuttered tiendas, stray dogs darting through trash piles. Every second corner feels like an ambush waiting to happen.

Finally, they turn down a backstreet and roll into the mouth of an underground garage. A steel door shudders closed behind them. Inside, the light is dim, the air close with oil and dust.

Peter kills the engine. The van ticks in the silence, cooling metal echoing off concrete.

They're in.

They haul their gear up a narrow stairwell, into a windowless apartment that smells of concrete dust and bleach. Inside are steel shutters, reinforced doors, cinderblock walls. Once the gear is stowed, Peter throws the deadbolt home.

Outside, bursts of gunfire rattle across the city, echoing like fireworks. Juárez gives a whole new meaning to the term 'the city that never sleeps.'

Two hours after their arrival, twilight bleeds across the skyline. Nothing reaches inside the safehouse. Instead, it glows with the dim light of laptops and satellite uplinks. Wires snake across the floor, antennae propped in the window wells, monitors humming.

Deacon leans over a keyboard, bringing up live satellite feeds.

One of their first problems will be finding the target. Because no one knows exactly where Miguel Sanchez lays his head. Not the CIA. Not the Federales. Even the cartels only whisper it among the highest generals of the Sinaloa cartel. They say his compound has a private bullring. Prize bulls for blood sport. And a church, built for Acosta, where the Narcosatánicos practice their rites. But no coordinates. Only rumors.

Peter scans the grainy feeds. "He's a ghost who lives like a king."

"Which means we don't chase the ghost. We chase the money."

Deacon clicks through until an area of industrial buildings fills the screen—vast, rectangular, lit by floodlamps. Warehouses stretch out across the desert floor, trucks crawling in and out like worker ants. Guard towers on each corner, machine guns bristling.

Peter studies it. "Distribution?"

Deacon nods. "That's what it pretends to be. Looks like a fulfillment center—groceries, electronics, online orders. But the trucks haul more than kitchen blenders. It's a processing hub. Drugs come in raw, go out refined. People too—migrants repackaged as mules, swallowed capsules in their bellies."

The feed zooms tighter: men unloading crates under the glare of arc lamps.

Peter's jaw tightens.

"This place is our first breadcrumb," Deacon says, voice low. "We sit on it, watch who shows. Maybe they lead us to Miguel himself."

The burner phone buzzes on the desk. Deacon checks the screen, eyes narrowing.

"It's my guy," he mutters. He snaps the laptop shut and grabs his coat. "We gotta move."

TWENTY-FOUR

THE IMPERIAL COUNTY Sheriff's Office smells of burned coffee and stale air-conditioning. A row of fluorescent lights hums overhead, casting everything in a flat, jaundiced glow. Michael and Mayu sit on metal chairs in front of a desk.

Mayu doesn't bother with patience. She leans forward, both palms flat on the surface, her voice cutting.

"What is being done about the little girl?"

The detective across from her, a tired-looking man in his fifties, exhales heavily. He glances at the paperwork scattered in front of him as if the answers might appear there.

"We've reviewed the hospital grounds. There's no CCTV covering the dumpster area—and the rest is fried. Can't make nothin' out. No eyewitness accounts either. At this stage..." He hesitates, then adds blandly, "We're not even sure how the body got there."

"She didn't put herself in that dumpster," Mayu snaps. "Somebody killed her."

Michael sits back, jaw tight, watching as the detective shifts uncomfortably in his seat.

"Look, miss," the detective says, rubbing his temples, "we're handling it. But without footage or witnesses, we don't have much to go on."

"Have you looked into cartel affiliates?" Mayu fires back. "You know they're using kids. You know they're running something through this town. What about the rumors we've heard about there being a tunnel?"

The word hangs in the air like a gunshot. At the back of the room, a young deputy pauses mid-conversation with a colleague, his head turning toward her. His eyes narrow, listening.

The detective shakes his head. "I can't discuss an ongoing investigation. That's procedure."

"Procedure?" Mayu's voice is sharp with contempt. "A child was butchered. A woman is dead. And your procedure is to sit here and shuffle papers while bodies pile up?"

The detective bristles. "That's enough. You may get away with speaking to the authorities like that up in New York. But down here, you show some respect. Now if you'll excuse me, I've got a job to do."

Mayu lets out a bitter laugh. "Yeah. Looks like it."

Michael rises, taking her by the arm. "Come on," he murmurs. "There's no one who can help us here."

Out in the harsh desert sunlight, they head down the courthouse steps, both exasperated. That's when the young deputy from inside appears at their side, walking quickly to catch up. He's wiry, with sunburned skin and a buzzcut that makes him look younger than he probably is.

"You wanted to know about that little girl?" he says, voice low.

Mayu stops cold. "Yes."

"You two were the ones who brought her into the hospital, right?"

Michael studies him carefully. "Yeah. How do you know that?"

"I was there. At the hospital. My partner and I answered the call. I saw you." He glances around the parking lot, eyes twitching nervously toward the passing patrol cars. "Look... my partner and me might've found something. Something you should see."

Mayu steps closer. "What?"

The deputy's gaze flits again, like a man afraid of being overheard. "Not here. Come on."

He leads them down a side alley that reeks of hot asphalt and garbage. At the end, a cruiser waits in the shadow of a wall, its windows tinted dark. A second deputy sits in the passenger seat, short and heavyset, his bug-eyes tracking them with an unblinking stare. The engine idles, low and steady.

The first deputy pulls open the back door. "Get in."

Michael stiffens. "Why?"

"Because I need to show it to you," the deputy says evenly.

"What is it?" Michael puts to him.

"What you mentioned."

"A tunnel?"

The deputy nods. "So you gonna get in?"

The hum of the cruiser's engine fills the silence. Mayu glances at Michael, uncertainty written across her face. Michael studies the deputy—his eyes, his stance, the way his hand rests just close enough to the butt of his holster.

Neither of them moves at first. Then Michael exhales slowly and nods once. "All right."

He gestures for Mayu to follow, and together they slide into the back seat. The door shuts behind them with a heavy, final thud.

TWENTY-FIVE

IN JUÁREZ, the black Chevrolet step van noses down a ramp into the bowels of an underground parking lot. The place stinks of oil and damp concrete. Fluorescent bulbs hang dead, leaving most of the level drowned in shadows.

At the far end, a pair of headlights blink twice. A signal.

Deacon kills the engine and rolls to a stop beside an SUV. Both vehicles sit there for a moment, engines ticking, the silence oppressive. Finally, the SUV's door opens, and a short, bald man steps out, his polished shoes clacking on the cement.

Peter slides from the passenger seat, circling around as the man wordlessly takes his place beside Deacon. Peter then slips into the rear, directly behind him.

"You alone?" Deacon asks, eyes sharp.

The man exhales through his nose, unimpressed. "What does it look like?"

"Good."

The man adjusts the mirror, catching Peter's cold gaze in it. "This your partner?"

"Yeah," Deacon says. "This is Peter."

The bald man nods once. "Hola, Peter."

Peter doesn't answer. His stare is unblinking, his silence heavier than words.

"Peter," Deacon says evenly, "this is Guilherme Hermoné. Head of the Mexican Federales task force in Sonora. He's the one who arranged the handover with Olivia."

Guilherme gives a thin smile. "I'm sorry about your girl. A terrible business."

"That's why we're here," Deacon says.

Guilherme's voice drops, almost sympathetic. "But I did warn your friend. Told her she would need more than two armed escorts. Told her this wasn't a job for tourists."

"No," Peter says flatly. "It wasn't."

A pause stretches. Tires squeak overhead on the ramps. Guilherme's hands drum nervously against the dashboard.

"So," he says carefully, "what can I do for you, old friend?"

Deacon leans back. "You tell us."

Guilherme forces a laugh. "What can I offer? Intel? Weapons? A squad of my men? It's about time your agency came down here and kicked the rattlesnake. Things are worse than they've ever been."

"Yes," Deacon says. "We noticed."

The silence this time is sharper. Guilherme shifts in his seat, visibly uneasy.

Peter leans forward into the rearview's frame. His voice is a whisper of ice. "Was it you who gave her up?"

Guilherme blinks. "I'm sorry? I don't understand."

Deacon's tone hardens. "Someone gave them the route."

"What—"

Before he can finish, Peter drives a syringe into the side of his neck, Deacon clamping his arms. Guilherme thrashes once, eyes going wide, then slumps as though all his bones have been sucked out of his body.

Peter withdraws the needle, expression unchanged.

Moments later, they're stuffing the limp Federale chief into the back, duct tape rasping around his wrists and ankles. The doors slam shut with a metallic finality.

Deacon wipes his hands on his jeans. "So much for old friends."

Peter heads back toward the front of the van, voice flat. "Let's go."

TWENTY-SIX

MICHAEL LEANS against the partition in the back of the cruiser, watching the desert unspool through the glass. Heat shimmers on the horizon. He shifts uncomfortably.

"Where exactly are we going?" he asks.

The deputy at the wheel doesn't look back. "Taking you to meet someone." His voice is calm, almost too calm.

Michael narrows his eyes. "Someone who?"

From the passenger seat, the partner twists around, bug-eyed face half-lit by the dash glow. "You wanted to know about a tunnel, right?"

Michael feels Mayu's gaze slide to him. "Yeah."

"So the person we're taking you to," the partner says, smiling faintly, "he can show you where it is."

Mayu leans forward, voice tight. "And can he tell us who killed the girl?"

"Yes," the driver says simply.

"Who is he?"

The two deputies glance at each other. A grin passes between them—private, ugly. They don't answer.

The cruiser veers off the main road and onto a half-paved track, tires crunching gravel. Before long, they're weaving into a skeletal housing estate, prefab shells crouching in the heat. Torn plastic flaps in the hot wind, snapping like gunfire. Window frames gape like eyeless sockets. The place looks abandoned, construction frozen halfway through, as if the money or the will to finish it had simply bled out.

But there is some life in the place.

Smoke curls lazily into the sky from somewhere deeper in.

Mayu frowns. "What is this place?"

The deputy behind the wheel lets his grin spread. "You'll see soon enough."

Michael shifts, unsettled. "This is bullshit."

Mayu takes out her phone, thumb flicking across the screen.

The partner barks a sharp laugh. "Oh, I wouldn't bother if I were you."

The driver adds mockingly, "Who you gonna call? The police?"

Both chuckle—low, knowing—and Mayu's stomach twists. Her screen shows nothing. No bars. No signal.

"That's right, little lady," the driver says, eyes dark in the mirror now. "They never put up a cell tower out here."

The laughter dies. Their faces flatten into something colder.

At the end of a cul-de-sac sits a house larger than the others but just as dead-eyed. Smoke drifts from behind it, gray tendrils curling into the sky.

The cruiser rolls toward it. The garage yawns open, swallowing them. They park beside two dusty pickups, oil stains on cracked concrete. The engine idles down as the door rumbles shut behind them, cutting off the last of the sunlight.

The deputies step out in unison.

Michael tenses as he tries the door: locked tight.

"What is this?" Mayu snaps, panic rising in her voice as she rattles the handle uselessly.

Michael grips her shoulder, steady, his voice dropping to something harder, colder.

"We need to fight now."

TWENTY-SEVEN

GUILHERME HERMONÉ WAKES up with a ragged gasp, his head jerking against the duct tape that binds him to the chair. A single bulb blazes overhead, its naked light searing his eyes. The room is featureless, the walls and floor covered in clear plastic sheeting. Every sound seems to echo. He can hear his breath in his ears.

Across from him, Deacon leans in a corner, arms crossed. Peter crouches nearby, working a jury-rigged device of wires and a crank telephone box—that old prison classic: the Tucker Telephone.

"You've been busy, Guilherme," Deacon says quietly, almost kindly. "Playing both sides like a champ. Giving up names. Selling routes."

Guilherme shakes his head, sweat already slicking his brow. "That's not true. You know me, Mark. We go way back—"

Deacon cuts him off with a sharp gesture. "Don't insult me. Olivia Wren is dead because someone sold her out. Sanchez's men knew the route she'd take to the border. And we both know who lined it up for her—who gave her that route. Federales." Deacon's expression sharpens. He stabs a finger at him. "You!"

Guilherme's lips tremble. "It wasn't me. I warned them she'd need more men. I—"

Peter suddenly jams the phone wires against Guilherme's thigh. Deacon cranks once. Electricity rips through Guilherme's body. He screams, bucking against the chair, veins bulging in his neck. The sound bounces off the plastic walls.

When the current stops, Peter leans in close, his voice ice-cold. "That one was just a preview. It had an element of mercy. The next one won't."

TWENTY-EIGHT

THE DEPUTIES HAVE VANISHED into the house, leaving them alone, locked in the back of the cruiser.

Michael's hands move quickly and precisely. He flips open a battered cigarette lighter, holding the flame under the seatbelt. Acrid smoke curls up as the nylon melts, softening, thinning.

Beside him, Mayu slips her keys between her fingers, knuckles white. Her breathing is steady, controlled—waiting.

The garage door swings open again. Footsteps. Multiple.

The deputies return, flanked by a couple of cartel muscle. Jeans, cheap leather jackets, gang tattoos curling up their necks, pistols loose in their hands. They grin at the sight of Michael and Mayu boxed in.

"Get them out," the partner orders, pointing to the back.

The driver steps forward, keys jangling. He stoops, jamming one into the rear lock.

That's when he sees it—the thin wisp of smoke curling out from inside the car. His bug-eyes widen. "Hey! They're burning my fucking cruiser."

He yanks the door open.

"Get the—"

The words die in his throat.

Michael bursts out of the car, exploding like a spring. The charred belt fragment flashes in his fist, slashing upward. The jagged nylon edge cuts deep into the deputy's neck. Blood sprays. The cop staggers back, gurgling.

Michael seizes him as he slips from the car, rips the pistol from his holster, and hauls him tightly as a human shield. He brings the weapon up in one fluid motion.

Crack. The partner is hit in the chest, his body thrown against the drywall.

Crack-crack. The two cartel men crumple before their guns clear leather. Forehead and neck.

The driver is still alive, gurgling, clutching his throat. Michael doesn't slow. He shoves him down hard onto the concrete, presses the pistol to the top of his head, and fires.

Silence for a breath. Just the hot stink of cordite, smoke, and blood.

Mayu surges out beside Michael, eyes like fire. He tosses her the pistol, and she catches it without hesitation.

Then Michael straightens, calm again, eyes scanning. He goes to work, stripping spare magazines from the homeboys and the other deputy. He slings an assault rifle off one of the cartel men, the weight feeling just right in his hands.

He tosses Mayu another magazine for the Beretta. "You're gonna need it."

Shouts echo from deeper in the house—more men, more boots on tile.

Michael chambers a round with a sharp clack. His voice is ice. "Now we finish it."

TWENTY-NINE

GUILHERME'S SOBS bounce off the plastic coated walls. Sweat slicks his face, plastering his thin, black hair to his scalp. His slacks are dark at the crotch, the acrid stink of urine rising with the heat. His body jerks against the duct tape as another jolt surges through the Tucker Telephone, veins bulging in his temples, teeth clenched so hard they could shatter any second.

Then it's cut, and he flops back down into the chair.

"Talk," Deacon growls, voice flat, unrelenting.

"I—I don't know—" Guilherme stammers, choking on spit. His eyes roll back, his head lolls.

Peter crouches in close, voice cold as ice. "You gave them the route. Didn't you?"

For a moment, Guilherme shakes his head weakly, lips quivering, denial breaking down into whimpers.

Another jolt. Another crackle of electricity tearing a scream out of him. His body bows against the chair, the scream raw, animal.

Afterwards, it takes him a while to get his breath back. Then he's ready to confess.

"Okay! Okay!" he blurts out, words spilling in panic. "I told them. I gave Sanchez the route. I had to—" He swallows, trembling so hard the chair rattles under him. "But San Diego... I had nothing to do with them finding her in San Diego. That wasn't me. That came from your side. It had to."

Peter straightens and meets Deacon's eyes across the room. No words—just the flicker of recognition between two men who've heard the same thing.

Not Mexico. Not Guilherme.

The leak is coming from their side.

Guilherme slumps forward, broken, sweat and piss dripping onto the plastic sheeting. His chest heaves, shallow and ragged. "It's done... I told you what you wanted. We're finished, sí?" His eyes shine with desperate relief, clinging to the idea that the nightmare might finally be over.

Peter's silence is answer enough. Deacon's hand hovers over the switch, calm, deliberate.

"Not finished," Peter says quietly. "We're just getting started."

THIRTY

THE SHOUTS GROW LOUDER. Boots thud against plywood and half-poured concrete, the whole structure echoing like a drum.

As they step out of the garage, the first man rounds a corner too fast, pistol up. Michael cuts him down with a controlled burst, the rifle's bark thundering in the narrow hallway. The man drops, chest cratered, blood slicking the exposed floorboards.

In the deafening silence that follows, Michael tilts his head toward the ceiling.

The unmistakable pad-pad-pad of feet on bare plywood upstairs.

Mayu hears it too. They glance across the half-built space at each other. Michael flashes two fingers, then points up. She nods once.

They split. He takes the stairwell on the left. She circles around to the half-finished frame that leads to the other side.

Upstairs, dust filters down as men hurry across. Muffled voices in Spanish—tense, uncertain. One shouts: "¡Por aquí! ¡Por aquí!"

Michael moves up slowly, rifle tight against his shoulder. A figure darts past the landing. Crack. Michael drops him, body tumbling down a set of stairs.

On the opposite side, Mayu edges toward a narrow corridor. A man steps out suddenly, shotgun held low at his side. His eyes widen as he sees her.

She doesn't give him a chance to lift the weapon. Two rounds hammer into his chest. He folds against the drywall, shotgun clattering.

She scoops it up, feeling the weight, the familiar heft. Racks a shell into place.

Two more men rush her position. She ducks into an alcove as four quick rounds tear into the drywall. Cutting through the next room, she pivots and comes up behind them. The shotgun booms like thunder, shredding the first man into the wall.

The second bolts for cover—scattering behind a half-built wall. Mayu swings the barrel, follows him across it, and pulls the trigger. The shot punches straight through the drywall, blasting him off his feet on the other side. Dust and blood mist the stale air.

Silence settles. The whole house smells of cordite, plaster dust, and copper.

Breathing hard, Mayu steadies herself. The shotgun smokes in her hands. She steps over the bodies, moving back toward the stairs.

She descends, boots thudding against raw timber, shotgun angled low but ready. The central hall yawns open before her—a skeletal frame of studs and beams, plastic sheeting fluttering where windows will one day be. A single work light dangles from a cable, swaying, throwing long shadows across the unfinished floor.

She slows.

At the far end, tucked half-hidden behind a leaning sheet of drywall, is a heavy steel door. Padlocked.

Her stomach knots. She calls out low, sharp. "Michael."

He appears a moment later, rifle gripped in his hands. His eyes follow hers to the door.

"What do you think is behind it?" Mayu asks.

Michael doesn't answer.

Because whatever's behind it, they both know, might just be worse than what they've already faced.

THIRTY-ONE

THE SWITCH SLAMS DOWN.

Guilherme jerks like a puppet on a wire, a strangled howl tearing from his throat. His legs thrash, heels hammering against the plastic-coated floor. The stink of piss and sweat thickens as his body bows against the chair, veins standing out all along his neck like vines.

Deacon holds it a beat too long, then cuts the current. Guilherme sags, chest heaving, eyes glassy and wet. A line of drool dangles from his chin.

Peter crouches in close, voice low, deliberate. "You're running out of time, Guilherme. You want this to stop? You want to see your kids again?"

The man shudders, nodding weakly, tears streaking his cheeks.

"Then give us something," Deacon says, tone hard but steady. "Something real. Miguel Sanchez. Where he moves, who he talks to, how we reach him. Anything."

Peter leans even closer, his breath cold against Guilherme's ear. "You help us, maybe you walk out of here alive. Otherwise..." He lets the silence stretch, the hum of the generator filling the void.

Deacon's thumb rests on the switch again, a promise of more pain.

Guilherme whimpers, swallowing blood and spit. "I... I told you... I don't know much."

"Let's start simple," Deacon says. "Where is he? Where's Miguel Sanchez's home? Which rock is he hiding under?"

"Nobody knows," Guilherme pants. "Not even me. His compound is hidden. Only his most trusted people are allowed inside. Even the men who built it were killed so that they would never reveal its location."

Peter slams his fist into the back of Guilherme's head. "Then you're useless."

"No! No—wait—listen!" Guilherme pleads, words tumbling out fast, desperate. "There are... rumors. Whispers. I heard them. They might help you."

Deacon crouches, studying him. "This better be worth your breath."

"They say—" Guilherme splutters. "They say Miguel... he isn't alone. He has a partner. A twin."

Peter and Deacon exchange a look.

THIRTY-TWO

MAYU STUDIES THE STEEL DOOR, shotgun balanced against her hip. The padlock hangs thick and rusted.

"This could be it," she says, voice hushed. "The tunnel."

Michael nods grimly. "Or something worse."

Mayu levels the shotgun, exhales, and squeezes the trigger. The blast rips through the lock, shards of rusted metal clattering to the floor.

Smoke curls into the hallway. They exchange a glance, weapons raised, and push the door open.

A stairwell yawns before them, the concrete steps slick with damp. The smell hits first—putrid, cloying. Copper and rot mingled into something almost chemical.

They descend slowly, boots crunching grit. The stench grows thicker, becoming almost suffocating.

At the bottom, Michael finds a switch on the wall. He flicks it. Strip lights snap awake overhead, buzzing to life one by one, throwing long shadows across the cavernous basement.

Mayu freezes. "Oh... my God."

THIRTY-THREE

"A TWIN?" Deacon says, skeptical. "That's your big reveal?"

"Yes. A twin separated in childhood from Miguel and Eduardo. They were in an orphanage in Juárez. I heard that Miguel's twin was adopted by a family in America. Then, some time ago, he came back... found his brothers. Brought with him money, influence, contacts. After that, Miguel rose like no one before."

"Fairy tales," Peter mutters.

Guilherme shakes his head, frantic. "No. He's real. I heard he's high up in the US government."

"CIA?" Peter puts to him.

"Maybe. Or worse. That's how Sanchez moves product so easily. That's how he's untouchable. Not because of that fucking clown Acosta and his bitch. No. American influence."

There's a silence. Peter watches him with flat eyes, weighing every syllable.

Deacon breaks it. "How'd you find out about this twin?"

"Rumors, mostly."

Deacon rolls his eyes. "Rumors!"

"But recently I heard more."

Both men narrow their eyes at him.

"Miguel's lawyer, Ramon Martinez. He's my contact, the Sinaloa's bag man. We meet up. Sometimes he stays for a drink. He likes to talk. Last time he told me that Miguel and his twin have fallen out."

"Over what?"

"Over Acosta," Guilherme says, voice breaking. "And the witch. The kidnappings, the rituals... the twin doesn't approve. Bad for business. They're at war."

"War," Deacon repeats. "Inside the cartel."

"Yes!" Guilherme seizes on the word. "That's why it's chaos now. That's why people vanish. They're feeding the rituals, and the twin wants it stopped."

Peter tilts his head. "Then give us a name."

"I don't know it," Guilherme whimpers. "But the orphanage. Casa Bethel. That was where they were. The records—they'll have it. Public files. Look there. Please. That's all I can give you."

Silence. The only sound is Guilherme's ragged breathing.

Deacon nods slowly. "You always were a talker."

Peter tilts his head, expression unreadable. He lifts the phone wires again and presses them back against Guilherme's neck.

Guilherme thrashes in blind panic. "No! Mark, you promised—you swore..."

Deacon doesn't move to stop Peter. He just watches, jaw tight.

"Me and my partner here made a pact before we came out," he says. "We'd burn anyone who had anything to do with Olivia's death." He leans in. "If you hadn't given up her route, she would have reached the border and the backup waiting there."

Deacon looks at Peter.

"No! Mark! Please—!"

Peter cranks the handle. Hard.

The current tears through Guilherme's body. His scream rips the air raw, filling the plastic-sealed room with a sound like an animal being slaughtered. His back arches, eyes bulging, spit flying from his mouth.

Peter keeps cranking, face blank, until the screaming stops. Until the body shudders, then slumps, smoke curling faintly from the singed tape around his throat.

The silence afterward is absolute, broken only by the buzzing bulb overhead.

Deacon finally exhales. "So much for old friends."

Peter wipes his hand on the plastic and turns away, voice flat. "He sold her out. He earned it."

THIRTY-FOUR

BODIES.

Dozens, maybe a hundred. Piled like refuse, limbs tangled, some stacked in heaps near an open furnace—the source of the smoke they saw on the drive in. Plastic bags cling wetly to heads, soaked dark with blood. Bullet holes puncture the shapes beneath.

Against one wall, a line of corpses that slump on gurneys, bellies slit open. The floor glistens black.

Michael swallows hard, his jaw tightening. "Drug mules."

Mayu turns to him, horrified. "What?"

He gestures at the carved torsos, the opened guts. "They swallowed product. Cartel cut it back out. Alive, dead—doesn't matter."

Her eyes flit across the carnage. Then she stops. She steps closer.

"No..."

It is the woman with the brand. The one they'd been told hanged herself in detention. Now here, head bagged, belly cut open like all the rest.

"She didn't kill herself," Mayu whispers, shaking her head. "They dumped her down here."

Michael's face hardens. "She wasn't the only one."

He points at another body—a man whose face he knows. "I treated him for dehydration. Four days ago, at the camp."

The silence after that is unbearable. Until—

Footsteps. Above.

Michael raises a finger to his lips. He moves like a shadow, rifle raised, climbing the stairs back toward the main floor.

From the cover of the doorway, he spots them: two men creeping through the shell of the house.

"They're all dead," one of the men hisses, glancing around the blood-slick rooms. "What the fuck happened here?"

The other shrugs, nervous. "I don't know. But we need to get the hell out of here."

"I agree."

From his hidden place, Michael watches them tear out. Seconds later, an engine growls to life outside. Tires spit gravel, then fade into the desert.

Michael slips back downstairs. Mayu waits in the glow of the buzzing strips, eyes wide with dread.

He tells her in a low voice, "Those weren't cartel guys. I recognized one of them."

"Who?"

"One of MacCready's deputies. Gary Stanton."

Her face tightens. "ICE?"

He nods. The two stand in silence for a moment, the weight of it all pressing down on them.

"So now what?" Mayu finally asks. "We can't go to the police."

"I know."

"And if we stay—"

"We can't."

She looks at him, desperate. "Then what?"

Michael exhales, the weight of it all pressing in. "We call my dad."

THIRTY-FIVE

PETER DROPS the scorched wires onto the plastic, flexing his hand once as if to shake off the residue of Guilherme's death. The smell of burned hair and ozone hangs heavy in the air.

"You believe that crap about the twin?" he asks, voice low and flat.

Deacon is already wiping sweat off his brow with the back of his hand, forcing his eyes away from the sagging corpse. "Sounds a little elaborate for buying time."

Peter stares at the body. "You think it could be our mole?"

"Maybe." Deacon shrugs, but his tone is tight. "But let's stick to the initial plan for the time being. Observation." He jerks his chin toward the mess. "And cleaning."

Peter doesn't argue. He just drags a tarp across the floor and goes about his work in silence, gloves pulling tightly over his hands.

Deacon crosses into the adjoining room, sits at the workstation, and fires up the satellite feed. The monitors flicker, resolving into a high-altitude view of the desert outside Juárez.

He pans the camera across a sprawl of industrial buildings—floodlit, with trucks moving in and out. The Sinaloa cartel's massive processing hub.

It's all a vast nothingness—until something moves.

"Hey," Deacon calls, sharp. "Come here."

Peter emerges, wiping his hands on the tarp. He leans over the monitor.

A convoy of buses crawls across the sand, dust plumes trailing behind them. They swing into the fortified compound, passing through an armed checkpoint beneath looming gun towers.

Peter and Deacon watch as hundreds of people are ordered off the buses at gunpoint. Herded like cattle into a massive warehouse at the far edge of the facility. Deacon zooms in, pixels sharpening into images of men with rifles escorting lines of migrants. Even from orbit, the terror is obvious in the way the people move.

"You remember that migrant caravan they were talking about on the radio?" Deacon says grimly. "I think we just found it."

He toggles another feed. The camera catches a figure stepping down from an SUV, massive shoulders filling the frame. El Monstruo.

Peter leans closer, eyes narrowing. "That's the big guy from the video. The one leaving Olivia's safehouse."

The confirmation lands like a weight in the room.

Deacon doesn't look away from the monitor. "You think this place could lead us to Miguel Sanchez?"

Peter shakes his head slowly, gaze still locked on the feed. "It might." His voice is ice. "Only one way to find out."

THIRTY-SIX

THE PICKUP they took from the garage rattles as Michael steers it out of the cul-de-sac, tires spitting gravel and dust across the half-built estate. Mayu sits rigid in the passenger seat, shotgun resting across her knees, her face pale in the glow of the dash.

Michael glances at her, jaw tight. "We'll need to dump this truck as soon as possible. Somebody's gonna notice it missing."

She doesn't look at him. "We killed two cops, Michael."

His hands tighten on the wheel. "We killed two cartel stooges wearing badges. There's a difference."

"Doesn't matter they were cartel," she says. "On paper, we shot two deputies. That's a death sentence if anyone finds us."

The suburb of ghost houses falls away behind them, a sprawl of skeletal structures with torn plastic flapping in the night wind —like dead animal hides drying out in the desert. At the edge, Michael pulls over beside a storm drain. Without a word, they both take out their phones and hurl them down the black grate. The clatter echoes a long time.

Back in the cab, Mayu digs through her bag. She pulls out a wad of crumpled bills and counts it fast. "Three hundred, maybe three-fifty."

Michael exhales half a laugh. "That buys us a couple nights in a motel. And some food."

"We'll need more than food," she mutters.

"Yeah," he agrees. "We'll need a burner, too. Only way to call Dad."

For a long moment, neither of them speaks. The desert road stretches ahead, an endless line of darkness broken only by their headlights.

Michael takes an old dirt trail, steering them toward El Centro. The truck jolts and bumps, suspension groaning, dust roiling in the beams of light.

Mayu stares out into the desert void, voice low. "What do we do if we can't reach him?"

Michael keeps his eyes ahead. "One step at a time. Right now, we keep moving."

Neither knows what waits for them out there. Only that going back isn't an option.

It's a death sentence.

THIRTY-SEVEN

THE WAREHOUSE STINKS of diesel and sweat, the air so thick with fear it's almost liquid. Bare bulbs hang from chains, swaying in the heat, casting long shadows that jitter across the corrugated walls. Hundreds of migrants crowd together on the concrete floor, herded into ragged lines by masked gunmen with rifles slung loose but ready.

Plastic-wrapped bundles the size of cocktail sausages sit in crates. One by one, the packages are forced into trembling hands. Men, women, children are ordered to swallow, guards barking in rapid Spanish. Those who gag or hesitate are beaten with the stocks of rifles until their bodies obey.

Near the front of the line, Rosa clutches her daughter Alma tightly. The girl is barely six, her hair matted with dust from the desert, her wide eyes fixed on the men with guns. Rosa whispers in her ear, frantic comfort. "Just be brave, mi vida. Do what they say. Just be brave."

Beside them, the American volunteers huddle together, still in their faded NGO shirts from Border Aid International. They'd been handing out bottles of water in Sonora only hours before. Now their faces are ashen, their hands shaking.

Lauren, pale under the harsh light, drags trembling fingers

over the welt burned into her chest where her shirt sticks with sweat. The faint outline of a goat's head is raw against her skin. A migrant woman nearby scratches at the same brand on her forearm until it seeps. Everywhere, migrants shift and twitch, the fresh burns itching like fire, the marks seared into them a reminder of ownership.

Darius, the eldest of the volunteers, stands taller than the rest, his beard soaked with sweat. He clenches his fists, muttering under his breath.

"First they brand us like cattle. Now they force us to be mules. Enough," he growls, stepping forward. "They're children. You can't do this to children."

The guards turn, rifles snapping up like the jaws of wolves. The room stills. Darius spreads his arms, chest heaving. "Kill me, fine. But you're not gonna shove that shit into a six-year-old girl."

He steps in the way.

For a heartbeat, silence reigns. Then a pistol cracks. The round takes Darius square in the forehead. He drops like an empty suit, blood spreading across the concrete.

Alma screams. Rosa clamps a hand over her mouth, sobbing silently into her daughter's hair.

The guards drag Darius's body out by the heels, leaving a long smear of red. The migrants' eyes follow, wide and hollow, until the doors slam shut again. A command is barked. The process resumes, more brutal now—the packages are shoved into mouths, water bottles upended to force them down.

In the corner, the Americans huddle smaller, staring at the space where Darius fell. One of them whispers, almost to himself, "God help us."

Outside, the desert night closes in fast. A violet sky bleeds into black, the horizon broken by jagged silhouettes of scrub and distant ridgelines. From his prone position in the dirt, Peter barely breathes. Through the green haze of his thermal NVGs, the warehouse glows like a furnace—bodies moving inside, heat signatures clustering like trapped animals.

"Comms check." Deacon's voice comes soft through the earpiece. Calm, steady. The old soldier's cadence. "You there, Lone Wolf?"

"I am," Peter murmurs, eyes never leaving the compound. "You have eyes on me?"

"I do. Ready to proceed when you are."

Less than a mile away, Deacon sits hunched in the surveillance van, the matt black Chevrolet P30 swallowed by shadow. Before him, satellite feeds flicker in ghostly light. He sweeps the cursor wider, widening the frame. Something catches.

"I got movement," Deacon mutters. "Three SUVs approaching from the southwest." His voice tightens. "You clocking them?"

Peter slides the NVGs up and raises his thermal imaging field glasses. The desert yawns empty, then dust plumes ghost upward, headlights flickering low and fast across the scrub. He locks on to them, tracks the convoy's heat signature as it glides across the sand and straight through the compound gates.

Doors open. Figures spill out into the floodlights.

Peter exhales slowly, jaw tight. "I see them."

Javier Acosta steps into view first, his silhouette sharp even at a distance: tailored black suit, white shirt unbuttoned to the chest, the swagger of a preacher king. The floodlights catch his gold crucifix as it swings across his chest. His eyes are almost black, as black as his raven-colored hair.

Beside him floats La Bruja. Tall, lean, draped in a shawl of deep crimson that drinks the light. Her hair is jet, her face pale as bone. She glides rather than walks, her followers scuttling behind with gold-plated Uzis held across their chests like holy relics.

And then him.

El Monstruo. A hulking shadow that dwarfs them all, long, shaggy black hair gleaming in the light, muscles swelling beneath a black shirt stretched to its limit. His gait is a predator's, each step radiating brutality. Even at this distance, Peter can feel the weight of the man who murdered Olivia.

Inside the warehouse, the migrants sense it too. Their muffled whimpers reach even the walls—a rising tide of fear as the Narcosatánicos enter, gods of blood and terror come to choose their offerings.

Peter swallows, eyes hard behind the glass.

Deacon's voice cuts in, lower now: "Eyes on the devil."

Peter doesn't answer. His breath clouds faintly in the NVGs, his trigger finger twitching against an unloaded rifle. He simply stares at the trio stepping into the floodlight glow and knows with icy certainty: the night has just become sacred ground for killing.

Back inside the warehouse, the air is stifling—sweat, fear, and the sour tang of unwashed bodies. The migrants huddle shoulder to shoulder, children pressed into their mothers' skirts, men ordered forward by rifles to swallow the capsules one by one. The crinkle of plastic water bottles and the crack of fists across faces punctuate the silence.

Then the ripple begins. A shadow falling across the packed crowd.

Acosta enters first, his presence sucking the life out of the room. His black velvet suit gleams under the bare bulbs, crucifix bouncing against his chest as if mocking Christ himself. His smile is broad, practiced, the smile of a televangelist who knows damn well the devil is his business partner.

La Bruja glides behind him, crimson shawl trailing, bare feet silent against the concrete, her eyes fixed and burning. She moves like smoke, her followers scurrying in her wake, their gold-plated Uzis glinting under the electric light.

And looming at their rear is El Monstruo. His bulk casts a huge shadow over the cowering migrants. He scans the mass of bodies with the eyes of a butcher weighing meat, pausing here, lingering there, as if already choosing who will be broken first.

The crowd recoils instinctively from him, as though the devil himself moves among them. Mothers clutch children tighter. Even the guards go rigid, knuckles whitening around their weapons.

La Bruja's gaze settles on Alma.

The little girl is frozen, wide-eyed, her mother Rosa clutching her arm tightly. Alma whimpers and tries to hide, but La Bruja only smiles, kneeling so her pale face is level with the child's.

"You don't want to eat the nasty medicine?" she asks softly, voice thick with honeyed Spanish.

Alma shakes her head, tears trembling in her lashes.

La Bruja extends her hands, fingers delicate, beckoning. Rosa panics, clutching her daughter tighter. But Alma is already being drawn forward, her small body pulled like a moth toward the flame.

Then—a shift.

La Bruja's head turns. Across the crowd, the American volunteers are pressed against the wall under guard. Pale skin. Light hair. Blue eyes.

Her smile widens.

"Ah..." she purrs, rising to her full height. "Better."

She waves a languid hand, dismissing Alma as if swatting away a fly. Rosa grasps her back into her arms.

La Bruja steps toward the Americans.

Having noticed them as well, Acosta's grin grows wider, and even El Monstruo lets out a low chuckle, a sound that makes the air vibrate.

"Gringo flesh," La Bruja says in English, her accent sharp, deliberate. "One gringo is worth a hundred migrant children. Their blood sings louder. Their bones burn brighter."

La Bruja steps daintily toward them, her eyes never leaving the remaining Americans. She claps her hands once, sharp as a pistol crack. "Take them," she commands.

The followers surge forward, dragging the NGO workers into the shadows. Their shouts and screams echo as the migrants cower, heads bowed, praying to gods who have long abandoned them.

Alma buries her face in Rosa's chest, trembling. Rosa whispers to her, voice breaking. "Don't look, mi vida. Don't look."

Through the green glow of his NVGs, Peter watches the convoy form up. The warehouse doors gape wide as La Bruja steps into the open, her tall frame draped in crimson, flanked by her gold-plated Uzi carrying followers. El Monstruo lumbers just behind her, a wall of muscle and tattoos.

The NGO workers are dragged forward, shoved hard toward the Narcosatánicos' SUVs. La Bruja's lips curl into something like joy. The witch takes Keisha by the chin, studying her pale face, smiling into her green eyes.

Orders bark. The Americans are loaded at gunpoint, their wrists bound, their eyes wide with terror. The witch climbs in after them, her shawl a red slash in the night.

Other migrants are herded into vans, packed so tightly Peter can see shoulders jammed to glass. Engines cough and roar. The convoy begins to roll, dust pluming behind it in the desert wind.

Peter lowers his glasses, eyes narrowing. His voice into the comms is clipped and cold. "We need to follow them."

Deacon's voice comes back steady, almost casual. "Copy that. Return to the road. I'll pick you up."

Peter stays crouched a beat longer, watching the last taillights vanish into the horizon before turning and disappearing into the dark.

THIRTY-EIGHT

SAN DIEGO. Midnight.

The church is dark but for a handful of guttering candles throwing shadows up against the whitewashed walls. Marble saints loom in the niches, their stone eyes forever raised to heaven. A lone woman kneels at the altar rail, head bowed, whispering a prayer only she and God can hear.

She strikes a match, lights another candle, and sets it beneath a photograph propped between votive glass. A young man's face smiles back—Felix Carmichael, twenty-one, the woman's only child. The photo is flanked by wilting lilies.

Her hands tremble as she crosses herself. "Bring him back to me," she breathes. "Please."

The sound of hinges groaning cuts through the silence. The church doors ease open. She stiffens but doesn't rise until measured footsteps carry down the aisle. A familiar voice.

"Ma'am. They're here."

Senator Carmichael lifts her eyes, jaw tightening, as her personal assistant appears out of the dark. He gestures toward the narthex. Reluctantly, she snuffs her match and rises. Together, they walk out into the cool night air.

Waiting beyond the steps is a black limousine, its paint

glinting beneath the streetlight. Two figures sit inside, their silhouettes sharp against the pale leather interior.

Inside the car, Special Agents Moorling and Patrick greet her with cool nods.

Moorling speaks first, his voice as flat as paperwork. "So. We did what you asked. We gave him everything we had on Acosta."

The senator slides into the seat, adjusting her blazer, her eyes sharp and cold. "And is he what you say he is? This... Black?"

"An assassin," Moorling confirms. "Trained from the age of nine. He's a ghost in daylight. If anyone can cut through that cartel circus, it's him."

Patrick leans forward, his smile thin. "Trust us, Senator. He's a one-man army. Doesn't matter if Langley signs off or not. He'll go in."

The senator studies them, face unreadable in the dim glow of the overhead light. "Good."

Moorling clears his throat. "There's something else."

Her gaze sharpens. "Oh?"

"Yes. We've since discovered that Black's son is here. Working as a volunteer at the detention center at Otay Mesa."

For the first time, Carmichael shows a flicker of surprise. "His son?"

Patrick nods. "Kid's no lightweight, either. Pretty handy in his own way. Not agency-trained, but he doesn't need to be. Black raised him."

"We were thinking of bringing him in," Moorling says carefully.

The senator's tone cools to frost. "For what?"

Patrick doesn't hesitate. "Collateral. Something to keep Black in line, in case he decides to go off-script."

A beat of silence. Then Carmichael leans back against the leather, and a slow smile touches her lips.

"So. Finally. Someone who can kick the rattlesnake nest."

"Yes, ma'am," Moorling says. "And if anyone can get to the people who took your son, it's Peter Black."

THIRTY-NINE

THE CHEVROLET VAN grinds to a halt on a narrow dirt track, engine ticking in the mountain air. Beyond the windshield, the desert night stretches black and endless—except for one place.

On the monitors, bathed in ghostly satellite feed, the compound glows like a cancer in the wilderness. Walls stretch wide, enclosing manicured lawns and gleaming lights. Swimming pools shimmer under floodlamps. Tennis courts lie empty, painted lines glowing like burn scars. At the edge rises a massive bullring, its stone terraces a circle of shadow. And everywhere are guards with rifles slung, patrols pacing, watchtowers etched against the stars.

Deacon exhales slowly, leaning back in his chair. "The lion's den," he mutters.

Peter studies the screens without blinking. His jaw is set, his face pale in the green glow.

They watch as the convoy they've been tailing snakes through the main gates. SUVs glide across the courtyard. Doors open. Acosta steps out first, wrapped in black velvet and dark charisma. La Bruja follows, her movements flowing, her otherworldly presence enough to make the guards keep their distance. And towering behind them, El Monstruo lumbers into view, his bulk making even the gunmen shrink away.

The migrants are herded out under floodlights. Thin lines of shadows against stone.

Deacon nudges the cursor across the glowing sprawl, the camera panning slowly over terracotta rooftops and courtyards. Guards pace in their loops. Spotlights sweep. The image drifts past the swimming pools and manicured lawns until it settles on the bullring at the edge of the compound.

Within the circle of stone, figures move. At the center stands a man in a white suit, wide-brimmed hat cocked low, the posture of someone who owns everything he sees. Even from orbit, his presence is unmistakable—Miguel Sanchez. El Lobo.

He leans on the rail, watching two bulls crash horns in the sand. Men laugh nervously at his shoulder, rifles slung, eager for his approval. A plume of cigar smoke rises from his hand, curling like a banner above the goat's skull ring.

Deacon's voice drops. "There he is."

Peter doesn't answer. His eyes stay locked on the screen, jaw tightening as if he's been waiting to see this man all his life.

Deacon breaks the silence. "So what's the plan?"

Peter's eyes don't leave the screen. "You think I can get in there and take him?"

"Dead or alive?"

"Alive."

"Maybe." Deacon glances at him. "Why?"

"If we could get hold of him," Peter presses, voice quieter now, "we might finally pin down our mole. We drag Miguel out, we get the truth with him. We'll know who really sold Olivia out."

Deacon nods slowly. His gaze flicks to footage of the chapel. "Okay," he says at last, his voice low, cold. "Let's see."

The satellite camera lingers on Acosta and La Bruja disappearing into their church. The image sharpens, the resolution flickering like a bad omen.

The whole compound seems to pulse with menace, alive with watchful eyes.

Peter slips from the van and vanishes into the darkness like a man born in it—returning to it. A crepuscular creature made of the darkness itself. The desert night clings to him, the crunch of gravel underfoot dampened by discipline and years of training. Ahead, El Lobo's compound breathes light and movement. Guards patrol in twos, rifles slung loose, cigarettes glowing like fireflies. He ghosts past them, staying low, slipping between patches of shadow cast by floodlamps.

Deacon's voice murmurs in his earpiece, steady and cool. "North tower's got two on rotation. Wait until they turn."

Peter freezes against a wall. Two guards pivot lazily, chatting. Cigarette smoke drifts. Their backs turn.

"Clear," Deacon whispers.

Peter moves. Silent. A shadow swimming through a sea of shadows.

He edges along the side of a large stone building.

Movement.

At the far end, a figure emerges. El Monstruo. His bulk fills the night, shoulders hunched. In one fist, he clutches something—Olivia's rosary beads, the silver chain glinting faint in the dark. He runs them between his thick fingers, as though savoring the memory of her death.

Peter goes still, hidden in the shadows. His breathing becomes nothing. He follows the colossus across a courtyard, sticking to the edges, weaving between pools of light, close enough to hear the scrape of the big man's heavy boots.

Ahead, the church looms—whitewashed walls, candles glowing in every window. A procession moves toward it: Acosta, La Bruja, and their followers, shepherding captives. The air is alive with chanting—low voices rising and falling, carried on the desert wind.

Inside the church, the Americans are stripped down to their underwear. Their clothes are piled in a corner. Devotees smear ash and blood across their bare skin, painting crude symbols. The Americans whimper and shiver, muttering prayers under their breath.

La Bruja moves between them, her hands steady, her gaze as sharp as a knife. She chants softly, the words sliding like oil over the captives' ears. Acosta takes a blade and slices the arm of one volunteer—Martin—who cries out as his blood spills. Acosta cups it, lifts it to his lips, and drinks. The congregation erupts into a frenzy of guttural chants, stamping feet echoing off the stone walls.

Peter crouches in the dark outside, watching through a round window.

"You seeing this?" he whispers into his comms.

"I see it—too much heat in that chapel."

"They're preparing them. Sacrifice. This is no narco-theater. This is real."

"Stay sharp, Lone Wolf. Remember the mission."

Peter doesn't answer. His gaze lingers on the terrified faces of the Americans, the cold ecstasy on La Bruja's face, the blood running down Acosta's hand. He grips his rifle tighter, every instinct begging him to storm the place.

Instead, he waits. A hunter biding his time.

In the van, Deacon hunches over the satellite feed, watching Peter's heat signature creep along the edges of the compound. He glances at another monitor, adjusting the zoom on the infrared sweep. Too much activity near the chapel. Too many guns. He mutters into the mic, "Stay outside the light. I don't want you boxed in if it goes loud."

But before Peter can answer, something happens. A sharp knock rattles the van's rear door.

Deacon freezes. The external cameras should be picking up anything within twenty feet—but the monitors show only empty desert, the compound glowing in the distance.

Another knock. Softer this time. Almost polite.

Deacon unclips his pistol, easing it free. "Peter. Someone's knocking on the van."

"Repeat that," comes back through his headset.

"Someone's outside the van," Deacon whispers. "I'm going silent."

He kills the lights inside, bathing the van in darkness. He pads silently to the back door, heart steady but every nerve on alert. He edges closer, pistol raised.

The knock comes again, right in front of him now.

He yanks the door open—

A hand is already there. A pistol barrel presses cold against his temple before he can breathe.

"Easy," a voice drawls in the dark. Calm. Confident.

Inside Miguel Sanchez's compound, Peter ghosts closer to the chapel wall, low and silent. Through his NVGs, the world is pale green fire.

Movement catches his eye. At the far end of the courtyard, a knot of men approaches—the gait unmistakable. Miguel Sanchez, white suit bright even through night vision, flanked by two bodyguards in tailored black. They cut across the courtyard with the slow arrogance of men who never hurry, the chapel bells tolling faintly as they draw near.

Peter's breath stills. He tracks them through the green haze, watching as Sanchez adjusts his cufflinks, head bowed just enough to pass for reverence. The guards push open the chapel doors, and light spills onto the flagstones. Inside, Acosta is already leading chants, La Bruja's painted arms rising toward the rafters, the Americans stripped down, shivering as sigils are scrawled across their skin. One of them—Lauren—whispers prayers through broken sobs.

Peter's jaw locks. His trigger finger twitches. He's thirty yards away—he could end this, stop it before the ceremony begins.

Then, just as Miguel Sanchez is about to step inside, he hesitates. A vibration in his pocket. He pulls the phone free, frowns, and lifts it to his ear. His bodyguards hang back by the door as he peels away from the procession, irritation flickering across El Lobo's face.

"What do you mean he's missing? ... His wife called?"

He turns from the chapel lights, stepping into shadow. Alone. Exposed.

Peter glides after him, low and silent, each footfall measured, breath locked down to nothing. Miguel's voice rasps in the night, the words sharp in the stillness.

"Well, have you searched the whorehouses, Ramon? ... You've checked with everyone? ... Come on, Ramon. Guilherme Hermoné doesn't just disappear. Who the hell was he meeting?" Sanchez pauses, shoulders rigid, cigar glowing briefly as he pulls on it. His tone drops, darker. "Find out who it was—and find him. I don't care how. He must be found."

Peter inches closer, eyes fixed on the vulnerable nape of Sanchez's neck, syringe in his palm. He can smell the cologne, hear the saliva click in Miguel's throat as he speaks.

"Could it be the Federales? A move against us? ... A power grab?" Sanchez's hand clenches the phone. "That would be bad, Ramon. You understand? A vacuum in Sonora means instability. And instability costs us."

He paces farther into the shadows, unaware of the hunter at his back. Peter moves with him, no more than a breath away now, muscles ready to drive the needle home. One step, one thrust, and the empire begins to crack.

But then the voice in his ear cuts through, cold and urgent. Deacon.

"Peter. Abort. Come back."

Peter freezes. His pulse hammers. His finger flexes around the syringe.

Silence on the line for half a beat. Then Deacon again, harder, edged with iron.

"Phase three is dead. I'm serious. Turn around."

A sharp click follows, unmistakable—the hammer of a pistol.

Deacon again, tighter now, "You more than anyone should know what that was."

Then another voice takes over, smooth as cut glass.

"You do anything, Mr. Black, and your partner's brains paint the inside of this van."

Peter's hand tightens on his weapon. He holds, unmoving. From the chapel, faint chants swell, the sound of fear sharpening under ritual. The Americans. Still alive—for now.

Slowly, deliberately, Peter eases back. No words, no argument. Just the careful retreat of a man who knows the game has shifted.

When he reaches the van, rifles are already trained on him. Shapes resolve in the dark—disciplined, not cartel thugs. One man steps forward, lowering his mask.

Peter recognizes him.

Jonny Hernandez.

Hernandez grins at him, a predator's grin.

"Easy, Black. We're friends here."

Peter whispers, low and cold, "There are US citizens in there. About to be butchered."

A pause. Then the same calm voice. "I know."

"And what?"

"And we have to leave them. Because in war, there are losses on both sides. Plus—we do warn them not to come."

Peter holds Hernandez's gaze, jaw tightening, but says nothing. Slowly, deliberately, he lowers his weapon.

FORTY

EL GUSANO DRIVES the truck through the dark, hands
loose on the wheel. The road cuts through tracts of abandoned
suburbia, rows of half-built houses swallowed by dust and silence.
Two men ride in the passenger seat—young, lean, their bravado
worn thin. Every so often they steal nervous glances at him, as
though it's not the night or the job that scares them but the man
driving.

The truck growls into a cul-de-sac. At the far end sits the
house. Plastic sheeting flapping in the windows. The chimney
cold. No smoke now.

Gusano kills the engine. The men climb out with him, boots
crunching gravel. Wordless, they suit up—rubber coveralls pulled
on, hoods zipped, gas masks snapping tight with hollow breaths.
Their silence is ritual, drilled into them.

They open up the back of the truck and roll the first barrels
down off the bed.

Inside, the air still reeks—copper, char, rot beneath bleach.
Plastic sheeting hangs limp. The floor is sticky. They crack open a
barrel. The stench billows. One man turns his head, gagging
behind his mask. Gusano doesn't even blink.

They get to work using machetes. Dismemberment by

routine. Arms, legs, torsos fed into the open mouths of the barrels. Once filled, each is sealed, dragged, and heaved into the back of the truck with dull metallic booms.

Downstairs, it is worse. A basement stacked with what's left of the migrant drug mules. They muscle barrels down the narrow stairs, bones scraping against concrete as they shovel remains inside. It is mechanical. Efficient. A cleanup, not a crime.

When the last barrel is sealed and in the back of the truck, Gusano orders them back inside. They strap on backpack sprayers, fogging the walls, the floors, the banisters with ethanol. The house becomes a giant wick.

Outside, they strike the match. Flames roar through windows, greedily devouring plaster and beams, collapsing the roof in on itself. The men watch from the driveway, masks hanging loose now, their faces pale in the firelight.

Gusano's expression never shifts.

An hour later, the truck pulls into San Diego docks. Under buzzing sodium lights, cranes swing overhead. Gusano directs as the barrels are offloaded, one by one, into the yawning mouth of a shipping container. The scrape of metal on metal echoes across the pier. When the last barrel is stacked, the doors slam shut, bolted, sealed. The shipment is set for Peru.

He claps his men once on the shoulders—dismissal, not thanks. They peel off into the night. Gusano drives the truck alone to a wrecking yard. He stands smoking as the crusher folds the vehicle into a block of twisted steel, headlights blinking out like dying eyes.

A short while later, he pulls out the satellite phone and dials.

A woman answers.

"It's me," Gusano says. "Did she get to sleep okay?"

"Yes. She went out like a light."

"You read her her story?"

"Of course. Do you think she would have let me get away without it?"

A rare smile flickers across Gusano's face. "She can be persuasive."

"Just like her granddad. Are you on your way home?"

"Yes. Twenty minutes."

"Then I'll call my dad. He can come pick me up."

The line clicks dead. Gusano dials again.

"Hello?"

"It is done."

"Good. No problems?"

"No problems."

"Okay. Well, my old friend, I have another job for you."

"Cleanup?"

"You could say that. But this time, they're alive. Two targets. Male and female. I'll send you the details."

The line goes dead.

Gusano pockets the phone, lights another cigarette, and walks off, the night swallowing him whole.

As though welcoming back one of its own.

FORTY-ONE

THE DESERT NIGHT is thick with silence when Michael and Mayu roll into El Centro. They leave the pickup at the edge of a darkened street—no fingerprints, no plates, nothing they can be tied to. Michael tosses the keys into a storm drain, watching them vanish with a clink.

There's no going back to their motel in Chula Vista. No using their cash or credit cards. No traceable phones—hence why they dumped them at the estate. Even using their real names at check-in is too dangerous. They pay in cash at a roadside motor court—a faded neon VACANCY sign sputtering above the office. The clerk doesn't ask questions.

Inside, the room smells of bleach and desert dust. One bed. A single buzzing light. Curtains that don't quite close.

Michael sits on the edge, flipping open the burner phone they bought at the 7-Eleven. Dial tone, voicemail. *Hi. You've reached the voicemail of Peter Black. Leave a message after the tone...*

He ends the call with a snap, frustration hard in his jaw. "Still nothing," he says.

Mayu stands at the window, two fingers pulling down the blinds just enough to peer into the parking lot. The room they chose is at the end—only one neighbor and a concrete wall for cover. Still, it feels exposed.

"This is going to be one uneasy night, Michael," she says quietly.

Michael lays the weapons out on the bedspread. A Beretta with half a mag. A shotgun with four shells. A hunting knife. Not much. Not against what's coming. He checks the Beretta, sliding the mag back in with a click.

"Come away from the window," he says.

Mayu lets the blinds fall and joins him on the bed. For a moment, neither speaks. The hum of the air conditioner fills the silence. Michael wraps an arm around her shoulders. She leans into him, their bodies pressed close, both acutely aware of how thin the motel walls are and how close the world outside is.

For now, all they can do is hold each other and wait.

FORTY-TWO

THE CONVOY CUTS through the desert night, engines low and steady. Sand stretches endlessly in every direction, the sky a vault of stars.

Deacon leans back beside Peter, voice flat. "Hernandez and I go way back. South America, dirty wars, ops that don't make history books. He's one of those they never let come home. Too wild. Too dangerous. So they just keep him fed out here. Budget, leash, and as much desert as they can get between him and home soil."

Peter glances at Deacon. "And his men?"

"Ghosts," Deacon mutters. "Ex-cartel sicarios, old Colombian paramilitaries, a couple of FARC commanders, war veterans burned too deep. Every one of them carrying a vendetta. Hernandez gives them direction—targets to point their guns at. It's his little dirty army of ghosts."

Lights bloom on the horizon—white squares etched against the dark. A compound rises from the sand: high fences, guard towers, stark floodlights sweeping.

Peter sits forward. "You recognize it?"

"Oh yes," Deacon says grimly. "Charles Rush's place. Should've known."

The SUVs grind to a halt at the gate of the familiar compound. Armed silhouettes melt from the shadows. Charles Rush himself waits under the lights, his tan face split by a practiced smile.

"You ratted me out, Charlie," Deacon calls to him as he climbs out.

Rush shrugs. "Only to your own people, Mark. Only to your own people."

A voice cuts in, smooth but edged. "Charlie was only being a patriot."

Jonny Hernandez steps into view, flanked by his men. He's lean and dark-haired, skin weathered by sun and dust. There's something in his features—set of the jaw, shape of the eyes—that echoes the cartel men he hunts, though nothing you could point to outright. His expression is calm, but his eyes are alive with calculation.

"Now come on," he says.

They're herded inside. Rifles hang loose in every hand but never far from firing position.

Peter realizes that they're not trusted.

A warehouse door slides open with a groan. The lights slam on. As they walk inside, Hernandez moves without warning.

He grabs Deacon by the lapels and hurls him back against the wall. The crack of impact echoes.

Peter takes half a step forward, then hears it: the hard click of safeties being flipped, barrels lifting all around him. Hernandez's men don't twitch. They don't need to. They've done this before.

Peter freezes, eyes narrowing, pulse steady.

Hernandez leans in close to Deacon, voice low. "You got a lot of explaining to do, old friend." His grip tightens on Deacon's lapels, knuckles white. "Why the fuck am I only just hearing about you in my AO? Who sent you?"

Deacon stays calm, voice measured. "It's off-books."

Hernandez sneers. "They're all off-books."

"This one's buried deeper than most."

"What is this, Mark? You breeze into my desert without so much as a courtesy call, step on my operations, and expect me to smile? You should've let your old friend Jonny know he had company in his backyard."

Deacon doesn't blink. "We're here for Miguel Sanchez. Nothing else."

Hernandez studies him, eyes narrowing. "This got anything to do with the mess at the border four nights ago?"

Deacon tilts his head. "What do you know about that?"

"Two DEA escorts shot to hell moving Eduardo Sanchez. One CIA asset made it out. Olivia Wren." His voice hardens, almost mocking. "They got to her stateside. You out here looking for whoever carved her into a witch's relic?"

Deacon's silence is answer enough. Hernandez finally releases him, shoving him back against the wall and stepping away. The tension in the room slackens by a fraction, weapons dipping but not lowering.

Hernandez fishes a battered pack from his jacket and lights a cigarette. Smoke curls. "I met her, you know. Out here. Sinaloa side. I walked her into a migrant camp that doesn't exist anymore."

Peter steps forward, voice cold. "You were in contact with Olivia?"

Hernandez exhales smoke. "Escorted her in myself. Got her settled with some local traffickers. She wanted to document the camp—thousands scraping by in the dust. Then one day... it was gone. No bodies. No fight. Just clothes and shoes scattered like they'd been swallowed whole by a tornado."

Peter's jaw hardens. "And what did Olivia do?"

"She dug in. Put pressure on some cartel captains till they talked. I helped with that."

"That's how she got to Sanchez."

Hernandez shakes his head. "No. That's how she got to Acosta and his Narcosatánicos. Sanchez came later."

Deacon cuts in. "And were you still with her then?"

"No," Hernandez says evenly. "When our missions started to clash, I warned her off. Told her this was bigger than trafficking. Went deeper. Told her to go home, write her report, leave the war to me."

"And did she?"

A slow shake of the head.

Deacon leans forward. "Funny thing, Jonny. Before coming here, I read every report the Agency has on Miguel Sanchez."

"Oh?"

"And you know what I didn't find?"

"What?"

"His location."

"You wouldn't have. It's not in there."

"Right. But the second Charlie told you we were here, you knew exactly where to go."

A grin breaks across Hernandez's face.

Deacon rolls his eyes. "How long have you known?"

"Long enough."

"In all those reports—nothing. Not a whisper of a confirmed location."

"That's because I don't report to the same people you do."

"So the man at the top of the DEA's top-ten most wanted has been on your radar, and you kept it quiet? Never passed it up the chain?"

"Not your chain."

"Then whose?"

Silence. Hernandez stares through the smoke trailing from his cigarette, unblinking, the grin gone.

Peter breaks it. "Tonight, you stopped me. Why?"

Hernandez turns. "Because this country's already carved up enough. Sinaloa. CJNG. Gulf. Northeast. Even the splinter crews —Los Chapitos, Los Viagras. Miguel's got the biggest slice, sure, but it's still less than a fifth. He wants to be king, but he's not there yet. Take him out now and you don't end the war—you just kick the hive. His territory fractures, and every crew comes swarming. That's not control. That's chaos."

Deacon's brow lowers. "You're trying to start a cartel war. Aren't you?"

Hernandez's grin returns, wolfish. "It's already started. I'm just stoking the fire."

Peter's voice is iron. "And us?"

"You're here. That makes you mine."

Deacon narrows his eyes. "So what are you planning, Jonny?"

Hernandez drops his cigarette, crushing it under his boot. Then, with a smile that doesn't reach his eyes, he says, "How about I show you?"

FORTY-THREE

THE MORNING SUN cuts hard over El Centro's sprawl, washing the suburb in flat, unforgiving light. Rows of one-story houses squat in the dust, air conditioners humming, dogs barking behind chain-link fences.

El Gusano rolls slowly through the neighborhood in a nondescript sedan. He's been tracing the missing Ford since dawn, the truck that was gone from the house. He noticed immediately. Cartel vehicles never vanish without him knowing. That's why they carry trackers—so the men behind the wheels can be accounted for, like cattle.

The last ping leads him here, to a quiet street where sun-bleached flags sag from porches. And there it is—parked halfway down the block, the Ford. Left in the open like a carcass on the roadside.

He stops, eyes narrowing. Stepping out of the sedan, he scans the street. From the Ford's flank, he lifts his gaze and spots it: a porch-mounted CCTV lens fixed over a garage, with a perfect view of the whole street.

He switches the jammer on in his pocket. The air fills with a faint static hiss. Then he walks up the drive with measured steps, knocking once on the door.

A man answers. Thick arms, trucker cap, belly pushing against a faded T-shirt. His eyes flick to the badge Gusano is holding—San Diego PD.

"Morning," Gusano says in flat English. "My name is Detective Reyna. Gonna need to take a look at your security feed. Ongoing case."

The man frowns, lips pulling back. "This ain't San Diego. You got no jurisdiction here. This neighborhood ain't your business." His tone sharpens, chest puffing up with a petty defiance that has carried him through years of arguments at county fairs and HOA meetings. Sovereign citizen, Gusano thinks. The type who thinks laws bend around him.

The fake badge won't work here.

Gusano exhales quietly and slides the badge back into his jacket.

His emptied fingers close on something else.

He produces the silenced pistol and fires in one single movement. It's so smooth, the guy doesn't even flinch. The round punches through his forehead, dropping him back into his hallway with a wet crack. A scream follows—high, panicked. The wife. She freezes in the kitchen doorway, hair in curlers, spatula in hand. Gusano turns, raises, and fires again. She falls face-first on the linoleum.

He closes the door behind him, muffling the outside world. The smell of bacon clings to the air. A pan hisses on the stove. He moves into the kitchen, shuts off the burner, then checks each room in silence. Empty. Just the two occupants.

On the counter sits an iPhone. He lifts it and scans the dead man's face with practiced patience until the device unlocks. He pulls up the CCTV app, scrolling. Rewinds the night. Watches Michael and Mayu abandon the Ford pickup. They then lurch out of the frame, heading east. He switches between cameras, wondering if there might be another external camera. There is. It sits underneath the eaves at the end of the house. It captures

Michael and Mayu walking off, tracing them all the way down the block until they vanish left at the end of the street.

He opens a map on the phone, pulling up the local area, and types without hesitation. Motels. He looks for those in the direction they were going. Then he checks them. Filters by the kind of places that take cash, no ID, no questions. He jots the names into a small notebook, neat and methodical.

He wipes the phone down, then sets it back down beside the cooling bacon. Seconds later, he leaves, stepping outside into the sharp desert light, and walks back to his car.

The engine turns over smoothly. El Gusano flips open his notebook, eyes the first name on the list, and puts the car in gear.

Time to check the nearest motel.

FORTY-FOUR

MORNING BLEEDS OVER THE DESERT, turning the ridgeline a pale bone-white. The convoy of black Durangos crunches to a halt on the edge of it, dust settling in slow clouds. Men spill out—Jonny Hernandez's ghosts, scattered in formation with practiced ease. Their rifles sweep the horizon as if danger might rise out of the sand itself.

Hernandez stands at the edge, coat flapping in the wind. He raises a pair of field glasses, squints, then wordlessly hands them to Deacon.

Deacon presses the glasses to his eyes. "What am I looking for?"

"Due east," Hernandez mutters.

Deacon shifts, then takes in a sharp inhale. Below, a sprawling compound stretches across the desert floor. On first glance, it could be a military base—rows of floodlights, towers topped with heavy machine guns, patrols crisscrossing the perimeter. But the details don't fit: stacked shipping containers, armored trucks with cartel markings, the gleam of razor wire fencing meant to keep secrets in, not out.

"What the hell is that?" Deacon murmurs. "Some kind of government storage site? A federal reserve?"

Hernandez chuckles, low and dry. "Mexico doesn't have a federal reserve. That," he says, nodding toward the fortress below, "is where the cartel keeps their gold. Their lifeblood."

Deacon lowers the field glasses and turns to him. Hernandez is smiling—wolfish, thin.

"And you're planning to rob it?"

"You bet your ass I am," Hernandez says, lighting a cigarette against the wind. His eyes cut toward Peter. "And you and your quiet friend here are gonna help. You can see we'll need all the hands we can get."

Peter studies the fortress below without answering.

Deacon lets out a dry laugh. "You're not kidding. To take that place down you'd need a goddamn tank."

The cigarette dangles from Hernandez's grin. "Funny you should say that, Mark," he says dryly. "Funny you should say that."

FORTY-FIVE

IT'S a pale morning across El Centro. The motel room is heavy with sleepless hours. Mayu stands at the window, eyes rimmed red, peering through the blinds.

"I think someone's coming," she whispers.

Michael sits up, instantly alert. "Who?"

"Looks like the janitor."

Down the walkway, a hunched man in a cap and overalls pushes a squeaking trolley up to their door. He stops, sets the brake. Knocks once with the side of his fist.

"Cleaning," he calls, voice rough and flat.

"We don't need any," Mayu calls back.

The man doesn't move. "Cleaning."

Michael frowns. "We said no."

"Cleaning."

Mayu's voice softens, trying to defuse. "Please—it's okay. We'll clean the room ourselves."

Still: "Cleaning."

Mayu glances back at Michael. "Maybe he's hard of hearing."

Michael strides to the door and yanks it open. "Look, buddy—"

He freezes. The badge glints up at him.

Special Agent Moorling tilts his chin so Michael gets a clear view of his face. His other hand rests easy on the butt of his holstered pistol.

Michael's eyes dart to Mayu, then to the bathroom window. The curtain ripples in the breeze, an open escape route begging to be taken.

But a shadow shifts there first. Special Agent Patrick, leaning against the frame, gun in hand, gives Michael a wink.

"You're trapped, kid," Moorling says evenly.

Michael turns back, jaw tight.

Moorling smirks. "There any reason why local PD is crawling all over your motel room back in Chula Vista?"

Michael just stares.

"And why the two of you aren't there but hiding out here instead?"

Mayu holds her breath.

Patrick joins Moorling at the door. "We gonna do this inside or out?"

Michael backs up, lets them in.

"How'd you find us?" he asks.

Moorling shrugs. "Pretty easy when you keep trying to call your old man. We've been monitoring calls to his number since Olivia Wren went missing. You bought a burner with cash at a 7-Eleven last night. Cute idea, but the moment you dialed, the tower lit you up. You're lucky local PD doesn't have that reach." He spreads his hands. "Nevertheless, we do."

Mayu steps closer, voice sharp. "What are the police saying?"

Patrick leans against the wall, casual. "Not much. Just that a couple of their officers are missing after a run-in with two people." He raises a finger, a faint grin tugging at his mouth. "Here's the funny part—their descriptions sound a whole lot like you two."

"You've also been booted from your volunteer posts at the detention facility," Moorling adds. "Looks like you've got a real mess on your hands."

Michael and Mayu stay silent, tension humming between them.

"Cat got your tongues?" Patrick says, amused. He nods toward Michael. "Look at them. They don't know who to trust."

He steps forward and lowers his voice. "Do you know where your old man is?"

Michael shakes his head.

"Well, we do," Moorling says. "He's across the border. Neck-deep in the same shit you've been stumbling into. You wanna help him?"

Michael nods.

"Then trust us," Patrick says smoothly. "We're on the same team."

"Come with us," Moorling adds. "You've been sniffing around. That's why local PD are hot on you—this whole place is cartel-owned, both sides of the border. You're looking for a tunnel? So are we. Help us and we'll help you."

Patrick gestures to the table. "Leave the burner. It's already compromised."

Michael moves toward the door.

"Michael," Mayu says in a low voice. "How do you know we can trust them?"

He takes her hand, leans close, whispering, "I don't. But whatever it is... it's the next step."

And with that, they follow the agents out into the blazing morning.

FORTY-SIX

BACK INSIDE CHARLES RUSH'S compound, it smells of oil and iron. Fluorescents buzz overhead, throwing pale light over three hulking vehicles lined up side by side. Eight wheels apiece, armored hulls painted desert tan, each one bristling with mounted M2 heavy machine guns.

Rush lingers in the background, hands folded behind his back, a faint smile playing under his neatly trimmed beard. He watches, silent, as though this is all a showroom tour.

"Technically," Jonny Hernandez says, almost casually, as though he's giving a lecture, "they're not tanks. They're armored personnel carriers—APCs. Mexican military issue. Design's based on the old Soviet BTR-60. Tough, fast, reliable."

The insignia on their flanks gleams under the lights: *Policía Federal*. Stamped, stenciled, convincing enough to pass in the chaos of gunfire and dust.

Peter's gaze drifts to the table nearby. Stacks of body armor, helmets, and black SWAT uniforms lie in neat rows. Alongside them are crates of rifles, shotguns, and sidearms—all exact matches for the kit Mexican Federales carry.

Deacon studies it all with a slow shake of his head. "This is how you start your war, isn't it?"

Hernandez doesn't answer immediately. He just watches them, lighting a cigarette with the ease of a man who has thought this all through a hundred times before.

Blowing out smoke, he says, "The Federales have been a thorn in my side for years. Crooked, lazy, feeding intel to whoever pays best. You offing Guilherme Hermoné has actually helped because now the chicken's running around headless. The power struggle's already breaking out. Some of the officers are drifting to CJNG, others staying tied to Sinaloa. No one knows who's in charge. Everyone's jumpy."

Deacon glances at Rush, voice sharp. "You helped him get all of this, Charlie?"

Rush doesn't flinch. "I helped my country."

"Helped yourself, more like," Deacon mutters. "I guess when things go to shit even worse, your clients will be willing to pay more. Am I right?"

Rush smiles thinly. "Entrepreneurialism is the lifeblood of America, Mark."

Deacon rolls his eyes.

Hernandez flicks ash onto the concrete. "If we roll up in Federales kit, take Sinaloa's gold, and leave a trail of bodies, every side is gonna point fingers. It'll tip the balance. Blow the whole thing open."

Peter speaks for the first time, his voice flat. "All we want is the people who killed Olivia."

Hernandez looks at him—long and unreadable. Then he smiles thinly again. "Yeah. Well. This is how you get them. All of them. We're about to set the field on fire—wait for all the snakes to come crawling out. You in?"

The silence stretches. Deacon meets Peter's eyes, searching. Both men are weighed down by the inevitability of it.

Finally, Peter gives a slow nod. Deacon mirrors it. They both turn back to Hernandez.

"Okay," Peter says. "We're in."

Hernandez's smile widens as though it has been inevitable all along.

FORTY-SEVEN

IN HIS CRAMPED office at the far end of the El Centro motel, the clerk curses under his breath as he smacks the side of the console. The security monitors have suddenly begun to flicker, lines of static rippling across their black-and-white feeds. Nothing but fuzz. Even the television on the shelf above hisses into snow.

Out in the lot, a black sedan drifts in, engine purring low.

El Gusano steps out, shutting the door softly behind him. He scans the lot without hurry, dark eyes moving over rows of faded doors. Most rooms are empty. Two glow with weak lamplight and open curtains, tenants visible inside. One at the far end sits in shadow, curtains drawn tight.

He moves toward it. Produces a thin pick. The lock yields after a click. Inside, the stale room smells of smoke and detergent. He checks the nightstand. Finds the burner phone. He exhales through his nose—an audible sigh. Nothing else. But he knows by instinct that they were here.

He leaves the room, pulls the door shut behind him, and looks up at the camera mounted over the lot, its red eye blinking.

Inside the office, the clerk is still bent over the scrambled monitors when the door creaks. He looks up, sweat dampening his shirt.

"Do those still have the recordings for the last twenty-four hours?" Gusano asks, voice flat.

The clerk frowns. "Yeah. Sure. Why?"

Gusano's hand dips into his jacket. In one solid movement, the silenced pistol appears.

Pfft.

The clerk's head jerks back, a hole neat as a penny in his forehead. He slumps sideways in his chair.

Gusano closes the blinds, locks the door, and yanks the wire from the corner camera. The hum in his jacket dies as he shuts off the jammer.

Calm, precise, he drags the body off the chair and sits down. Rewinds the footage. Watches until he sees them: the two DEA agents arriving, Michael and Mayu stepping into their car. He notes the plates.

Then he takes the satellite phone, calling a number.

"Who is it?" a voice answers.

"Me."

"Okay. Sure. What do you need?"

"You still got access to the ANPR cameras in Imperial County?"

"I do."

"El Centro?"

"Sure."

"I need you to run some plates. See if they've been spotted anywhere."

"Okay. I'll make it a priority."

"You do that. I'll call back soon."

He hangs up and moves to the clerk.

Taking the keys from the dead man's belt, he flips the sign on the door to CLOSED, steps out, and locks it. He then tosses the key down a storm drain.

The sedan slides from the lot, leaving the office dark and silent behind.

FORTY-EIGHT

THE DRIVE IS long and silent, desert sun glaring off the hood as the DEA sedan cuts through the wasteland. Dust devils spin across the flats, thorn brush clawing at the edges of the road.

Michael leans forward from the back seat, eyes narrowing. "Why am I starting to feel like we've been tricked again?"

Patrick chuckles from the passenger side. "Relax, kid. We're not setting you up. We're taking you to someone who needs your help."

"Forgive me if that doesn't fill me with confidence," Michael mutters.

The road finally dips into a canyon, where manicured palms and stucco walls rise like a mirage out of the desert. The sedan noses through a gated arch cut into the canyon rock. Beyond it sprawls a desert fortress disguised as a mansion. The house crouches low against the earth, all sharp concrete angles and wide glass panes, as if the architects carved modernity into the bones of the red stone. A swimming pool glints in the back like an oasis.

As they're walked inside, the air is cool and dry, scrubbed of the dust outside. The ceilings stretch high, polished concrete floors reflecting recessed light. The kind of house built to impress and intimidate in equal measure. A place that says power lives here, power sleeps here.

But in the living room, power looks fragile.

Candles flicker on a console table beneath a framed portrait of Felix Carmichael—smiling, hair neatly combed. The picture is ringed with flowers, fresh and wilting, replaced daily by staff. A shrine.

Senator Carmichael stands before it, head bowed. She doesn't turn right away when the agents bring Michael and Mayu in. Only when she exhales, her fingers brushing the picture frame, does she pivot toward them.

Her face is polished steel, but her eyes are rimmed red, the practiced composure of a woman who has spent years on podiums and in hearing rooms barely holding on against something raw. She carries herself with the poise of office, tailored suit immaculate even here in the half-light, but grief has carved fine lines around her mouth, softening the severity of her posture, adding a few more strands of gray to her chestnut hair.

"You're Felix Carmichael's mom," Mayu says quietly, almost reverently. "Senator Carmichael. I saw you on the news."

The woman gives the faintest smile. "Then you know what I've lost."

Michael nods. "Who doesn't? It's been all over the country. He was kidnapped in Tijuana. The news says it was Mexican cartel."

Her jaw tightens. "They don't just kill each other anymore. They hunt our children, tourists, agents. It makes no difference. Americans are commodities now. Ransoms, leverage, sacrifice. Look."

She lifts a slim black remote from the console and points it at the wall. A flat screen hums to life, spilling harsh light into the dim room.

The news is already rolling: the border crossing at San Ysidro, a cluster of microphones crowded around a group of exhausted, weeping parents. Reporters jostle for space, flashes going off. A woman clutches a photograph in both hands, raising it high so the cameras can see. Blond hair, twenty years old, smiling in her NGO T-shirt. Lauren.

Her mother's voice trembles but carries. "My daughter went to Mexico to help people. She was volunteering with a migrant caravan. She's been missing for days. Please—please—if anyone knows anything..."

Beside her, a father's voice cracks as he appeals directly to the US government: "We just want our kids home. We need help. We can't do this alone."

Senator Carmichael watches the screen in silence for a long moment, her face unreadable, then clicks the remote. The TV dies with a faint pop.

"It isn't safe anymore for Americans to go into the badlands," she says flatly. "Not for tourists. Not for idealists with bottled water. Not for children who still believe the world can be fixed."

Her eyes shift back to Felix's portrait, softening at the edges. She brushes a knuckle across the frame as if the glass were his cheek.

"Especially not for my son." She turns to face them. "I heard what they did to that little girl at the hospital dumpster... and I wonder if my son suffered the same. I pray every night that he died quickly."

Silence lingers. Michael clears his throat. "Why are we here, Senator?"

Carmichael straightens. The stateswoman returns. "Because I think you can help me."

She leads them into a study lined with photographs and maps. On the desk are glossy prints of half-built housing developments, skeletal shells of concrete and rebar stretching across desert flats.

"This looks like the place they took us yesterday," Mayu says at once.

"Yes. You must've stumbled into cartel real estate." Carmichael's voice cuts sharp. "You have to understand—this isn't America anymore. Not really. Not since the southern border became the gateway for the biggest movement of narcotics in the entire world. A trade route worth billions. Enough to own every sheriff, every border agent, every council seat from here to Texas. They wear badges with our nation's name, but their loyalty's bought."

Michael narrows his eyes. "And what about you, Senator?"

Her lips thin. "I told those bean-eating bastards where to go. For that, they took my son." Her voice breaks, just for a heartbeat. "They don't forgive women who say no. Not down there. Not here, either."

Mayu whispers, "So you're waging war."

"No, child." Carmichael's eyes glisten but harden again. "We're already at war. America just hasn't woken up yet. They talk about tariffs and trade deficits on TV? If only we could tariff cocaine, opioids, methamphetamine. That's the deficit that's killing us."

She stabs a finger at one of the photos. "These estates— they're built with cartel money, abandoned on purpose. Used for things worse than housing."

"Incinerators," Mayu says quietly.

Carmichael points at her. "Exactly. But also staging grounds. And tunnels."

Michael and Mayu exchange a glance.

The senator goes on, her voice low and dangerous. "They move most of their product through one massive tunnel. Protected at both ends. Bring that down, you don't just hurt Miguel Sanchez—you cripple his entire empire."

Michael leans forward. "So why us?"

Carmichael glances at the agents.

Moorling steps up. "Michael Black. Son of Peter Black. Went on the run with him at fourteen. Your father trained you for five years. You've got confirmed kills, even if they don't sit in official files."

He turns to Mayu. "Mayu Tanaka. Daughter of Koji Tanaka and Yūki Yokashina. Born to money and murder. Trained with weapons since you were ten. You both know how to survive in ways others can't."

Patrick folds his arms. "Which brings us to yesterday. What exactly happened with the San Diego PD?"

Michael exhales, rubbing his temple. "We tried to find out about the girl."

Carmichael's eyes snap to him. "And?"

"They stonewalled us. No cameras, no witnesses, no leads. Just shrugged us off."

Mayu adds, voice tight, "Then this deputy—he overheard us. Said he knew something. Offered to help. Took us to meet his partner. Next thing, they're driving us out into some half-built suburb in the desert."

Carmichael's expression hardens. "Cartel real estate."

Michael nods. "They drove us straight into a trap. A house with smoke pouring out of it. Cartel men waiting inside."

Patrick shifts against the wall, his jaw tight. "And?"

Michael's voice goes flat, stripped of anything but fact. "We killed them. Deputies, cartel muscle, everyone in that house. Burned our way out before they could bury us."

Mayu cuts in, softer but no less chilling. "That's when we found it. The incinerator. Piles of bodies. Drug mules with their stomachs cut open. The woman who brought us the girl—branded, executed, carved open like the rest. It was a slaughterhouse."

The room goes quiet. Even the agents glance at one another.

Carmichael's face doesn't change, but her hand clenches over Felix's photograph. "And you're both still breathing."

Michael meets her gaze, unflinching. "Barely."

"Your father must be as good as they say to have trained you so well. Do you know where he is?" Carmichael asks.

Michael shakes his head. "Special Agent Moorling here mentioned they're monitoring calls to his number. What does that mean?"

"It means your father is right now in Mexico, fighting the same rot we are. It's why you haven't been able to reach him."

"Are you in contact with my father?" Michael asks.

"Not at the moment, but I hope to reach him soon. First I need your help. Is there anything else you saw at that place yesterday?"

Michael nods. "Yes. One more thing. On our way out, two men showed up. One of them I recognized."

Patrick straightens. "Name?"

Michael nods once. "Gary Stanton. He's an ICE agent. Works at Otay Mesa. Deputy out of MacCready's outfit."

Patrick leans in. "If we help you find him, you think you can make him talk?"

Michael's face goes still. "I can try."

FORTY-NINE

THE INSIDE of the APC is a furnace of sweat and gun oil, the air heavy with the metallic taste of anticipation. Peter sits wedged between Deacon and a scarred mercenary with dead eyes, all three kitted out in black Federales body armor. The insignia stitched across their chests looks convincing enough to fool a drone flyover —or a panicked guard glimpsing them under floodlights.

The diesel engine growls beneath their boots, rattling the steel deck, a beast straining against the leash.

The comms crackle in their ears. "ETA, sixty seconds."

Nobody speaks. Hernandez's men check and re-check their weapons—chambering rounds, clicking safeties, tightening straps. Peter rests his gloved hands on his rifle, his face impassive behind the visor. His mind is cold, mechanical: entry, clear, kill, survive.

The engine surges, roaring to fever pitch as the driver puts his foot down. The APC lurches forward with bone-jarring force. Peter's shoulder slams against Deacon's. Outside, the night explodes in searchlights and klaxons as the compound looms up from the desert floor.

"Thirty seconds."

The gunner up top braces. Then the first heavy thumps of the M2 rip through the night. The weapon chatters like thunder, .50

caliber rounds tearing through the darkness, stitching glowing arcs across the walls.

Men on the gate scatter, some diving for cover, others too slow—cut down in sprays of dirt and blood. Alarms howl. Floodlights blink awake, flooding the yard in harsh white glare. Armed guards pour from the barracks, weapons barking.

The APC doesn't slow.

The driver swings hard, and instead of ramming the reinforced gates, they veer toward the weaker wall just beside it. The concrete erupts on impact, shattering in a roar of dust and debris. Masonry collapses inward, burying the guards who are crouched behind it for cover. Screams are swallowed beneath tons of rubble as the eight-wheeler claws over them, crushing bone and masonry alike.

The entire vehicle shudders as the wheels chew through fallen brick. Bullets hammer against the hull, sparking off the armor, deafening inside the cabin. The gunner swivels the turret, his tracers walking across the yard, cutting down the men firing from behind sandbags.

The other two APCs hit the compound from different angles, each crashing through with equal violence. The defenders are caught in a three-pronged assault, their defensive line shredded before it can solidify.

Inside the rattling steel beast, Hernandez barks over comms, his voice iron calm, "Here we go."

The APC screeches to a stop in the heart of the chaos. Smoke and dust curl in the floodlights. Peter feels his pulse slow, not quicken. War is the one place his body knows how to breathe. His heart had beat faster during dinner with Lena.

Hernandez turns in the dim red glow of the cabin, mask hanging around his neck, visor lowering. His grin is wolfish. "Remember—no inglés. Español only."

The rear ramp slams down. Gunfire and screams flood in like a tide.

Peter, Deacon, Hernandez, and the ghost army spill out into the inferno.

FIFTY

THE LAST ORANGE of the day fades into a gray-blue dusk over suburban San Diego.

Michael crouches behind a Ford pickup at the end of a driveway, heart thudding. He slides the tracker into place beneath the rear wheel arch, sticky magnet clicking home. He wipes his hands on his jeans, glances once up the quiet street, then jogs back to the waiting sedan.

Inside, the air is thick with coffee and the stink of old takeout containers. Moorling grips the wheel, eyes on the house. Patrick balances a laptop on his knees, the glow painting his face sharp in the dark. A black antenna box—the IMSI catcher—hums faintly beside him, its screen alive with scrolling signals.

Michael and Mayu lean forward from the back.

The front door of the house opens. A man steps out, locking up behind him.

"That him?" Moorling mutters.

Michael nods. Mayu does too. "Yeah. That's Gary. MacCready's right-hand man."

They watch him climb into the pickup. The engine growls. Gary settles in, pulls a phone from his pocket, and presses it to his ear.

Almost instantly, Patrick raises a finger. "Incoming." A number flashes across his screen, intercepted mid-call. He clicks, and MacCready's gravel-thick voice fills the sedan in tinny bursts.

"...load's ready. Pick it up at the facility. Deliver straight to our friends. No mistakes this time."

Gary's muffled voice replies, too faint to catch. Then MacCready again, harder now: "You know the drill. Don't fuck it up." The line clicks dead.

Patrick leans back, eyes flicking to Moorling. "A load?" he says slowly.

Moorling gently shakes his head. "And who the hell are their friends?"

On Patrick's laptop screen, a blinking red dot appears on the map, fixed over Gary's truck. It shifts and begins to crawl down the digital street. Patrick's mouth curls into a thin smile. "Let's go see."

Moorling eases the sedan into gear, headlights off, slipping into the current of the night.

The chase begins.

FIFTY-ONE

THE YARD HAS ERUPTED.

Gunfire rakes the night in a storm of tracers and muzzle flashes. Hernandez's ghost army fans out, disciplined in their chaos, rifles barking in controlled bursts as they sprint from cover to cover.

Peter moves like a blade through the din, snapping up his rifle and cutting down a guard scrambling toward the barracks door. He ducks behind a stack of oil drums, bullets hammering the metal.

Deacon is already moving, rolling to a knee and dropping two more with precision shots. "Flanco izquierdo!" he barks into comms.

Left flank.

The M2s above them thunder, chewing holes in guard towers. Concrete and flesh spray outward as spotters topple from their nests. The heavy guns sweep arcs across the rooftops, suppressing the cartel's counterfire.

Still, the defenders aren't amateurs. The cartel's men regroup fast, barking orders in Spanish, laying down crossfire from sandbagged positions. One of Hernandez's mercs breaks cover too early—his chest jerks, crimson sprays, as he crumples into the dirt.

"¡Tejado!" someone yells.

Roof.

Two cartel snipers crawl into position on the far barracks, rifles just dipping into line. But before they can fire, two sharp cracks roll across the desert night. The rounds hit home with surgical precision—both men's heads burst in red mist, their bodies tumbling down the tiles.

Out on the ridgeline beyond the compound, ghost army marksmen settle back behind their Barrett M82s, smoke drifting from the massive rifles. A calm voice cuts into the comms, accented but unhurried.

"El techo está desalojado."

Roof's clear.

"Copia eso," another voice answers, steady.

The ghost army pushes forward, pressure unrelenting. Grenades arc into windows—detonations rock the compound, rattling the ground under their boots. Guards scream inside.

Peter vaults a low wall, firing as he lands, his rounds smashing into a man trying to shoulder an RPG. The rocket clatters harmlessly to the ground before it can be fired.

The defenders begin to break, falling back into the main building. Hernandez doesn't let up. "¡Métanlos adentro! ¡Arrástrenlos hacia abajo!"

Drive them inside! Put them down!

They chase the retreat, boots pounding down concrete corridors slick with blood. Rooms erupt in close-quarters carnage—ricochets shriek off plaster walls, smoke burns the air. One mercenary is cut down in a doorway, his helmet rolling across the floor. Peter steps over him, face cold, rifle barking.

Inside, it becomes room-to-room slaughter. Cartel soldiers pop out from stairwells, from doorframes, from behind overturned furniture. Peter catches one through the throat, feeling the spray hot against his face as he pushes deeper. Deacon drops another with a clean double-tap, then shoves a grenade down a hall and clears it with one thunderous detonation.

Step by step, floor by floor, they herd the defenders downward, always downward.

The air grows cooler. The walls thicken, reinforced concrete leading into the underground. The last stand happens in the stairwell—two cartel gunmen laying down punishing fire, refusing to give ground. A merc takes one in the face, another in the gut. Blood soaks the steps.

Peter dives, rolls hard, and flanks low. He empties his magazine into the gunmen's legs, dropping them screaming. A mercenary finishes them with a burst to the chest. Silence falls for a breath.

They push through the final steel door.

And there it is.

A vault the size of an aircraft hangar, lit by white industrial lamps. Piles of gold bars stacked like bricks of bread. Pallets of cash wrapped in plastic, millions upon millions lining the floor. It looks obscene, like a dragon's hoard in the heart of hell.

Hernandez steps inside, smoke curling from the cigarette clenched in his teeth. His grin is feral. "You wanna hurt Miguel Sanchez?" He spreads his arms wide. "This is a damn good start."

Peter doesn't smile. He scans the shadows, rifle still tight in his grip. The war isn't over. It's only just begun.

Once the last pockets of resistance are crushed, the work begins. Flatbeds rumble in, tires squealing on the concrete. Gold is heaved onto them in backbreaking loads. Cash is tossed into crates like garbage. Hernandez's men chant and laugh, adrenaline bleeding out of them.

Peter just watches. Eyes hard. Because all this wealth, all this blood, is only fuel for the war to come.

FIFTY-TWO

THE SEDAN HUGS the dark edge of the road, headlights off as Moorling eases it to a crawl. Ahead, Gary Stanton's pickup turns through a gate, its taillights flaring red for a heartbeat before vanishing behind razor-wire fencing.

Michael presses his face to the glass. "That's the detention facility."

They park half a mile out, tucked behind a rise of scrub and dirt. The night hums with insects, the faint stink of dust and diesel carried on the wind.

Patrick pops the glovebox, retrieves a pair of night-vision field glasses, and hands them into the back. Mayu takes one, Michael the other. The lenses bloom green as they lower the windows and raise them to their eyes.

Through the scope: floodlit yard, migrants herded like cattle. Shackled wrists, hunched shoulders. Guards shove them toward the back of a waiting truck.

A figure steps into view. Square jaw, buzz cut, hands planted on his hips. MacCready. His ICE jacket gleams under the sodium lamps. He barks an order, and Stanton moves to obey, climbing up into the cab of the loaded truck.

Michael exhales sharply. "Why's MacCready handing him a truck full of migrants?"

"Good question, kid," Moorling whispers. "But the better one is—where are they taking them?"

No one answers. The only reply is the low rumble as Stanton drops the truck into gear. The chain gang of migrants lurches forward in the back, their silhouettes shivering beneath the tarpaulin.

Moorling turns the key, the sedan rumbling back to life. He kills the headlights, then rolls them forward into the dark.

Patrick snaps the laptop shut. After all, the tracker is locked to Stanton's empty Ford at the edge of the lot—not the truck.

"Stay sharp," he mutters as they ease after the departing convoy. "From here on, we don't have a safety net."

FIFTY-THREE

THE VAULT IS a cavern of wealth—stacks of bullion, bricks of cash, the air stale with the musk of paper and dust. Hernandez's ghost army grunts as they load pallets of cash and gold onto flatbeds, the metallic screech of forklifts echoing against the concrete walls as they haul it all away.

Peter drifts at the edge of it all, eyes scanning. Something gnaws at him. The scale of it, maybe. The sheer arrogance. Then, as he stares out across the vast space, he sees it—at the far end of the vault, half-buried in shadow.

A house.

Not a shack, not an office—an honest-to-God two-story house, built brick by brick inside the belly of the massive vault. Painted stucco walls, curtained windows, a tiled roof that makes no sense beneath the dripping air-conditioning pipes running overhead.

Peter slows. "What the hell is that?"

Deacon follows his gaze, muttering, "Looks like somebody decided to move in with the money."

Peter catches movement—shadows behind glass. He unslings his rifle, slides his visor down. The tension in his shoulders tightens like wire. "There's someone in there."

They move as one, crossing the vault floor in silence, keeping low behind stacks of gold bars and crates. Up close, the place is stranger—a house in the belly of a cavern, absurd and domestic, its front door standing ajar like it's been waiting for them.

Peter signals. They advance, slipping inside. The air changes immediately—cooler, faintly sharp with disinfectant. Carpets underfoot, furniture neatly arranged, a lamp glowing in the corner. It's obscene, this slice of suburbia hidden inside a tomb of billions.

They creep through the first rooms, muzzles sweeping, breaths shallow. The place is quiet—until a door bangs open.

A man bursts out, sidearm raised. Peter doesn't hesitate—two shots crack through the silence. The man jerks back, blood spattering the pale wall as he collapses.

They drag him out of sight, deeper into the house. At the end of a narrow hall, something looms: a sealed steel door, thick as a vault, set flush into the wall. Beside it, a glowing biometric palm reader hums faint green.

Peter grabs the dead man's wrist, slamming it onto the plate. The scanner blips, light turning blue. With a hydraulic hiss, the door grinds open.

"Stay sharp," Deacon mutters, covering the hallway as Peter slips through.

Inside, the room is plain. A bed. A desk. A frightened young man in his early twenties, dark hair, hollow eyes.

He jolts upright when Peter enters.

Peter frowns as recognition sinks in. "Felix? Felix Carmichael?"

The young man stares, trembling. His lips part, but before he can answer, the air shifts.

A shadow swallows the doorway to their left.

"Watch out!" Felix shouts.

Peter whips around. El Monstruo fills the frame—massive, hunched shoulders, eyes burning. Peter swings his rifle up, but the giant is already there, slamming into him with the force of a truck.

Peter smashes into the steel door, the impact slamming it shut behind him, locking Deacon out.

He rolls aside, weapon half-raised, but El Monstruo rips up a table, wood splintering as bullets chew through it. With a roar, the giant hurls it across the room. The table smashes Peter's rifle from his grip, slamming him hard against the wall.

Peter draws his pistol—but Monstruo stomps down, his boot smashing the gun aside. It skitters across the floor.

Peter's hand finds his knife. He rolls as the giant's foot slams into the wall, plaster cracking under the weight.

They face each other now—predator and predator.

Peter lowers his stance, knife in hand, eyes never leaving the monster's. His voice is low, steady. "Find somewhere to hide, kid."

Felix Carmichael nods and runs out of the room.

The fight. Is. On.

FIFTY-FOUR

THE DESERT IS black glass under the moon, broken only by the hazy glow of floodlights bleeding over the horizon. Michael, Mayu, and the two DEA agents sit in the sedan pulled onto a dirt shoulder.

Through the windshield, they stare at a looming CEMEX plant on the edge of a canyon, a skeletal sprawl of conveyors, towers, and rumbling cement trucks. The yard is alive with harsh white light and the ceaseless grind of machinery, drowning the desert night.

Only one minute ago, they watched Gary Stanton drive the truck through its gates.

Moorling's jaw is set as he grips the wheel, headlights still off. "We stay here. Too many eyes if we push closer."

Michael presses a pair of binoculars to his eyes, elbows braced against the window frame. The floodlit yard swims into focus—cement trucks rumbling in and out, workers drifting like ants between pools of glare. But the detail is useless. He lowers the glasses and flips on the thermal scope. Colored blobs writhe across the screen, indistinct and meaningless.

"From here we can't see anything," he mutters. "We need to get inside."

"Out of the question," Patrick says firmly. "That place will be full of cartel soldiers. We're not walking you into a kill zone."

Michael's hand is already on the door handle. He shoves it open. "Then I'll walk myself."

"Michael—" Mayu scrambles after him, catching up in two quick strides.

"Goddammit," Moorling mutters, slamming a palm against the steering wheel as the two of them vanish into the desert scrub. He starts to reach for his own door, ready to follow, but Patrick throws an arm out, stopping him. "See where it leads," he says, eyes never leaving the canyon lights.

Michael and Mayu crouch low, creeping along a dry drainage ditch that snakes toward the quarry at the back of the plant. Gravel crunches under their boots, every sound magnified. At the lip of the canyon, they flatten themselves against the earth and peer down.

The plant spreads before them, lit up like a stadium. They spot Gary's truck. Migrants shuffle in a line, heads down, corralled at gunpoint. The guards bark orders in Spanish, shoving them into vans. Some stumble, some cry out. A child is slapped back into place.

Michael's gut twists. "Jesus…"

Then movement near the hangar makes his blood run cold. Gary Stanton. He steps out of the shadows, ICE windbreaker zipped up, clipboard under his arm. His posture is casual, as though this is routine.

They watch as Stanton counts heads, then produces a folded sheet of paper. He hands it over to one of the cartel men like it's nothing. The cartel man scans it with his eyes, nods once, then pockets it.

"Tell me I'm not seeing this," Mayu whispers.

They can't deny it. ICE isn't just turning a blind eye—they're funneling the mules straight back into cartel hands.

"That's what the brands are for," Michael murmurs.

Mayu blinks at him. "What?"

"The brand on that woman," he says. "It marked her out. So if ICE picks them up, they know exactly which ones to return. Which ones are carrying product."

More migrants are prodded forward. The guards bark for them to move faster, kicking stragglers. Stanton doesn't even flinch. He watches like a foreman overseeing a shipment.

Then a low groan rattles the air. A freight elevator big enough for an eighteen-wheeler shudders as it rises out of the earth. Chains clank, steel grinding, dust boiling into the night sky like the breath of some buried beast.

The platform crests level with the yard. Trucks sit heavy on it, beds packed with migrants. Guards swarm the cargo, barking orders. The crowd is split in two with ruthless efficiency—mules from those who paid their crossing. Branded from unbranded.

Those with the goat mark are herded toward waiting vans, crammed shoulder to shoulder with others just like them. The unbranded are shoved onto a separate bus, faces pressed to the glass as the doors slam shut.

Michael's throat tightens. "Oh my God..."

Mayu's whisper is a tremor. "It's real. The tunnel."

The elevator platform rattles once more, beginning its slow descent back into the earth.

Michael's voice is barely audible, horror catching in it: "A highway under the desert."

FIFTY-FIVE

PETER RIPS a chair from the floor and smashes it across Monstruo's back. Wood splinters like kindling, the crack echoing off the vault walls. The giant barely flinches. He wheels around, swiping a paw the size of a sledgehammer. Peter slips under it, driving an elbow strike into Monstruo's ribs, then a sharp front kick to his knee. The big man staggers but doesn't fall.

Felix presses himself against the far wall, eyes wide, trapped between terror and disbelief, the fight having managed to find him inside the large kitchen.

Monstruo snarls, seizes the refrigerator by its handle, and tears the entire door free with a screech of metal. He heaves it like a discus. The slab smashes into Peter's chest. Air bursts from his lungs.

He twists and shoves it aside just as Monstruo barrels in.

Peter ducks. Just in time. The giant's fist punches through plaster where his head was a heartbeat ago.

Having lost his knife some time ago, Peter has to improvise. He snatches a lamp from a side table and smashes the bulb across Monstruo's face. Glass bursts, light flares, and for a split-second the giant reels, blinded. Peter doesn't waste it—he drops low, hooks Monstruo's ankle with his foot, and sweeps with a leg take-down. It takes all his strength.

The floor shakes when the big man crashes down. But Monstruo is up again almost instantly, blood streaking his cheek. He lumbers forward, a raw, bare-knuckle brawler, swinging with meat-hook fists that smash through tables and tear gouges in drywall.

Peter shifts into tighter form—boxing guard, then seamlessly into Krav Maga. He drives a hammerfist into Monstruo's temple, following with a knife-hand strike to the throat. For anyone else, it'd be enough to end the fight. Monstruo just grins through blood-streaked teeth, grabs Peter's wrist, and slams him back-first through a wooden cabinet.

Felix has to duck out of the way, crying out as splinters rain down on top of him.

Peter grits his teeth, rolls with the impact, and plants a knee into Monstruo's gut. The giant doubles slightly, only to slam Peter bodily into a table, snapping it clean in half. Furniture shatters, blocking escape paths and cutting off corners. Monstruo is herding him, using his sheer bulk like a wall of flesh.

Outside the metal door, Deacon curses under his breath. He jams the dead guard's palm onto the reader again. Nothing—red light. Monstruo must've locked it down the moment he saw Peter slip through.

Deacon tries again. Still locked. "Come on, come on," he growls, listening to the thundering fight vibrating through the steel frame.

Inside, Peter and Monstruo circle, two predators locked in a cage—one a colossus of raw muscle, the other a calculating fighter bloodied but still standing.

Monstruo feints left, then surges forward with terrifying speed for his size. Before Peter can reset his stance, the giant's hands clamp around his throat. Thick, callused fingers dig in, crushing his windpipe, lifting him clear off the ground.

Peter claws at the grip, his boots kicking against Monstruo's shins, but it's like fighting an iron vise. The giant snarls, hot breath washing over Peter's face as he squeezes harder, the edges of Peter's vision already going dark.

Felix shouts something, but it's muffled, distant. All Peter can hear is the thunder of his own heartbeat. His vision tunnels. Then he sees them—swinging against Monstruo's chest in the flicker of the overhead light: Olivia's rosary beads. Her rosary, soaked now in sweat and blood, desecrated on this monster's neck.

Through clenched teeth Peter forces out, "It was you... you butchered her?"

The words hang between them, his voice flat, American vowels cutting through the tension.

Monstruo's eyes narrow. He was under the impression from this man's uniform that he was State Police. He leans closer, nostrils flaring as though scenting prey. His voice comes out low, in Spanish.

"¿Americano?"

Peter's lips curl into something that isn't quite a smile. He forces the words out, Spanish rough but deliberate. "Sí. Estoy aquí para vengar a la mujer que asesinaste."

Yes. I'm here to avenge the woman you murdered.

For a moment there's silence. Then Monstruo grins. A cruel, wide thing that shows broken teeth.

"The American agent?" he says in English.

Peter says nothing. Just glares at him.

Monstruo smiles. Leans in. "Ahora está con nosotros."

Now she is with us.

The rosary beads swing from his neck as his grip hardens.

Something shifts in Peter. Rage stiffens into ice.

He jabs his forehead forward like a piston. The headbutt smashes into Monstruo's nose. Cartilage crunches. The giant reels, loosening his grip. Peter drops, snatching up a jagged table leg from the wreckage at his feet. He drives it into Monstruo's ribs with all his weight behind it. The nails poking out the end of the wood sink deep, piercing the thick muscle of his torso.

Monstruo bellows and rips it free, blood flowing down his side.

Peter doesn't stand his ground. He moves. Bolts down the nearest hallway, dragging his sleeve across his mouth, blood smearing. He knows brute force won't win this. Not against this beast. He needs to get him outside. He needs the help of the others.

Peter finds Felix huddling in the corner of a room, trembling. "Stay in there. Don't move," he orders, shoving the boy into a wardrobe.

But before the latch clicks, the wall explodes inward. El Monstruo bursts through the drywall in a storm of dust and plaster. His roar drowns Felix's gasp.

He seizes Peter like a doll, lifting him off the floor and charging forward into the next wall. Drywall and studs give way like tissue, the two of them crashing through one room, then another, plasterboard raining down, furniture splintering under their weight.

At last, Monstruo drives him to the ground, straddling him, massive hands clamping around Peter's throat.

The pressure is merciless. Peter thrashes, clawing at the giant's wrists, but it's like grappling with iron. His vision narrows. A high ringing fills his ears. Olivia's face flickers behind his eyes. The rosary beads sway inches above him, taunting.

Deacon's muffled curses filter through the metal door beyond the wrecked wall, the palm reader still rejecting him. He pounds uselessly at steel.

Peter's world fades to a suffocating tunnel. He feels himself sinking through the floor.

And then Monstruo shudders. His grip falters. His brows knit. Confusion flashes across his brutal features. Slowly, his hands loosen from Peter's neck.

The giant rises, staggering back, one paw reaching for the nape of his own neck.

Peter rolls to the side, gasping in precious air, just in time to see Felix Carmichael standing behind the beast, knife handle trembling in his white-knuckled grip.

The snapped-off blade juts from the base of Monstruo's skull.

The monster turns, eyes gone incandescent with rage, and lurches toward the boy. His steps thunder, hands stretching wide like the jaws of a beartrap.

"Run!" Peter barks, trying to haul himself up.

But Monstruo only makes it halfway. One step, two steps, three steps, then his knees buckle. His body heaves once, then collapses forward, crashing face-first into the dust and rubble.

Dead.

Peter staggers upright, swaying. Amid the wreckage, his eyes catch the pistol glinting in the debris.

"Now I find it," he mutters as he lurches forward.

He snatches the gun up, steps to the giant's fallen bulk, and without hesitation empties the magazine into his back and skull. Each shot slams into the silence like a hammer blow, driving the point home: stay down.

Felix clamps his hands over his ears, eyes squeezed shut, rocking against the wall.

The slide clicks empty. Peter lowers the weapon, chest heaving.

He bends, rips the rosary beads from Monstruo's thick neck, and stuffs them into his pocket.

He then staggers toward the steel panel beside the metal door, squinting at the scanner. No keypad. No lock. Just the slick plate glowing faint red. He frowns, trying to work it out.

Felix, pale in the corner, swallows hard. "His hand," he whispers. "That's how he opened it."

Peter exhales, ragged. He trudges back to Monstruo's corpse, grabs the wrist, and heaves.

Grunting, muscles screaming, he drags the giant's bulk across the wreckage, leaving a red smear in his wake.

Lifting the arm up, he plants the hand on the scanner plate.

Deacon yells beyond the door, voice muffled by steel and concrete. "Talk to me, Black! What's going on? Say something!"

"Give me a minute," Peter calls through the door.

The plate flashes green with a hard, clinical beep. Peter hears the lock release inside the mechanism—a metallic click, then a grinding that starts soft and climbs into a full-throated groan as the door's deadbolts slide free.

"What was he doing here anyway?" Peter mutters as they wait for the locks to disengage.

"He came to get me," Felix replies sheepishly. "Got here just before you."

"Where was he going to take you?"

"I don't know."

Peter thinks he does. Thinks he knows where they were heading.

Acosta.

At last, the door grinds open, and Deacon nearly barrels through, gun raised—then freezes at the sight inside. His gaze flicks from the wrecked room, to Peter's blood-streaked face, to the dead giant, to Felix Carmichael, trembling in the corner.

"Is that...?"

Peter nods once, curt. "Yeah. They've been keeping more than gold down here."

FIFTY-SIX

THE DESERT NIGHT is still but for the rumble of trucks and the throb of machinery from the CEMEX plant.

Michael and Mayu break from the drainage ditch, breath ragged, legs heavy. Ahead, the DEA sedan is a dark shape against the canyon rim. Moorling and Patrick step out as they emerge from shadow.

"You two could've gotten yourselves killed," Moorling snaps, jaw clenched.

Michael blurts out, chest heaving, "We found it. We found the tunnel."

Moorling's eyes brighten. "You found—"

His skull bursts forward as a suppressed round punches through the back of his head. His body jerks, then crumples.

Muzzle flashes strobe the desert black.

Michael and Mayu hit the dirt as rounds hiss overhead. Suppressed, surgical, untraceable.

Patrick dives for cover, pistol out. He barely clears the door when the fire finds him—cheek, shoulder, chest. He jerks like a puppet, collapsing in a spray of grit and blood.

Michael makes out the faint tap of a falling magazine hitting the dirt. He grabs Mayu, dragging her into the scrub before the next one is snapped in. Bullets snap and whip around them. One grazes his leg, fire ripping across his thigh, but he keeps moving.

They tumble into a dry gully, skidding down sand and rock, gravel shredding palms and knees. Above them, rounds chew the rim.

The CEMEX plant looms closer as they slide down, a hulking fortress of concrete and light. Floodlamps bleach the dust pale. Cement trucks thunder past like mechanical beasts.

Michael and Mayu keep low, pressing into the ditch that snakes along the perimeter fence. The chain-link above rattles faintly with the vibration of trucks passing through the gates.

"Stay tight," Michael whispers, half dragging Mayu along. They crawl in the narrow gully, shoulders brushing rusted tin cans and broken bottles tossed down by workers. Every so often, headlights sweep the fence line, but the ditch holds them in shadow.

They reach the main gate. A flatbed truck idles there as it waits to be waved in. Guards in reflective vests mill around, clipboards in hand, pistols holstered. Michael doesn't hesitate. He nods once, then hauls Mayu forward.

The two of them slither under the truck's chassis, pressing themselves flat against grease-streaked steel. Their hands find struts and pipes slick with oil. Mayu clamps her jaw shut against a grunt as the hot metal bites into her palms.

The truck lurches forward. Both of them cling harder, muscles screaming, their bodies swaying inches from the grinding wheels. The wound on Michael's leg drips blood. The driver, oblivious, rolls the truck through the gate, passing under glaring floodlights, into the yawning yard beyond.

Behind, El Gusano emerges from the desert like a phantom. Silent. Unhurried.

He holsters his pistol and walks calmly toward the gatehouse, dust swirling around his boots. He produces an ID, placing it in the guard's hand. The guard glances once—recognition, respect, fear—then waves him through.

Inside, Gusano stalks the yard with mechanical precision. No wasted movements. He studies the spatter of blood on gravel, the faint drag marks. He follows without hesitation.

Climbing onto the running board of a passing truck, he hangs one-handed from the door. His eyes rake the convoy of trucks, calculating.

He drops off beside a parked trailer, crouching low. He sees the dark patch of blood beneath the belly of the truck. The trail continues.

It leads him to the service elevator inside the canyon. He's too late. It groans as the doors close. Chains grind, gears shriek. Gusano is just in time to watch the platform sink into the earth.

Too late.

Deep below, Michael and Mayu cling to the rear axle of a descending truck, having moved to this one not long after entering the yard. The elevator screeches, cables rattling, the shaft swallowing them whole.

The platform shudders as it reaches the bottom, opening into a cavern vast as a cathedral. Rock walls curve overhead, lined with humming ventilation fans and fluorescent strips that stretch into infinity.

The truck growls forward into the tunnel's throat.

Michael and Mayu drop down, boots sinking into dust, the smell of oil and earth filling their lungs.

The tunnel stretches on and on. An artery under the desert.

Mayu whispers, voice breaking, "What now?"

Michael shakes his head, eyes wide with equal parts fear and awe. "I don't know. But we can't go back."

FIFTY-SEVEN

THE COMPOUND OUTSIDE is alive with movement. Trucks idle with engines growling, flatbeds piled with crates of cash and gold already being loaded. Hernandez's ghost army moves in tight formation—disciplined, efficient, the kind of men who've done this before. The air reeks of diesel and sweat, and somewhere in the distance, gunfire still pops from scattered resistance being mopped up.

Hernandez stands in the middle of it all, cigarette burning between his fingers, barking clipped orders. When he sees Peter emerge, he takes one long look at the blood, the split lip, the stiffness in his movements.

"Christ, Black," he says with a low chuckle. "You look like you got hit by a train."

Peter wipes blood from his mouth, his reply flat, gravel-edged. "That'd be about right."

Hernandez's eyes slide past him, fixing instantly on Felix. That half-smile flickers. "Well, well. The senator's boy."

Felix stiffens. "You... you know my mother?"

Peter studies Hernandez carefully. No surprise in the man's face. No flicker of recognition denied.

Hernandez doesn't answer Felix. He turns instead to Deacon,

voice steady. "Do you have any idea what kind of bargaining chip this is?"

Peter snaps before Deacon can. "He's not a chip. He's a kid. And I didn't drag him out of there just so you could sell him back to his mother."

Hernandez doesn't bristle, doesn't even raise his tone. His smile thins, his eyes sharpening. "Listen, Black—you're playing checkers in a chess game. That boy is leverage. With him, we can turn half of Washington against Sanchez."

The rift is instant, cold and sharp. Peter's jaw is granite. Hernandez's pragmatism is unflinching.

Felix swallows, his voice cracking. "Please... I just want to go home."

No one answers him.

Engines roar louder as the last crates of gold and bundled cash are muscled onto the waiting flatbeds. The ghost army works with mechanical efficiency—boxes slammed down, tarps thrown tight, rifles never far from hand. The vault compound reeks of smoke and cordite now, echoing with the shouts of men finishing their work.

Behind them, the dead are left sprawled where they fell, their black Federales uniforms soaked and torn. Hernandez glances once at the bodies, then flicks his cigarette into the dirt.

"Leave 'em," he orders. "It'll make it more convincing."

His men understand. Those corpses, dressed in the State Police's colors, will serve a new purpose: evidence planted in blood, a story written in uniforms.

Doors slam, engines rev. One by one, the trucks rumble to life, headlights knifing across the compound. The three APCs growl into formation, their turrets swinging as though daring anyone to give chase.

Deacon ushers Felix into the back of one vehicle, Peter climbing in after him, his movements stiff with pain. Felix huddles close, knees drawn up, eyes darting between the strange soldiers moving around them like shadows.

As the convoy rolls out, the desert swallows the compound's noise. They leave behind only the firelight of smoldering wreckage and the scattered dead.

Felix breaks the silence at last, his voice small but cutting through the engine's roar. "Who are you guys, anyway?"

Hernandez leans into the open doorframe, his face lit by the glow of his cigarette tip. He exhales, a curl of smoke vanishing into the night.

"Don't worry about it, kid."

The words hang cold as the convoy disappears into the desert, engines fading to a low growl against the vast emptiness.

FIFTY-EIGHT

THE AIR IS DAMP, humming with the grind of generators and the drone of fans. Michael and Mayu move slowly, backs to the excavated wall, their footsteps drowned out by the rattle of conveyor belts.

Ahead, the tunnel bends and widens. A line of men shuffle in single file, shirts clinging with sweat, faces hidden by dust masks. Their bellies bulge unnaturally under loose clothing. Drug mules. Guards with rifles walk the line, barking orders at the sheep to keep the rhythm.

Michael tugs Mayu into the shadow of a column. A guard's flashlight sweeps past, lingering on the wall just feet from them. They don't breathe until it moves on.

The tunnel forks. Painted arrows slash across the floor: blue pointing left, green pointing right. The blue lane groans under the weight of bricks wrapped in tape, carried by men like they're handling explosives. The green lane is worse—pallets stacked with cash in shrink-wrapped bundles, forklifts whining as they ferry the money toward a distant freight elevator. Every bundle is escorted by armed men in body armor, eyes cold and alert.

Mayu whispers, "It's like a city."

Michael can only nod. The scale of it presses down on him—

factories, payrolls, smuggling routes—all carved under the desert like a hidden country.

They slip left, hugging the edge of the green lane. A forklift lurches by so close Michael feels the heat of the engine. The driver spits, glances toward them, and keeps going, unaware.

The tunnel climbs, opening into a cavernous warehouse. Sodium lamps buzz overhead, washing the space in yellow haze. Trucks idle in rows, their trailers yawning open. Men in gloves and balaclavas heave bundles of cash inside, the sound of ratchets snapping down echoing like machine-gun fire.

A guard turns suddenly, scanning the upper walkway. Michael yanks Mayu behind a stack of pallets. The guard pauses, cigarette tip glowing red, then flicks ash and keeps walking.

Michael exhales, barely a sound. "This way."

They skirt the trucks, keeping low, shadows stretching long under the buzzing sodium lamps. Diesel fumes and the acrid bite of hot rubber cling to the air. Michael leads Mayu along the far wall until they find a service stairwell, its metal door half-hinged and dented.

Michael eases it open. The hinges groan like a warning siren, loud in the hush. He freezes. No shouts. No footsteps. Just the distant roar of forklifts and shouted orders from the warehouse floor.

"Go," he whispers.

They slip inside. The stairwell is narrow, caged in rusting steel. Concrete steps spiral upward, the walls streaked with oil and handprints. Their boots echo faintly as they climb, breath quick and ragged.

Halfway up, Mayu stumbles, catching herself on the rail. Michael glances down. Below them, through the grated stairwell gaps, the warehouse hums with activity. Cartel men haul crates of bundled cash. Others herd mules with backpacks heavy with drugs. It looks endless, a living artery pumping contraband in both directions.

They keep climbing, legs burning. The air grows hotter, the smell of dust and diesel pressed into the walls.

At the top, Michael shoulders the exit door. It resists, swollen from years of desert heat. He shoves harder. With a groan, it gives way, a rush of night air spilling in—dry, sharp, stinging with sand.

They step out onto a concrete ramp. The desert yawns before them, black and endless, the stars burning low along the horizon.

Behind them, the warehouse hums on, oblivious, its glow pooling against the night.

Mayu glances back once, eyes wide. "We should move. He'll be coming."

Michael doesn't answer. He knows she's right. Whoever is hunting them isn't gone. He's only somewhere in the dark, already closing in.

FIFTY-NINE

DAWN BLEEDS INTO THE DESERT, pale and unforgiving. The vault lies open like a wound. Cartel soldiers fan out through the wreckage, boots clanging on the steel floor, rifles slung, eyes restless.

Miguel Sanchez stands at the edge, fists clenching and unclenching. Beside him, Javier Acosta mutters Palo Mayombe prayers under his breath while La Bruja drifts around like smoke, her shawl dark against the first light.

Before them is the body of El Monstruo. The giant lies broken in a pool of shadow, his head twisted, flies already gathering at his slack mouth.

Miguel trembles. His lips move, almost too soft to hear. "I feel them here with me. Feel them seeing into me. Through my eyes."

Acosta steps close, voice firm. "I told you, Miguel. The spell I cast shields you. Your twin is blind to your fortune."

But his gaze lingers on the giant's corpse at their feet. "Still," Acosta whispers, "we are dealing with something supernatural. Only a demon could bring El Monstruo down. No man could defeat him."

Miguel's mind is elsewhere. He shakes his head, staring off into the empty vault. "We spent nine months together in our mother's womb. Fed at her breast. Side by side. That bond cannot be severed." His gaze snaps to Acosta, sharp and accusing. "Are you sure your spell is working?"

Acosta does not flinch. "I am sure. This has nothing to do with your twin. This—" He gestures at the corpses in stolen Federales uniforms. "This is the work of Guilherme Hermoné. His men died here, in your vault, stealing your money. He has not disappeared. He hides—waiting for his men to return to him with your gold."

Miguel's jaw tightens. "Are you certain?"

"I warned you about Hermoné," Acosta says. "His spirit was always clouded. Too obscure to read during the rituals."

Miguel breathes deep, forcing calm, though the tremor in his hands betrays him.

La Bruja tilts her head, eyes lingering on Felix's absence. "It is a shame the gringo boy was taken. His blood would have made a strong spell."

Miguel growls. "I told you. He wasn't for the altar. He was leverage."

"It no longer matters," La Bruja says, shrugging. "The enemy has him now."

Miguel shakes his head, muttering, "They have taken everything."

Nearby, soldiers huddle around the vault's surveillance monitors, salvaged from the wreckage. The grainy footage plays back in silence: the fake State Police storming in, gunfire crackling; Peter Black grappling with El Monstruo, steel against brute force; Felix dragged away into the dark.

Miguel's hands tighten as he watches, rage coiling. He wheels on Acosta, eyes wild. "You swore the spirits favored us. You swore your protections held. But I see now—maybe they have turned their faces. Maybe they favor my enemies instead." His glare cuts to La Bruja. "Maybe they no longer favor you."

La Bruja stiffens, shawl tightening about her shoulders, but says nothing.

Acosta raises both hands, a calm in the storm. "Miguel. Listen. You must trust in the work. The spirits are not soldiers who march in straight lines. They weave, they circle, they test our faith. Fate itself is a braid, Miguel—it tangles before it pulls taut."

Miguel's chest heaves, his rage a fire barely contained. He looks back to the screen, at the image of Peter dragging Felix away, and his lips peel back from his teeth.

"They want to test me? Then let them. I will show them what happens to those who cross me." He turns, voice thundering across the steel chamber. "I will light a fire under every bastard who ever stood at Hermoné's side. I will burn them all until he comes crawling from his hole!"

Soldiers lower their eyes. Acosta and La Bruja exchange an uneasy glance, though neither dares to speak it.

Miguel Sanchez stands in the wreck of his fortune, trembling with fury, already plotting the next bloodletting.

SIXTY

THE CONVOY ROLLS EAST, engines growling, tires grinding the sand flat. Dust trails rise behind them, curling in the pale dawn. Peter sits in the back of a dust-caked Suburban, Felix pressed nervously at his side, Deacon across from him with arms folded. Up front, Jonny Hernandez rides shotgun, window cracked, cigarette smoke curling out into the desert air.

Conversation drifts back at first—scraps of talk about fuel, checkpoints, schedules. But then Hernandez exhales smoke, glancing into the rearview. His voice drops almost lazily.

"Funny thing about leverage," he says. "It's never the gold, never the cash. It's people. People are what move the world." His eyes linger in the mirror, fixing on Felix.

Felix stiffens, his shoulders tightening as though he's just been struck. Peter catches it and leans forward. "The kid isn't leverage," he says flatly.

Hernandez smirks. "Everything's leverage, Black. Question is whether you know how to use it."

Felix looks from one man to the other, panic flickering across his face. Deacon shifts, his expression tightening, but he says nothing.

The desert stretches out wide and empty, endless scrub

broken only by the rise and fall of distant ridges. The sun lifts slowly, painting the horizon in pink and gold. The convoy veers off the dirt track, bumping into open ground where the sand stretches unbroken to the edges of sight.

Engines cut. The silence is sudden, almost crushing. Doors slam. Men spill out, rifles slung, boots crunching.

Truck doors swing open. Bundles of shrink-wrapped cash are heaved into the sand, each stack landing with a heavy thud. More follow—thud, thud, thud—until a mountain of US dollars rises from the desert floor, obscene and glittering in the dawn light.

Deacon steps closer, brows furrowed. "So what? You got choppers coming to pick it up?"

Hernandez climbs down slowly, sunglasses flashing in the morning sun. He smiles wolfishly. "Not quite."

His men haul jerry cans from the trucks, red plastic sloshing. The smell of gasoline floods the air as they splash it over the pile. The money darkens, soaking through, bills dripping until the whole mountain glistens like little green fish.

Deacon stares, disbelief raw in his voice. "You're gonna burn it all?"

Peter shakes his head, weary, already seeing where this is going. "Figures."

Hernandez doesn't bother with a speech. He just flicks his cigarette into the pile.

The ember arcs through the air.

WHOOMPH!

The mountain erupts. Flames leap high, devouring the bills in seconds. Heat lashes across the sand, smoke billowing upward like a signal fire.

It is a signal. A signal of the war to come.

Peter throws an arm across Felix's chest, pulling him back from the blaze. "Step away, kid."

Felix stares, wide-eyed, as black ash spirals into the dawn.

Hernandez stands at the fire's edge, grinning, his face painted gold in the inferno's glow. "The gold I'll keep," he says. "Easier to move, harder to trace. Arms dealers like it better."

Deacon narrows his eyes. "Does Charlie prefer it?"

Hernandez doesn't blink. "Among others."

Peter steps forward now, heat blazing across his face, eyes locked on Hernandez. "And who's this war between?"

Hernandez turns toward him, the firelight snapping in his lenses. His grin never falters.

"Chaos and order."

Peter's jaw tightens. "Chaos and order?"

Hernandez nods once.

"And which one do you fight for?" Peter asks.

Hernandez lowers his shades, eyeing Peter over the rims. "Isn't it obvious?" he says casually.

The two men hold each other's gaze, silent, the roar of the flames between them.

And Peter feels it in his gut. Hernandez isn't just reckless. He's something else. Something worse.

SIXTY-ONE

THE DESERT IS AWAKE NOW. Heat rolls off the dirt in shimmering waves, every cactus throwing a sharp shadow. Michael and Mayu trudge across the arid flats, lips cracked, shirts sticking to their backs. They glance behind them every few steps, but the horizon stays empty.

After what seems like an endless march, Michael lifts his head. A pickup sits in the distance, parked by a half-strung barbed-wire fence. A man in a straw hat works the posts, hammer ringing in the stillness.

They stagger closer. The man looks up, frowns, and walks briskly to his truck. He reaches into the bed, his hand closing on a rifle.

He doesn't aim it at them, but he does hold the weapon across his chest. On show. Ready.

Michael raises both hands. Mayu too. They keep walking, slowly, their exhaustion obvious. The man studies them, his suspicion hard. This is cartel country. He's seen neighbors vanish from fields just like this, never to return.

But as they close the distance, he sees what they are: not sicarios, not scouts. Just two desperate gringos burned raw by the sun.

He lowers the rifle to his side.

Water first. The man tosses the rifle back into the pickup bed and pulls a plastic jug from behind the cab seat. He pours a little into a dented tin cup and hands it to Mayu.

She drinks deeply, throat working, every swallow like fire and balm at once. Relief floods her body, almost painful in its intensity. She gasps and passes the cup to Michael, who drinks slower, savoring each mouthful as though it might be his last.

The man studies them in silence, his brow furrowed.

Having wet his throat, Michael is able to speak.

"¿Telefónico?"

Without another word, the man motions them into the truck.

The road winds through scrub and stone into the foothills of low mountains. At the end of a dirt track sits his home—a squat, one-story building of sun-cracked plaster and tin. The yard is bare dust, chickens scratching at nothing. A chained dog barks, straining at the links, until Mayu crouches low and murmurs to it. The dog presses its muzzle against her leg, tail wagging as her fingers graze the coarse fur.

Inside, the air is cooler, shaded. The rooms are sparse but lived-in—crosses on the walls, a clay pitcher in the corner, the faint scent of woodsmoke clinging to the rafters.

His wife appears, her face lined from sun and work, apron dusted with flour.

"I found them in the desert," the man says in Spanish, voice low but steady. "They were lost."

Her gaze lingers on Michael, then Mayu, their clothes torn, skin burned red from the sun. She exhales, shaking her head. "Lost out there, they're lucky to be alive."

"They need the telephone," he says.

"And food," she adds, already pulling a pot from the stove. "They must be hungry."

Without hesitation, she sets down tortillas, beans, and a wedge of salty cheese at the rough wooden table.

Michael and Mayu eat quickly, almost guiltily, while two

young boys sit at the end of the bench, wide-eyed, staring at these pale strangers with mouths full.

The man and his wife listen as Michael and Mayu speak. Their Spanish is steady but clipped, the story simple: lost while hiking in the desert.

The husband and wife trade looks across the table. This is not hiking country. Too close to the border, too dangerous. People who wander here don't wander back.

Still, despite her reservations, the woman softens. She nods once and gestures toward the phone on the counter—an old land-line, its cord knotted and frayed.

Michael rises, every muscle heavy, and dials. The line crackles, a low hum riding beneath the rings. Then a voice answers, clear, familiar, commanding.

"This is Senator Carmichael."

"It's me," Michael says, breathless. "We need help."

There's a pause on the line, then Carmichael's tone sharpens, though still calm. "Michael? Where are you?"

Michael grips the handset tighter, the cord coiling around his wrist. "We found the tunnel," he blurts. "Patrick and Moorling— they're dead. The man who killed them chased us down there. We made it through... we're in Mexico now." He glances at Mayu, then adds, "We're with a family. Poor people. Somewhere near El Pinacate."

Static hisses between her words. "Listen to me carefully," Carmichael says. "You cannot trust anyone there. Do you understand? That is cartel country. Every door, every pair of eyes—they could belong to them."

Michael swallows hard. "So what do we do?"

"You stay where you are," she orders. "I'll send someone to collect you. Someone I trust. Until then, you do not leave that house, no matter what."

Michael presses, voice low. "And you?"

A pause, then, "I'm on my way. I've already crossed the border. I'll meet with you soon."

The line crackles once more, then goes dead.

Michael lowers the receiver slowly, the weight of senator's words heavy in the air. Behind him, Mayu's eyes search his face, waiting for an answer.

"We wait," he says.

SIXTY-TWO

THE AIR in Charles Rush's compound feels heavy, like it's carrying weight no one wants to name. The walls are bare, the furniture functional—more a barracks than home.

Felix sits on the edge of a couch, bouncing one knee, glancing at the door as if expecting danger to come bursting in any second. Peter leans against the wall, arms crossed. Deacon paces, restless.

"When do you think I'll get to go home?" Felix asks, voice thin.

Deacon exhales. "I'm not sure, kid."

Felix looks up at him, eyes wide and tired. "I mean, I haven't even called home. Shouldn't we be calling? Just to let them know I'm okay?"

Peter pushes off the wall, comes in close to Deacon, voice low but sharp. "The kid's right. He should be on his way home."

Deacon shrugs, uneasy. "I'm sure Jonny will contact someone soon."

Peter's eyes narrow. "Then what was all that leverage crap?"

Deacon opens his mouth to answer, but the sound of a knock cuts him off.

The door swings open. Jonny Hernandez steps inside,

cigarette smoke clinging to him. A smile that doesn't reach his eyes.

"Mark," he says. "Can I have a word in the other room?"

"Sure," Deacon replies.

Peter moves to follow, but Hernandez blocks him with a hand. "In private."

The two men stare each other down for a beat. Then Deacon nods at Peter, a small signal: *Let it go.*

Peter backs off, staying with Felix as Hernandez leads Deacon out, the door clicking shut behind them.

The main operations room hums with low chatter and the clink of glass. Ghost soldiers drift about, restless, checking rifles, cleaning pistols, leaning against the walls like shadows.

Charles Rush sits alone in a corner, smile fixed, eyes glassy with satisfaction. His fingers tap a rhythm on the armrest, the kind of rhythm that comes after counting money—or weighing gold.

Hernandez strides in with Deacon at his shoulder. He doesn't waste time. "We've all been talking," he says. "The kid. He's too valuable to just let go."

Deacon's jaw tightens. "I'm already not liking where this is going."

Hernandez's smile widens, wolfish. "Resources are hard to come by out here, Mark. This war I'm waging—it needs money. And I can't be expected to steal all of it. So I had a little look into our senator."

He paces, the cigarette glowing between his fingers. "She's rich. Real rich. Comes from old money. Family runs a warehousing dynasty, now the biggest e-commerce outfit in Southern California. She's been a senator for ten years, and some say she's locked on for the primaries in three. A real shot at the White House."

Deacon watches him, expression flat. "And what? You're going to kill her son and make it look like the cartel did it?"

Hernandez stops pacing. He just stares.

Deacon shakes his head slowly. "You're insane."

"She could be a strong ally," Hernandez says, almost conversational. "But if she gets her boy back, then what? She'll walk away from the war. Thankful she's got her baby safe. And that'll be it. But"—he flicks ash onto the floor, voice sharpening—"if we place fire in her heart, if we give her something she can never forgive, then she joins the fight for good. She becomes the war."

The room goes still. Even the ghosts are listening.

Deacon shakes his head, stunned. "What is it you're actually doing out here, Jonny?"

Hernandez exhales smoke, his smile thin. "I told you. Bringing order."

Deacon steps closer. "By kidnapping kids? Burning money? This isn't order—it's lunacy."

Hernandez tilts his head, almost amused. "Think back, Mark. When we were in our twenties, running ops in South America. The Medellín cartel. We thought they were monsters, and they were. But even those butchers had a system. Bursts of violence, then ceasefires. Settlements. There were rules to the game. You could measure the blood. And know it would stop before the whole thing bled out."

He paces the room, voice sharpening. "But out here?" He gestures toward the desert beyond the walls. "Violence is the point. It doesn't end. No rhythm. No rules. Just chaos chewing through human meat."

Deacon folds his arms. "And you want the Medellín cartel back?"

"I want order back," Hernandez says. His eyes glint, fevered. "We never understood the real monster back then. It wasn't Escobar. It wasn't the sicarios. It was the market. It was demand. Dollars flooding south, insatiable. The junkie with a needle in his arm, the coke-snorting yuppie, the meth head twitching through another night. That hunger makes monsters out of everyone."

Deacon's lip curls. "So what's your fix?"

Hernandez grins. "There's an organization waiting in Colombia. Ex-Medellín, ex-FARC generals, some Brazilians, a few Bolivians. A council with government backing. They'll regulate it. Streamline it. No more butchered families on back roads. No migrant caravans dying in the dust. Just product, moving clean. Controlled."

Deacon stares at him. "You're turning into a narco yourself."

"Don't be naïve, Mark." Hernandez leans in, lowering his voice. "Unless you can get one in five Americans to quit using, this is the only hope we've got to stop all-out war."

The room hangs silent. Even the ghosts have stopped moving.

Deacon's voice cuts through the quiet. "You know about the tunnel, don't you? It's not just Sanchez's location—it's the tunnel, too. You know everything. You're not out here trying to stop it. You're trying to control it."

Hernandez doesn't blink. "And that's a bad thing?"

"I was right. You really are becoming a narco."

He chuckles. "And I was right, too. You really are naïve, Mark, if you think this can all just be stopped."

Deacon steps forward, eyes narrowing. "You're him, aren't you?"

"Who?"

"The twin."

For the first time, Hernandez's smile falters. His eyes sharpen to slits. "Whose twin?"

"Miguel Sanchez's."

Hernandez gently shakes his head. "Been listening to ghost stories, Mark? Did Guilherme Hermoné whisper that in your ear?"

The two men lock eyes, the air between them charged.

"So," Hernandez begins, voice a low growl. "Does this mean you don't agree with me using the kid?"

Deacon shakes his head, jaw tight. That's when he notices them—the three closest ghosts, stepping in, silent, hands hovering near their weapons.

Hernandez gives a small nod. The men move at once, grabbing Deacon, wrenching his arms behind him.

"Go get the kid," Hernandez orders flatly. "And take care of Black."

Six men march out. Boots echo down the hallway.

Moments later, they return. "He's gone."

"What do you mean gone?"

"Room's empty."

At that moment, boots echo down the hallway. A ghost pushes through the doorway, face pale under the sweat.

"Boss," he says, voice tight. "One of the SUVs just pulled off the lot. Headed east."

Hernandez's grin returns, slow and dangerous. He stubs out his cigarette on the table, the ember hissing.

"Well now," he murmurs, glancing back at Deacon, still pinned between two men. "Looks like your pal just left you in the lurch."

Deacon shrugs. "Looks like it."

"Where could they be going?"

"You think I'd tell you?"

"Mark!" Hernandez snaps, pulling a knife from his belt and quickly pressing it to Deacon's throat. "This isn't a game. Where are they going?"

Deacon stares back, steady. "No idea."

Before Hernandez can answer, Charles Rush saunters forward, holding up a phone with a smug grin. "Don't worry. That SUV has a tracker on it."

On the glowing screen, a small dot crawls east across a digital map.

SIXTY-THREE

THE AFTERNOON HEAT hangs heavily over the yard. The chickens peck at the dirt, their clucks carrying under the shade of a large cypress. Michael and Mayu sit on a low wall at the back of the property. The two boys kick a ball between them, laughing, their voices rising above the stillness.

Through the open windows of the house comes something else—raised voices. The man and his wife, sharp words in Spanish, the tone unmistakable.

The back door bangs open. The wife emerges, yanking her arm free from her husband's grip. She hurries toward Michael and Mayu, face pale, eyes darting.

"I am so sorry," she says in Spanish, voice breaking. "My husband has done something terrible. He has informed his bosses that you are here."

Michael frowns. "His bosses?"

"Yes. They are looking for you."

Mayu steps closer, her voice low, urgent. "Who are his bosses?"

The wife glances back at the house, then at her sons. "Narcos."

The husband bursts through the doorway behind her, fury in his eyes. "Be quiet! You'll put the children at risk!"

The couple argue, voices colliding. Michael and Mayu don't wait. While the man is turned toward his wife, Michael's hand darts out. He snatches the keys hanging from the man's belt.

"Come on," he hisses.

Michael and Mayu sprint across the yard, scattering the chickens, and dive into the pickup. Dust rises as Michael jams the key into the ignition—

"Stop!"

Michael freezes.

The husband stands at the driver's window, rifle raised, muzzle inches from Michael's head. His hands shake, but his eyes are hard.

"Please, señor," he says, his voice ragged. "They called me. Said they were looking for two people. If I protect you, my family dies. I cannot risk them."

Michael swallows, heart hammering. He looks past the rifle at the man's face—the same man who gave them water, whose children watched them eat at the table.

He answers in Spanish, steady and calm. "Señor, I'm going to assume you're the warm, good family man I've seen today. I'm betting you're not the type who paints his own truck with a stranger's brains."

And with that, Michael twists the key. The engine roars. He slams the truck into gear and drives, the rifle still aimed at his head.

The man doesn't fire. Michael was right. He isn't the type to murder an innocent stranger.

The pickup fishtails down the dirt track, tires spitting gravel. Michael's hands grip the wheel so tightly his knuckles blanch. Mayu braces against the dashboard, her breath sharp.

The road twists around a rock outcrop. Michael yanks the wheel—then slams the brakes.

A black SUV looms ahead, grill snarling, blocking the track. The two vehicles come to a sharp stop nose to nose.

Behind the windshield sits an old man, calm, unblinking.

El Gusano.

For a beat, the world holds still. Michael and Mayu lock eyes with him through the glass, and in his lined face, they see something worse than recognition—certainty.

He knows them.

Gusano's hand slips inside his jacket. Comes out with a pistol.

"Down!" Michael shouts.

The windshield erupts in spiderweb cracks. Bullets punch through the glass, whine past their heads, and hammer the upholstery. Mayu covers her face as shards rain down on top of her.

Michael slams the gearshift into reverse. The pickup lurches back, tires skidding. He doesn't see the bank until the truck drops, crunching down in a spray of dust and scrub.

The SUV surges forward, trying to pin them, but Michael spins the wheel, flooring the accelerator. The truck whips in a half-circle, sliding broadside before snapping straight. He guns it, roaring out into open desert.

The SUV follows.

Dust clouds bloom behind them, engines screaming. Michael jinks left, right, throwing the truck over ridges, through dry gullies. Gusano stays with them, unhurried, steady, like a predator running its prey to ground.

Ahead, the scrub thins. Asphalt appears, sun-cracked and lined with market stalls. Michael jerks the wheel, and the pickup bursts from the desert into the edge of a town.

People scatter in their wake. Vendors leap aside, shouting. Chickens explode into the air, feathers drifting down as tires shriek against the baked road.

Behind them, Gusano's black SUV howls into the street, locked on to their tail.

The battered pickup howls through the streets of the sun-blasted border town. The engine knocks, and the windshield is webbed with cracks and holes, but he keeps his foot welded to the floor.

Mayu clutches the dashboard, white-knuckled. "Left! Left!"

Michael jerks the wheel, missing a fruit cart by inches. A child darts across the street, and he swerves, the truck skidding so close that the mirror scrapes a wall. Sweat stings his eyes, but he doesn't blink.

Behind them, Gusano's black SUV moves with mechanical precision. He threads through obstacles without panic, eyes calm, lips almost smiling.

The satellite phone on his dash begins to chime—a childish ringtone, bright and out of place amid the wail of horns and the crack of gunfire. Gusano presses a button and answers on speaker.

"Abuelito?" a girl's voice chirps.

A smile flickers across his lips. "Hola, mi princesa. Did you do well in your play last night?"

Inside the pickup, Michael floors the accelerator. "He's still on us!" he growls.

Mayu twists around in her seat. The SUV is closer now, impossibly steady, even as Michael whips through traffic.

On the speaker, Gusano's granddaughter chatters proudly.

"Abuelito, I was the fairy queen! I had wings and everything. Everyone clapped."

Gusano guides the SUV with one hand, eyes calm as he weaves through the chaos of the chase. "Wings?" he says warmly. "Ah, mi princesa, I wish I had seen them. Did you smile, like I told you?"

"I did! Wide and proud. And mamá said I spoke so clear."

"Of course you did," he says, his voice soft. His other hand slips the pistol from his jacket. He leans out the window, the wind tearing at his face.

CRACK-CRACK-CRACK. A burst of shots slaps into the pickup's fender ahead. The truck shudders, sparks spitting from the wheel well.

There's a pause on the line. "Abuelito... what was that noise?"

Gusano pulls back inside, steering steady, voice never losing its warmth. "Ah, nothing, cariño. Just some boys with a car stereo. Playing music too loud."

On the road ahead, the battered pickup jerks away, tires screeching. Gusano smiles faintly, eyes locked on the chase even as his granddaughter continues.

"They said I can be in the Christmas play too. Will you come?"

"Of course," he murmurs, pistol still in hand. "If work allows it, I will be right there, front row."

Michael curses, jerking the wheel. Bullets shriek off brick walls, sparks snapping in the corner of Mayu's eye. She ducks low, heart hammering.

On the line, the little girl hesitates. "What was that noise?"

"Music, cariño," Gusano answers lightly, slipping the pistol back into his jacket. He guides the SUV around a panicked bus, voice never faltering. "Those pesky boys playing their rap music too loud. You know how it is."

Michael forces the pickup through a plaza, tires chewing stone. Mothers scream, children scatter. He clips a fruit stand, bananas and oranges exploding across the road. Mayu shouts, bracing herself as the truck fishtails.

Still, the SUV follows. Always steady. Always closing.

On the speaker, Gusano's granddaughter chatters proudly, her voice bright and sweet. "I wish you could have been there, abuelito!"

Michael jerks the wheel, swerving around a toppled cart. In the rearview mirror, he catches sight of Gusano, lips moving softly into the phone, eyes calm, guiding the SUV with absolute precision. The sight makes Michael's stomach knot.

"And your mamá took pictures, sí?" Gusano says gently, as though he isn't thundering through a street littered with fruit and debris. "I want to see them."

"Yes, mamá took lots of pictures," the girl's voice chirps. "She says she will send them to you."

With genuine warmth, Gusano replies, "Oh, I look forward to seeing—"

The world detonates.

A delivery van barrels out of a side street, slamming broadside into Gusano's SUV. Metal screams, glass bursts outward in a glittering rain. Both vehicles grind to a stop in a tangle of wreckage.

Michael doesn't look back. He guns the pickup, careening into an alley, Mayu pressed against the seat. They vanish into the maze of streets and out toward the desert beyond.

Pinned by the airbag, Gusano calmly retrieves the phone from the floor. Blood drips down his temple.

"Abuelito?" the girl gasps. "What was that? Are you okay?"

His voice is smooth, almost tender. "It's nothing, princesa. Just a car exhaust backfiring very loudly. Don't worry. I'm fine."

She sniffles. "You promise?"

"I promise. Now go help your mamá with breakfast. I'll call soon. I love you."

"I love you too, abuelito."

The line clicks dead.

Gusano sits still a moment. The smile fades. His eyes turn cold again.

He pushes the door open, wipes the blood from his brow, and steps out of the twisted SUV. The delivery van steams in ruin beside him. Ahead, the horizon shimmers, dust trailing faintly where the pickup has gone.

He pockets the phone. And begins walking.

SIXTY-FOUR

OMAR MANERO STEPS OUT of the Sonora State Police command center into the bright morning glare. A briefcase in one hand, his phone in the other, he pauses to check the screen before heading toward his car.

The street is alive with the bustle of workers and vendors, the air hot with diesel fumes. He adjusts his tie, distracted, already thinking about his next meeting.

That's when the van slides to the curb. Dark windows. Engine idling too long.

The side door slams open. Two men in masks leap out, fast and precise.

The first seizes him by the collar, wrenching him sideways. The second jams a pistol into the air, firing two silenced rounds. The *thup-thup* sounds wrong, soft—but it's enough. The crowd scatters, screaming, ducking for cover.

Omar's briefcase spills, papers fluttering across the sidewalk like frightened birds. He thrashes, gasping, trying to yell, but a sack drops over his head, rough cloth clamping down the light.

His cry is muffled. His knees buckle as the men drag him toward the open door. Boots pound the pavement, his heels scraping concrete, then metal. The van door slams shut behind him. He hears only the guttural growl of the engine, tires squealing as the van lurches into traffic.

The city noise fades, replaced by the pounding of his own heart inside the stifling dark.

Like so many people throughout Mexico each year, Omar Manero has been kidnapped.

———

FRANCESCO GARCÍA SITS at a café table under a faded awning, sipping bitter coffee, the morning paper spread before him. He lingers over the headlines—*Sonora State Police Chief Missing*— the smell of fresh tortillas wafting from the corner stall.

He doesn't notice the black SUV rolling to a stop across the street.

Two doors open. Sicarios step out—hard-eyed, fast-moving.

The first is on him before he can rise. A hand like a vise clamps down on his shoulder, pinning him to the chair. His coffee spills, steaming across the paper.

The second sicario smashes his head into the table. The sharp crack of bone on wood makes nearby customers flinch. Gasps ripple through the café. No one moves.

Francesco groans, stunned, blood running from his nose. The masked men haul him upright, dragging him past the frozen patrons.

One customer half rises, but a glare from the gunman keeps him rooted to his seat. The message is clear: stay quiet, stay alive.

Outside, the SUV door yanks open. Francesco is shoved inside, body crumpling against the seat. A rough sack drops over his head, plunging him into darkness.

The SUV peels away, tires squealing, leaving behind spilled coffee, a bloodied newspaper, and a café full of trembling silence.

———

Morning settles over the neighborhood, the air already warming under a pale sun. Birds chatter in the trees, a dog barks somewhere down the street. Alejandro Guitiérrez shuffles down his hallway in slippers, coffee steaming in his hand, the television murmuring from the kitchen. His wife is rinsing dishes when the front door crashes inward.

Masked men flood the house, black shapes moving fast.

She screams, a cup falling from her hands and shattering on the floor.

Alejandro freezes, stunned for half a heartbeat—then they're on him. One slams him against the wall, another clamps a hand over his mouth. His wife claws at them, shrieking like a banshee, but a rifle butt swung her way sends her sprawling.

They drag Alejandro through the doorway, his slippers skidding on the tiles. He thrashes, muffled cries spilling against the gloved hand over his face.

Outside, curtains twitch. Neighbors peer out from behind glass, faces pale, but no one dares step forward. They've seen this before.

The trunk of a waiting car yawns open. Alejandro is shoved inside, knees cracking against metal. A sack drops over his head, stealing the morning light away.

The trunk slams shut. The engine growls. Tires spit gravel as the car vanishes down the sunlit street, leaving the house in a silence broken only by the wife's sobs.

———

It is a few hours later when the sacks are torn away all at once.

Daylight stabs their eyes. The three men blink furiously, breath catching as the world comes into focus. They stand ankle-deep in dust and sand, the walls of a bullring rising high around them like an ancient coliseum.

The stench hits next—sweet and rotten, thick with flies. At their feet lie five corpses in decomposing State Police uniforms, the flesh sloughing from bone. Maggots writhe in sockets, buzzing clouds of flies lift into the air with every shift of wind.

The men recoil, gagging, clutching their bound hands to their mouths.

Above, at the rim of the ring, stands Miguel Sanchez. El Lobo. A dark silhouette against the glaring sun. Acosta and La Bruja flank him like carrion birds, Acosta's lips moving in a low prayer while La Bruja whispers to herself in the old tongue of Palo Mayombe. Soldiers line the walls, rifles angled down, waiting for a nod.

Miguel's voice carries, calm but laced with steel. "Do you recognize the uniforms?"

Omar Manero, trembling but defiant, steps forward a half pace. His voice cracks but grows stronger as he speaks.

"What is this, Miguel? Why are we here?"

His chest heaves, sweat running down his temples. He tries to hold Miguel's gaze, to sound more brave than he feels.

Miguel exhales slowly. "I won't ask again."

"This is madness!" Omar goes on. "We are servants of the state. You cannot treat us like this."

Miguel doesn't answer. He only tilts his head, the faintest gesture of disdain.

At the signal, a sicario raises his rifle. The muzzle flashes once.

The shot cracks the air. Omar screams, a raw, tearing sound as his leg buckles. He crashes to the ground, clutching his knee. Blood gushes between his fingers, soaking into the sand.

He writhes, bellowing through clenched teeth, his cries echoing around the bullring, high and desperate, carrying up to the rim where Miguel, Acosta, and La Bruja stare down with the calculating eyes of predators.

The other two captives flinch hard, faces draining of color, horror written across them as Omar thrashes in the dust, his screams filling the hot air.

Miguel leans on the railing, eyes fixed on them. "Do you

know where I found them?" He gestures to the corpses buzzing with flies.

Alejandro Guitíerrez and Francesco García exchange terrified looks, their heads shaking violently. "No, Miguel. We don't know."

His voice hardens. "I found them in my vault. My now empty vault. Where they died, stealing my money and my gold."

Francesco raises his hands as if to ward off the words. "Not ours. Not our men."

Miguel's eyes flash. "Yes. Your men. Guilherme's men."

"Guilherme is gone," the other protests, his voice breaking. "Someone has taken him. We haven't seen him in days. No one knows where he is."

Miguel's lip curls. "Liars!"

Alejandro and Francesco stumble toward him, shaking their heads. "We swear to you, Miguel. We knew nothing of this. No one would dare steal from you. It would be madness."

Miguel straightens, his voice sharp, accusing. "Madness? Yes. These are mad times. And you would not be the first madmen to stand before me with lies on your lips."

He points down at them, eyes burning with suspicion, his paranoia bleeding through every word. "You are guilty. And like Guilherme, you will pay in blood."

Miguel's knuckles whiten on the railing. His voice lashes down like a whip.

"Where is he? Where is Guilherme hiding? Where is my money?"

Alejandro stammers, his voice breaking. "We don't know where he is! We swear it. We've sent our own people looking— asking questions in Hermosillo, in Nogales. Nothing. Only whispers."

Francesco blurts, desperate to speak before Miguel's temper snaps. "They said he was meeting an old friend in Juárez. That's all we heard. An old friend! We don't know who, we don't know where."

Miguel's face twists, the mask of control shattering. He slams a fist against the iron railing, the clang echoing across the arena.

"¡Mentiras! Lies!" His roar carries over the hoof pounded sand. "There is no way you would not know. Your own men went into my vault. They bled out on my floor. And you—Guilherme's right hand, his shadow—you tell me you knew nothing?"

Omar writhes on the ground, his voice ragged with pain. "We didn't! Miguel, listen—we didn't know! If we had, do you think we'd be here? We'd have taken our share and run!"

Miguel spits down into the dust. "If you didn't know, then you should have. That makes you worse than guilty. That makes you incompetent."

The two men fall to their knees, pleading now, voices cracking in the heat. "Please, Miguel! One last chance—we will find him, we will find your gold—"

Miguel cuts them off, his voice suddenly cold, deadly calm. "This, here, is your last chance. Tell me where Guilherme and my money are."

The silence that follows is broken only by Omar's whimpering and the buzz of flies over the rotting uniforms. Alejandro and Francesco can only shake their heads, sweat streaking their faces.

Miguel breathes once, twice. Then gives the smallest nod.

The heavy doors at the far end of the ring grind open. From the shadows emerges a hulking bull. It lumbers into the ring, black hide rippling, horns glistening in the electric light of the sunken arena. It snorts, pawing at the sand, the air trembling with its rage.

The three captives go rigid with terror as the beast lowers its head, breath steaming in the morning heat.

Then it charges.

Wounded and on the ground, Omar barely has time to raise a hand before hooves slam down. His scream is cut short, crushed under the animal's weight, blood spraying into the dust.

The other two captives bolt in opposite directions, panic

ripping through their bodies. Their bare feet kick up sand, their cries echoing around the ring.

The bull wheels with terrifying speed, muscles rippling. It barrels into Francesco, horn punching clean through his chest, lifting him like a rag doll. He arcs high, limp by the time he hits the ground.

Alejandro stumbles and tries to climb the wall, fingers scrabbling at the rough stone. The bull slams into him from behind. Bones snap under the impact, his body folding, crushed into the dirt.

The arena falls silent except for the rasp of the bull's breath. It stands over the broken corpses, sides heaving, nostrils flaring. Blood streaks its horns, dripping into the sand.

It paws the ground, snorting, eager for more.

Above, Miguel watches with cold satisfaction, eyes burning with something beyond rage—paranoia, vindication, hunger for more blood to seal his power. Acosta's prayer rises louder, trembling, while La Bruja closes her eyes, smiling faintly at the slaughter as though feeding on its darkness.

SIXTY-FIVE

JUÁREZ SPRAWLS in dust and ruin. Graffiti scars every wall, old posters peel in strips, and buildings sag under the weight of years of neglect. Smoke from burning trash drifts across the streets.

Peter drives slowly, eyes sharp. Every alley, every rooftop, every shadow gets scanned. His hand never strays far from the pistol at his hip.

Beside him, Felix shifts uncomfortably, head darting from one chaotic corner to the next. A man hosing what looks like blood from the sidewalk. A pack of dogs fighting over scraps. The city hums with menace, and it's overwhelming.

Peter pulls into a line of parked cars and cuts the engine. "Rush will have a tracker on it," he says flatly. "So we'll need something else for the rest of the way."

Before Felix can ask, Peter is out of the SUV. He strides to another car, pulls a slim tool from his pocket, and works the lock with practiced ease. A moment later, the door pops open.

Felix hesitates at the curb, both impressed and unsettled, then climbs in beside him.

Peter crouches under the dash, wires sparking. The engine

coughs, then growls to life. He eases them into traffic without looking back.

"That should buy us a little time," he mutters, scanning the rearview.

The new car rattles over potholes, the suspension groaning. Felix stares out the window, his face pale.

Ahead, an underpass looms. From its beams hang bodies—men, stripped to the waist, arms and legs hacked off. A head dangles on a rope, turning lazily in the draft.

Felix stiffens, voice tight. "What is this place?"

Peter doesn't take his eyes off the road. "Juárez."

Felix swallows hard. He's heard the name before, whispered in news reports, splashed across horror stories. Now it's all around him.

He turns to Peter. "Are you taking me to my mom?"

Peter hesitates. The pause is long enough for Felix to notice. "We're on our way," Peter says finally. "But first, we need to stop somewhere."

"Where?"

"Casa Bethel Orphanage."

Felix frowns, confusion deepening. "What's there?"

Peter's hands tighten on the wheel. His answer is flat. "The truth," he says.

The car hums along, the engine the only sound. Dusty streets slide past the windows, but neither of them looks at the scenery.

A short while later, Peter breaks the silence. "I keep asking myself one question, Felix."

Felix glances at him, uneasy. "What's that?"

"Why were they keeping you there?"

Felix shrugs, shifting in his seat. "They never said. But they... they treated me okay. Fed me. Let me watch TV. Play video games."

Peter's eyes stay on the road, voice hard. "But the DEA thinks you're dead. As far as they told me, your family hasn't been contacted. No ransom. No threats. Nothing. Those two agents surmised that you'd ended up in Acosta's cauldron. But instead they were keeping you in some underground hotel. Why?"

Felix fidgets, staring at his hands. "They just said if I did what they told me, I'd be okay."

Peter glances at him. "But why keep you there? You think they called your mom? Asked for ransom? Is she the type of person to keep something like that quiet?"

Felix shakes his head, small and quick. "I don't know. They never told me anything."

Peter studies him for a long moment, eyes narrowing. Something about the kid's treatment doesn't fit. The pattern is wrong. But he lets it go, jaw tightening as he turns back to the road.

The car slows. Ahead looms a rust-streaked gate, flaking paint clinging to twisted iron. A warped wooden sign dangles from chains: *Casa Bethel Orphanage*.

Children's laughter drifts faintly over the wall—bright, innocent sounds that feel out of place against the desolate sprawl of Juárez.

Peter eases the car to the curb, cuts the engine. Silence folds in around them. Neither speaks for a long beat.

Felix finally says, "I still don't get why we're going to an orphanage."

Peter doesn't answer. He opens his door, scanning the street one more time before stepping out. "Come on."

Felix lingers a moment, nerves jangling, then follows him toward the gate.

Across the street, a dented sedan idles in a line of parked cars. Inside, a man in a ballcap and sunglasses lifts a radio to his mouth, voice low and flat. "They're here."

SIXTY-SIX

THE STOLEN pickup rattles to a stop beside a rusted payphone on a lonely desert crossroads. The sun bleeds low across the horizon, painting the dirt and scrub in gold. The wind hisses through dry grass, carrying only the faint growl of trucks far off on the highway.

Michael digs through his pockets, finding the handful of coins he discovered in the truck. His hands tremble as he feeds them into the machine.

Beside him, Mayu scans the horizon, her eyes wide, searching for the black shape of Gusano's SUV.

Michael dials, the numbers etched into his memory. The line crackles, thin and distant.

A calm, commanding voice answers. "This is Senator Carmichael."

Michael blurts out, words tumbling. "It's me—Michael. We need help. Please. The family we were with—they called the cartel. We barely got out. And the man hunting us... he found us. Chased us. We only just shook him."

There's a pause, then the senator's tone softens, just enough. "Where are you?"

Michael turns, squinting at a weathered gas station sign down the road, then a crooked highway marker.

"Agua Prieta," he says into the phone.

"Good," Carmichael says crisply. "Do you have transport?"

"Yes."

"Then keep driving toward Juárez. I'll give you an address."

Outside the box, Mayu catches Michael's eye through the cracked glass, mouthing silently: *Can we trust her?*

Michael doesn't answer. He scribbles the address Carmichael dictates across the back of his hand.

The senator's voice sharpens. "Where's your tail?"

Michael glances out across the barren desert, the memory of the SUV still fresh. "We don't know. But he won't be far."

A pause, followed by "Then you better get moving. Don't stop for anything."

The line clicks dead.

Michael and Mayu exchange a look. The silence around them feels heavier now, the desert stretching wide and hostile, an open hunting ground.

They climb back into the pickup. The engine coughs and catches. Michael pulls them onto the road toward Juárez.

Behind them, the payphone dangles from its cord, still swinging gently.

The wind stirs dust across the crossroads. No SUV. No sound. No sign of Gusano.

But the silence makes it worse.

He's out there. Unseen. Unhurried. Inevitable.

SIXTY-SEVEN

THE FRONT DOOR to the orphanage is tall and bleached bone-gray by the sun, its wood warped with age. A hand-painted sign above it reads *Casa Bethel*. From inside the walls, children's laughter drifts faintly, high and innocent, floating against the grit of Juárez's streets.

Peter knocks once, hard. His other hand hovers near his waistband, eyes cutting across the street, measuring every shadow.

The door creaks open, heavy on its hinges. A weary priest stands framed in the gap, robes dusty, eyes sunken with sleeplessness.

Peter gives a name that isn't his, then adds in Spanish, "We've been sent from the municipal office. Records division. We need to review your adoption files."

The priest's brows pinch together. His gaze flicks from Peter's face to Felix standing awkwardly behind him. "The city sends word ahead," the priest says flatly. "I've received nothing."

Peter presses, leaning on the frame. "This is urgent. Time-sensitive. The paperwork is already in motion—you'll have confirmation by tomorrow. All I need is a look at your files. Twenty or thirty minutes, no more."

The priest doesn't budge. His eyes narrow, suspicion seeping into his tired voice. "The Casa Bethel is not a library. These children are not your business. Without authorization, you will see nothing."

Peter forces a tight smile. "You know how the city works, Father. Half the time they lose the paperwork themselves. You'd save everyone trouble just by letting me in."

The priest's hand clamps harder on the door, ready to shut it. His voice sharpens. "I said no."

The smile drains from Peter's face. His jaw works, the faintest tremor of frustration. Slowly, deliberately, his fingers drift toward the pistol tucked in the back of his waistband.

Felix notices. Quickly, he lays a hand on Peter's arm and whispers, "Not here."

To the priest, Felix forces a shaky smile. "Sorry for the trouble, Father. We'll get that paperwork to you ASAP." He tugs Peter back a step.

The door closes again with a heavy thump.

Peter growls under his breath, "We don't have time for this."

Felix glances around, his eyes already moving, assessing angles. Quietly, he says, "Trust me. Just follow my lead."

Around the back, Felix leads Peter into a narrow alley choked with weeds and broken glass. He points up at a drainpipe that runs to a half-open window on the second floor.

"I spotted it earlier from the street," Felix says.

Before Peter can argue, Felix is already climbing, hands and sneakers finding purchase on the rusted metal. He moves with the quick, careless agility of a teenager, hauling himself up and slipping through the open window in one smooth motion.

Peter waits, tense, eyes flicking across the street.

Inside, Felix pads down the dim hallway, heart hammering. Murals of saints peel from the plaster, their eyes faded to ghostly smudges. The air reeks faintly of detergent and incense. His sneakers squeak once on the tiles, and he freezes—listening, pulse racing.

Sure no one's watching, he heads for the stairs.

But he's wrong. Someone is.

From within the gloom of a side corridor, the priest from the door lingers by a cracked window. His gaze fixes on Felix, the boy moving inside. The priest's lips move in a whisper, fingers tracing the sign of the cross before he slips deeper into shadow.

At the bottom of the stairs, Felix finds a heavy service door, bolted shut. He works the latch with careful fingers, the metal scraping softly. The door groans as it swings open to the alley.

Peter slips inside, silent as smoke, pistol tucked close at his back. He gives Felix a sharp look that's almost approval. "Not bad, kid," he mutters, brushing past into the gloom.

Felix grins despite himself, then sets his jaw, leading the way down the corridor.

The hallway narrows, plaster flaking from the walls, the air heavy with dust. Doors line the walls—bathrooms, medical office, janitor's closet, records room.

"This is it," Peter says, shouldering the door open.

Inside, rows of tall filing cabinets stand wall to wall, their metal drawers labeled in fading ink. The smell of paper and mildew fills the air.

Peter steps in, scanning the room, then nods once. "Let's get to work."

They split without another word. Peter yanks open a drawer, files rasping against their folders. Felix pulls another open, fingers darting through brittle stacks.

"Anything linked to Miguel Sanchez," Peter says, his voice low but sharp. "Especially adoption papers. If he's got a twin, there's a file—and it'll be in here."

Felix nods, his face set. He moves quickly now, determination overtaking nerves.

The only sounds are the shuffle of paper and the faint rustle of their breathing in the still air.

Outside, the priest has returned to his office. The blinds are drawn, the air stale. He presses a phone tightly to his ear, voice low, measured.

"Yes. He wanted to see the records. And you did say that if a gringo ever came asking, to let you know."

The voice on the other end is flat, dangerous. "Where is he now?"

The priest rolls his eyes, glancing toward the back hall as if he can see through walls. "They're in the records room."

"Okay," the voice says. "Keep them there if you can. We won't be long."

The line goes dead.

The priest sighs, slow and weary, and makes the sign of the cross.

He takes a heavy key from his desk and walks the quiet corridor. The echo of his steps is the only sound. He slips the key into the records room lock and turns it. The faint click is swallowed by the walls.

Inside, Peter and Felix keep rifling through drawers, too focused to notice.

The priest enters the main hall, where two nuns wait, pale-faced, hands wringing. He keeps his voice low. "Gather the children. Take them out the side gate. Do it as quietly as possible."

The nuns nod, scurrying away. Soon the hall is filled with the shuffle of small shoes, the hushed whimpers of children clutching each other's hands. One by one, they are ushered out into the day, their wide eyes glistening with fear.

The orphanage empties, room by room, until the building feels like a ghost ship waiting for the storm.

Outside, the watcher sits low in his dented sedan, binoculars resting on the dash. His eyes narrow as a line of children shuffles out of the orphanage's side gate, shepherded by nuns in pale habits.

He leans forward, listening. No sirens, no bells. Not a fire drill.

The watcher exhales slowly, suspicion hardening in his gut.

He picks up his radio.

SIXTY-EIGHT

THE PICKUP RATTLES as it crawls beneath an underpass. Above them, bodies hang from ropes like macabre Halloween decorations. Flies swarm the air, the stench pushing through the cracked windshield.

Mayu recoils, covering her mouth, fighting the urge to gag. Michael grips the wheel tighter, jaw locked, eyes fixed straight ahead. He doesn't let himself look.

Juárez sprawls out before them—a city of chaos and ruin. Burning trash barrels throw oily smoke into the air. Stray dogs gnaw on scraps in alleys. Walls are smeared with spray-painted tags, warnings and threats layered on top of one another.

They roll to a stop outside a run-down dry cleaners. The neon sign flickers weakly, buzzing, its red letters half-dead. Inside, a lone woman sits behind the counter, a cigarette dangling from her lips.

"This is it," Michael says, reaching for the door handle.

They enter the place. The woman barely looks up as they give the name Carmichael instructed.

Her eyes flicker with recognition. She grinds out her cigarette, then rises slowly. Without a word, she crosses to the windows, pulling the blinds down one by one. The shop dims. She throws the lock on the front door with a sharp click.

"Venir," she mutters.

She leads them into the back room. At the far wall looms a massive dry-cleaning machine, its front door streaked with rust. She grips a hidden latch and yanks. With a groan, the entire front swings open on heavy hinges, revealing the mouth of a steel cage elevator inside.

She gestures with a jerk of her chin. "Entra."

Michael and Mayu step inside. The metal door slams shut behind them.

The elevator shudders, then begins to ascend. It rattles and hums as it rises, climbing higher and higher, until at last the cage doors grind open, and Michael and Mayu step into a world that doesn't belong to Juárez.

Marble floors gleam under chandelier light. Leather chairs sit in neat arrangements. Expensive paintings hang in gilded frames —landscapes, portraits, things stolen or bought with old money.

Around the room, suited men lounge with rifles slung across their chests. They lower their voices as the newcomers enter, eyes sharp, watching every move.

At the center, in a high-backed chair, sits Senator Carmichael. She wears a black cloak draped across her shoulders, her posture regal, a faint smile curving her lips.

"Welcome," she says.

Mayu leans close, almost whispering. "What is this place?"

Carmichael's voice is smooth, assured. "A little residence of mine, tucked away. A secret from anyone who would do us harm."

Michael steps forward, tension in his jaw. "What's our next move?"

"Our next move, Michael..."—Carmichael's smile widens, eyes glinting—"...is to rendezvous with your father."

Michael frowns. "My father?"

"Yes, Michael. Your father is in Juárez at this very moment."

For the first time in days, Michael and Mayu feel something verging on relief. As the two turn to one another, they feel it—a flicker of purpose. As if, at last, everything is moving toward an end.

However, that relief may be short-lived. Because in the shadows of a nearby alley, Gusano waits.

The dry cleaners glows faintly across the street, neon stuttering in the midday sun. Gusano leans against his car, cradling his arm. The bone is fractured, pain gnawing at him with every movement—but it is only pain. His face remains calm, eyes flat and cold.

The front door of the shop opens. Armed men emerge and climb into a waiting convoy—three armored Hummers, engines rumbling low.

Gusano straightens. He wonders where they're headed, considers following, then decides to stay on his true targets. Michael and Mayu.

As the convoy disappears down the road, his eyes drift back to the dry cleaners.

Following. Silent. Inexorable.

SIXTY-NINE

MIDDAY. The sun burns white overhead, the light harsh enough to bleach color from the world. Heat shimmers off the cracked asphalt, distorting the air.

The watcher sits hunched in his dented sedan, sweat darkening the band of his ballcap. His binoculars stay fixed on the orphanage entrance—its gates closed, its façade still and silent.

The targets are still inside.

The passenger door creaks open. Jonny Hernandez slides in, smelling of smoke and sweat, his shirt collar damp. He settles into the seat with a grunt, fishing for his cigarettes.

"You were right," the watcher says, eyes never leaving the gates. "He came straight here. But there's more."

Hernandez cups his lighter against the glare, sparking flame. "There's always more."

"About twenty minutes ago, the priest and nuns cleared the kids out. Locked the place down."

Hernandez drags deep and exhales through his nose, watching the thin stream of smoke curl toward the sunlit windshield. "Interesting. Sounds like I'm not the only one who's been tipped off. Anyone else turn up yet?"

The watcher shakes his head. "No. Just—"

A low rumble interrupts him. Heavy, mechanical.

"You spoke too soon," Hernandez remarks as he leans forward.

At the end of the street, an armored personnel carrier rolls into view, sunlight flashing across its steel skin. The vehicle growls forward, bristling with cartel insignia, tires chewing the pavement. Three armor-plated Hummers follow, each packed with soldiers.

The sedan vibrates as the convoy passes.

Doors slam open. Commandos pour out, boots striking in unison, weapons gleaming under the noon sun. Their movements are crisp and controlled. Ex-Mexican Special Forces—the best the cartel has on payroll.

The watcher's throat tightens. "Christ."

Hernandez narrows his eyes, cigarette clamped in his teeth. He leans back in his seat, watching the soldiers fan out. "Looks like we've got ourselves a good ol' confluence."

"A what?"

"A coming together of separate forces."

The watcher risks a glance at him. "What are you gonna do?"

Hernandez grins thinly, smoke curling from his lips. "For the time being, Carlo, I'm just gonna watch. See what happens."

One by one, men drop from the back of the APC into the sunlight. Black fatigues, armored vests, helmets strapped tight. Ex-Mexican Special Forces. They move with the precision of men long drilled, their rifles held low but ready.

The leader steps down last. His face is painted with a streak of camo under each eye, his jaw hidden behind a scarf. A patch on his vest bears the cartel's insignia, crudely sewn over an old military unit badge. He surveys the block in silence, scanning windows, alleys, rooftops. A single flick of his fingers, and his squad fans outward in disciplined arcs.

The orphanage doors creak. The priest steps out. His skin looks almost gray in the sunlight, sweat running down from his temples. His hands shake as he clutches a heavy iron key.

He bows his head as he approaches the soldiers. His lips move in a whisper, a prayer muttered between breaths.

When he reaches the leader, he doesn't meet his eyes. He simply holds out the key with both trembling hands.

The leader takes it without a word. The priest swallows, crosses himself quickly, then scurries away down the street, robes swishing in the dust.

The soldiers move into position with machine precision. One checks the perimeter, another secures the side gate the children slipped through earlier. Two kneel in the dust, rifles trained on the upper windows.

The leader raises his hand. His men freeze, silent, eyes locked on him. He keys his radio, his words clipped, sharp in Spanish.

"Recuerden. Paquete Azul, vivo. Paquete secundario, prescindible."

Remember: package Blue alive. Secondary package expendable.

Acknowledgements crackle back—low affirmations, each man's voice steady.

The leader lowers his hand. His squad shifts forward, boots crunching in unison on the gravel. The orphanage looms before them, its weathered façade hiding the two fugitives inside.

The siege has begun.

Inside, the records room feels like another century. Dust coats the air, filing cabinets groaning as drawers slide open and slam shut. Stacks of folders pile on a desk, spines splitting, loose sheets spilling to the floor.

Peter flips through one drawer after another, jaw tight. Felix kneels on the other side of the room, rifling furiously, sweat streaking down his temples.

Somewhere in the orphanage, a floorboard creaks. Then another. Slow, deliberate footsteps echo faintly down the hall.

Felix pulls a folder, eyes skimming the first page. He freezes. "I think I found it. Miguel Fernando Sanchez."

Peter snaps to his side, crossing the room in two strides.

"What does it say about his twin?"

Felix's eyes dart over the lines, lips moving as he reads. "Here. Dani Rio Sanchez. Given up along with their... wait. What?"

Peter's voice sharpens. "What does it say about his adoption?"

Felix frowns, his face draining of color. "This can't be right."

Peter grabs his shoulder, urgent now. "Felix. Who adopted him?"

Felix stammers, "Him?!"

"Was it a family by the name of Hernandez?"

Felix shakes his head, confusion spilling into panic. "Dani's not a—"

The door explodes inward.

BOOM. The frame splinters, shards of wood spraying across the room. Flashbangs clatter through the opening—white light detonates, a thunderclap hammering the air.

Peter jerks back, half-blind, ears ringing.

Felix screams, clutching his head.

Shadows surge through the breach—commandos in black armor, shields raised, rifles leveled. Stun batons crackle alive with arcs of blue electric.

The orphanage records scatter into the dust as the storm pours in, shields raised in a tight phalanx. The black slabs of reinforced plastic soak up Peter's pistol fire—*bang bang bang*—sparks flying as bullets glance off. They don't break stride.

"Felix, get down!" Peter snarls, shoving the boy back behind a cabinet.

The wall of shields slams into him, pinning him into a corner.

A crackle of blue light—*zzzzzt*—and a stun baton slams into his ribs. Pain floods his chest, muscles spasming. He roars through it, driving forward. His forehead smashes into the nearest visor. Glass spiderwebs as the man stumbles back.

Peter twists, firing his last shot into another shield before an armored fist bats the pistol aside. A second stun baton arcs across his forearm, nerves screaming. The gun clatters away.

Peter doesn't hesitate. Ducking back, then lunging, he grabs a commando by the wrist as the man swings at him and wrenches.

The commando howls, arm bent at a sick angle. Peter hurls him into the line, toppling two more.

Another swings a baton down. Peter sidesteps, traps the man's arm under his own in a clinch, and drives an elbow into his jaw. Blood sprays, the helmet spilling loose.

He feints right, ducks under a shield, then explodes upward, shoulder slamming into a chestplate. The man crashes back into his comrades, shields breaking formation.

"Stay behind me!" Peter shouts, teeth bared, blood on his lips.

The commandos regroup fast. Shields raise again. Two come in low, battering his legs, another high across his shoulders. Batons crackle as they rain shocks into him, electricity searing his nerves.

Peter staggers, spits blood, then surges again. He rips one man forward, drives a knee into his gut, then heaves him into another. The two crash into a filing cabinet, drawers bursting open, papers snowing across the room.

Another baton rakes his spine. His body jerks, muscles locking. He collapses to one knee. A shield slams into his chest, hammering him against the wall.

Still, he fights—swinging wild, elbows, fists, teeth. He's a rabid wolf in a trap, bloodied but unbroken.

It takes four men to bring him down, shields pinning his shoulders, batons slamming across his back again and again until his strength finally bleeds out of him.

Peter drops, panting, sweat and blood dripping to the dusty floor.

Felix bursts from cover, grabs a chair, and swings it with a scream. It shatters against a commando's shield. The boy is seized instantly and slammed to the ground, his arms wrenched behind him.

A rifle lowers, black muzzle pressing to Peter's head.

"No! Don't!" Felix cries out.

Peter simply closes his eyes.

But the bullet never comes.

"Wait," the leader snaps in clipped Spanish. "No. The boss said he prefers both of them alive. That way he can question the gringo."

The rifle eases back.

Peter lifts his head just enough to see Felix pinned to the floor, eyes wide with fear.

Plastic cuffs are shoved on both, biting into their wrists. Then they are yanked to their feet, boots scraping over the litter of torn files. The papers they fought to uncover lie scattered, useless, fluttering in the dust stirred by the commandos' boots.

They're marched down the corridor, past crucifixes on cracked walls and the smell of incense still clinging faintly in the air. Empty classrooms and dormitories echo with the sound of stomping boots, the children long gone.

Outside, the midday sun blazes white. The APC idles at the curb, armored plates humming, heat waves rising from its engine block.

The commandos shove Peter forward to the rear hatch. Felix follows, half-pushed, half-carried, his sneakers barely finding purchase.

The hatch yawns open. The air inside is thick with oil and sweat.

They're hauled up and shoved in, hitting the metal floor hard. The door slams shut, sealing them into the dark belly of the machine.

Engines roar, gears grind. The APC lurches forward.

Casa Bethel fades behind them, its secrets left half-buried in scattered pages.

From the sedan, Jonny Hernandez and the watcher sit in silence as the APC growls away from the orphanage. Its bulk shrinks down the sun-baked street, then swings onto the main road where the rest of the convoy waits—Jeeps and Hummers lined in formation. Engines rumble, dust stirs, and the armored column rolls out together, the APC swallowed among them.

The watcher breaks the quiet first. "So what now?"

Hernandez takes a drag, ember flaring, then flicks the ash out the cracked window. His grin is thin, sharp, eyes glinting with something between amusement and hunger.

"Looks like we're gonna need the big guns for this, Carlo."

Smoke curls around him as the street falls still again.

SEVENTY

IT'S nightfall when the convoy leaves Juárez and pushes down a desert highway. Six vehicles in line, dust clouds trailing. Headlights cut the dark, long beams flashing across scrub and stone.

Inside the armored carrier, Felix Carmichael sits hunched forward on the bench. He doesn't speak. Doesn't move. His hands are clasped together so tightly the knuckles shine.

Peter studies him from across the narrow aisle. The boy hasn't been right since Casa Bethel. Something he read there burned itself into him. Whatever it was, he hasn't let it out.

"You've been quiet a long time," Peter says, keeping his voice low.

Felix swallows, eyes fixed on the floor plates trembling with each grind of the treads. In the dim red light, his face looks older than his years—drawn, haunted.

Peter leans forward. "What is it? What did you see in that file?"

Felix's eyes flick toward him. For a moment, it seems like he might answer. His lips part, breath hitching.

"I know—" he begins.

The commando wedged between them shifts sharply. A jab of the rifle stock into Felix's chest. The boy chokes off mid-sentence and curls against the seat. The soldier barks something in Spanish, eyes flat in the glow.

Peter stiffens. He doesn't move, doesn't speak. But his stare stays fixed on Felix.

Felix looks back at Peter as if the words are still pressing against his teeth, begging to get out. But he clamps them down.

The carrier rattles into a shallow valley. The engine's growl deepens, the steppe rock walls bordering the road shaking with each jolt. Shadows gather beyond the edges of their headlights, unseen but felt.

Something in Peter tightens. A silence falls across the convoy, heavy as a held breath.

Then—

The night rips open.

A blast punches through the convoy's center—fireball blooming, metal shrieking. A Jeep flips end over end, spraying sparks as it cartwheels across the asphalt.

Screams, shouts, brakes howling.

Tracer fire slashes from the ridgeline. Three armored personnel carriers crest the rise, engines bellowing. Muzzle flashes strobe across the night.

Hernandez's ghost army is here.

A streak of fire arcs from the ridge. RPG. It slams into a cartel Hummer, detonating it in a blossom of flame. The explosion hurls jagged steel into the night, shrapnel screaming past. On the ridge, Jonny Hernandez himself lowers the smoking tube, cigarette glowing in the dark like a mocking star. His men roar as another rocket whooshes skyward.

Inside the carrier, the world erupts. A concussive thump rocks the hull, tilting it sideways. Peter and Felix are slammed against the benches as the carrier screeches, lurches, then topples. Metal screams as it rolls once and crashes hard onto its side. The red light swings wild, bodies flung, boots scrambling for balance.

The carrier shudders to a standstill.

Peter's ears ring. The world's a storm of smoke, shouts, the groan of stressed steel. The commando beside him shoves upright, weapon clattering as he braces against the wall-turned-floor. Felix is curled against the bench, pale in the flicker.

Outside, gunfire rips—staccato bursts, heavy machine guns pounding like war drums. RPGs howl, each impact a hammer blow in Peter's chest. Flames flicker through the vision slits.

In the chaos, Peter's hands scrape against something cold—metal. A fallen knife, lost in the scramble. He closes on it, wrists twisting against his bindings. The plastic bites deep, but the blade's edge reaches it and begins to saw.

Another blast shakes the carrier. Dust rains from the ceiling. Felix flinches, staring at Peter with wide, hollow eyes.

Peter doesn't stop. The convoy is dying outside. Inside, his chance has just been born.

At the rear of the carrier, commandos bark frantic orders, yanking open the hatch.

By the time Peter has the zip-ties cut, two cartel men are grabbing Felix by the arms. He thrashes, shouting Peter's name, voice drowned by gunfire and explosions.

Peter lunges across the bench, fingers stretching. They brush Felix's jacket for an instant, then the commando wedged between them drives the butt of his rifle into Peter's ribs. Pain detonates through his side. Felix is ripped away, dragged out into the fire and the night.

Peter snarls, twisting. The commando swings again, rifle butt arcing for his skull. Peter ducks low, the blow smashing sparks into the wall behind him. His hand finds the pistol on the commando's belt, yanks it free, and fires point-blank.

The man collapses into the footwell, chest blown out.

Peter scrambles through the open hatch into the storm. The night is alive with muzzle flashes, bullets whining past his ears, burning trucks hissing smoke.

Ahead is Felix. The boy stumbles, screaming, yanked toward a separate truck by two men. Peter raises the pistol, squeezing off two shots. One cartel soldier drops, tumbling into the dust.

Felix wrenches free for half a heartbeat—then another soldier clamps an arm around his chest, dragging him backward.

Somewhere on the ridge, a mounted gun roars. The highway is raked with fire. Peter dives behind an overturned Hummer, bullets sparking and whining off steel, the heat of passing tracers burning his face.

Ghost operatives move in with surgical precision, advancing in disciplined lines. Night-vision visors glow green, red lasers slicing through the dark. Suppressed rifles snap, each shot sharp and final.

Cartel escorts are shredded in seconds, cut down before they can regroup. One of the ghost APCs plows straight into a burning Hummer, pushing the wreckage aside with a scream of twisting metal.

Peter bursts from cover, pistol flashing. A cartel soldier drops, blood spraying the dirt. He keeps moving, eyes locked on Felix, who's being hauled toward a waiting Jeep.

He makes it within thirty yards—close enough to hear Felix screaming—when a cartel bruiser slams into him from the side. The impact rips the pistol from his grip, sending it skittering across the dirt.

The man is massive with shoulders like stone. As he lands on Peter, a fist smashes down, cracking across Peter's jaw. White light bursts behind his eyes. Peter snarls and drives a knee into his ribs once, twice, feeling the thud of meat and bone.

The bruiser roars, slamming his forehead down into Peter's face. Cartilage crunches. Blood spills hot over Peter's lips. He claws for the man's throat, fingers digging, but the bruiser wrenches free and hammers his forearm across Peter's neck, pinning him down.

Peter bucks, twisting, knees jerking up. He catches the man in the gut hard enough to stagger him back a step. Peter surges upright, swinging wild, a hook that glances off the man's cheek. The bruiser answers with a piston of a punch that drives into Peter's ribs, folding him sideways.

Boots scuff the gravel, more shadows rushing in. Two more cartel soldiers close fast. One smashes a knee into Peter's side while the other wrenches his arm back, forcing him down.

The bruiser spits blood, grinning through swollen lips. He draws a machete from his belt, raising it high. One soldier grinds a boot into Peter's chest, pinning him flat. Another jams the muzzle of his AK down against Peter's skull.

Peter bares his teeth, chest heaving, braced to die.

That's when headlights cut across the ridge—white lances through smoke and flame. Engines thunder, deep and snarling. Three armored SUVs and a ghost APC charge down the slope, suspension screaming as they hammer across the rocks.

Gunfire rakes the ground in a storm of sparks. A mounted DShK on the APC opens up, heavy rounds tearing the night apart. The bruiser and his men jerk and thrash as the machine gun scythes through them, blood and bone ripped into the dirt.

Peter rolls, the pressure gone, smoke and fire whipping around him as the ghost army drives past. For a moment, he just lies there watching it all, his head concussed, vision swimming.

Mounted gunners lean out of the windows, rifles barking, cutting swathes of fire through the melee. One APC slams into a cartel truck at full speed, flipping it in a shriek of steel and sparks, the wreck rolling end over end.

Peter claws himself upright, staggering, his ears ringing.

Farther ahead, headlights flare as an SUV fishtails around, doors flung wide. Peter sees them—two cartel men wrestling Felix inside, his arms flailing, mouth open in a scream Peter can't hear over the thunder. The vehicle slams its doors and rockets forward, tires spitting gravel as it tears into the desert night.

Commandos stay behind to cover the retreat. They throw themselves into the fray with suicidal resolve, opening up with rifles, RPGs whooshing into the dark. Explosions light the ridges, shockwaves rattling Peter's ribs. The ghosts answer with heavier fire, mounted guns tearing men in half, APCs plowing through.

Peter tries to run, legs weak, lungs burning, but he stumbles, dropping to a knee. The SUV with Felix vanishes, red taillights shrinking into the black horizon. He roars after it, a sound lost in the storm.

Rough hands seize him. Two men haul him up by the arms. He whips around, snarling, ready to tear them down—until he sees their faces. Not cartel. Not Hernandez's men either.

One of them shouts over the chaos, "We're with your son!"

Peter freezes. "Michael?"

"Yes," the man says, dragging him toward the shoulder of the road. "He's in Juárez. With Mayu. Come. We'll take you to him."

Gunfire rakes the highway behind them, the fight boiling on. Peter glances back once—Hernandez's APC is chewing through the cartel line, muzzle flashes lighting the ridge. The cartel commandos are dying, but the SUV with Felix is gone.

The men hustle him up the broken tarmac toward a black Hummer idling in the shadows. Doors slam, the engine revs, and they speed away, leaving the war behind. The echo of the firefight fades with distance, replaced by the steady drone of the highway pulling them back toward Juárez.

SEVENTY-ONE

THREE HOURS LATER, Felix is driven through the iron gates of Miguel Sanchez's compound. The gates loom tall, wrought iron worked into bulls and saints, and beyond them, the fortress sprawls. Armed men stand everywhere—at guard posts, on rooftops, along the walls—assault rifles gleaming under floodlights, body armor strapped tight, radios hissing static. Their eyes follow the SUV as it enters through the gates and then climbs the winding road.

The path leads upward, lined with torches and spotlights. To the left, a sprawling Spanish colonial mansion dominates the slope—arched windows and broad terraces, its roof a sea of terracotta tiles that resemble the scales of a dragon. Balconies are strung with lights, fountains spray into marble basins, and a cascade of manicured gardens spills down toward the valley. Farther off, silhouetted against the night, a vast bull-breeding facility spreads across the hillside: corrals crowded with massive black bulls, a training yard echoing with snorts and stamping hooves, and a full bullring carved into the rock like an arena awaiting spectacle.

The SUV halts before the mansion's grand portico, its columns pale and immense, flanked by guards in black tactical gear. The commandos pull Felix out and drag him up the steps, his sneakers scraping polished stone.

The doors swing open onto a hall dripping with obscene wealth. Chandeliers of crystal blaze overhead, throwing fractured light across gilded ceilings. Murals of conquistadors and saints cover the walls. Persian rugs smother the marble floor. Peacocks defecate on it all.

Felix is shoved forward through the hall and into a vaulted chamber. Javier Acosta stands waiting, shadowed, his eyes hard. Beside him drifts La Bruja, veiled in silks, her painted eyes unreadable as she glides over the floor. In one hand, she carries a cane crowned with a rattle bound in feathers, which she taps softly against the marble with each step. A low chant hums from her lips —Yoruba syllables stretched and repeated, hypnotic and steady, like a thread weaving through the room.

And at the far end, Miguel Sanchez rises from a leather chair. The cartel lord's presence fills the room, a man swathed in tailored black, heavy rings flashing as he spreads his arms in welcome. The air smells of cigar smoke and expensive perfume, the kind of opulence only a kingdom of blood can buy.

Miguel's gaze fixes on Felix with a hunger that isn't hunger. It is something colder, harder, more primeval.

He turns to Acosta. "Get him ready for the ceremony."

Acosta steps forward, face painted black and white, hands heavy as they land on Felix's shoulders. He begins to drag the boy away.

Felix stiffens. His throat is dry, but he forces the words out. "I know who you are."

Acosta falters. Miguel turns slowly, eyes narrowing.

Felix meets his gaze, chin trembling but unbroken. "I read the paperwork at the orphanage. Is that why you took me?"

The chamber stills. Even La Bruja's chanting seems to stumble.

Miguel stares back, unreadable, before giving a single nod. "Yes. It is. She wouldn't listen otherwise."

Silence stretches between them, heavy and suffocating.

Felix breaks it. His voice is quiet, stripped bare. "What happens now?"

Miguel steps close, so close Felix can feel the heat of his breath. His eyes blaze with feverish certainty.

"Now your blood will protect me from her."

The words land like a blade.

Miguel turns, dismissing him with a flick of his hand. La Bruja closes in, grip like iron on Felix's arm. She helps Acosta drag him toward the doors, her rattle hissing.

Drums throb in the distance as Felix is dragged into the dark. Behind him, Miguel lights another cigar, the smoke curling like a chanting prayer.

SEVENTY-TWO

THE SUV PARKS in front of the quiet dry cleaner's shop on the edge of Juárez. Neon buzzes in the window, half the letters burned out. Late night and the street is empty, save for a stray dog nosing trash.

Inside, the counter woman straightens as Carmichael's men herd Peter through the door. She forces a smile, but it twitches at the edges. A bead of sweat rolls down her temple.

"Señora," one of the men says warmly.

She nods, throat tight.

They move past her with mechanical familiarity, hands brushing past the racks of pressed shirts, the humming machines. At the far wall, the metal door disguised as a dryer swings open, revealing the narrow elevator beyond.

"Come," one of Carmichael's men orders. Peter steps in, jaw set. The doors grind shut.

Inside the shop, the hum of the rising elevator fills the air. The woman at the counter exhales, a ragged breath.

A shadow stirs beneath the counter top.

El Gusano uncoils from the floor, rising slow and deliberate from his hiding place, pistol in hand. His face is calm, eyes flat.

The silencer glints in the light. He presses the muzzle against the woman's forehead.

Her mouth opens, but no sound comes.

A soft *pfft*.

She drops behind the counter, blood blooming beneath her head. Gusano doesn't look down.

He steps out into the shop, shoes clicking on tile, moving with the patience of a man who knows time always favors him.

The elevator hums somewhere above, ascending into the hidden apartment.

Gusano stops before the closed doors, shoulders loose, pistol at his side.

He waits.

Upstairs, the elevator doors slide open. Peter steps into a narrow corridor, dimly lit, walls lined with screens. Security monitors flicker with static, the feeds stuttering—snow bleeding across the images of downstairs.

No one seems to notice the interference.

Two guards flank Peter as they march him forward. The rooms brim with armed men in tailored suits, pistols bulging at their waists and rifles resting within easy reach, their eyes following every step Peter takes. At the end of the corridor, a door opens into an opulent lounge: crystal chandeliers blazing above leather chairs and marble floors.

Michael is on his feet instantly. "Dad!"

Peter stops dead. His son crosses the room in two strides, Mayu just behind him. Both look worn—eyes hollow, smiles faint.

Peter grips Michael's shoulders, scanning his face as if checking for damage. "What the hell are you doing here? In Mexico?"

Michael manages a crooked smile. "Volunteering at the border got a little out of hand." He glances at Mayu.

She adds quietly, "We were pulled in, same as you."

For the next minute, Michael and Mayu spill their story. Peter just shakes his head, pacing, dragging a hand down his face. "Christ almighty," he mutters again and again.

Then a throat clears.

Senator Carmichael steps from the shadows—immaculate in a tailored suit, pearls at her throat, eyes cool and assessing.

Michael gestures. "Dad... this is Senator Carmichael. She—"

Peter cuts him off, his gaze locked on her. "I know who she is."

Carmichael inclines her head, the faintest smile curving her lips.

Peter's voice hardens. "I was with your son."

The room goes still.

Carmichael's composure cracks, just for a heartbeat. Her breath hitches, eyes widening. "Felix?"

Peter nods once. "He's alive."

Carmichael takes a step closer, the mask of control slipping. "Where? Where did you see him?"

Peter doesn't flinch. "On the road. He was in the convoy with me when we got hit. Cartel pulled him out, dragged him off kicking and screaming. Last I saw, they were hauling him into a truck."

Her hands clench into fists at her sides. "Where are they taking him?"

Peter's voice is flat, heavy. "Back to Sanchez's place would be my guess. It's where we were heading when Hernandez showed up."

Carmichael's breath comes sharply through her nose. For a moment, her veneer of power is gone, replaced by raw panic. She whispers, almost to herself, "Felix."

Then her chin lifts, spine stiffening. The mask slides back into place. Her voice steadies. "Then you'll get him back."

Peter narrows his eyes. "That's not how this works. I came here for my son. For Mayu. My priority is them right now. Your problems aren't mine."

Carmichael's stare is ice. "They are now."

Peter shakes his head. "No. I need to get my son and his girlfriend out of here. Then I need to find my partner. He's currently being held hostage by a man who may or may not be a cartel mole. You'll have to get your son back yourself, Senator."

Carmichael's jaw tightens. "But you lost him."

"I hardly misplaced him." Peter's tone is iron. "Look, this is no place for you, ma'am. And I mean that in the most respectful terms. But Juárez is—"

Her eyes flash. "Don't tell me about this place. I know this place better than most."

Something in her gaze makes Peter itch. A weight behind the words.

In the background, the elevator pings.

Carmichael steps closer, voice low and edged. "You can take my best men. But you are going to get my son back, Mr. Black."

Peter glances around. Her guards have shifted, shoulders tight, hands hovering near triggers.

"What if I don't want to?" Peter puts to her.

"There is no choice."

She nods.

In an instant, the room erupts in motion. Michael and Mayu are grabbed, guns jammed against their ribs. More muzzles swing toward Peter. He is unarmed, caught in the crosshairs.

"You will take four of my best men," Carmichael says, steady as stone. "But you will get my son back. Or I will take yours."

Peter studies the guards—hard faces, gang tattoos peeking under sleeves. He turns back to her, voice sharp. "And would your best men by any chance be cartel men?"

She doesn't answer.

"That's why the kid got all sheepish at the orphanage," Peter presses. "That's why Miguel was keeping him safe. He was using him to keep you in line. To keep his twin in line. Isn't that right, Dani?"

Her glare hardens into something venomous. "I always preferred Daniela. But Dani is okay."

Michael stares, confused. Mayu too, her breath caught.

The room vibrates with tension, on the edge of snapping—

And then the elevator doors grind open.

El Gusano steps out, silent, pistol raised, death walking into the room.

SEVENTY-THREE

THE FIRST SHOT IS MUFFLED—*THUP*—A
guard's head snaps back, spraying the antique mirror behind him
in crimson. Crystal shatters in a tinkling rain. Another two are hit
before Carmichael's men react.

The apartment explodes into chaos.

Gunfire rips across polished oak panels, shredding Persian
rugs. An antique cabinet bursts apart, china and crystal detonating in clouds of glass. The air fills with dust and shards, every
surface screaming under the onslaught.

Peter dives low, dragging Mayu with him, shouting for
Michael. Bullets chew through a leather armchair, stuffing spilling
like snow. Another guard goes down, chest punched open by
Gusano's silenced rounds.

Carmichael throws herself behind a marble column, clutching
her pearls like they'll shield her. Her guards are nothing but meat
—dropping one by one, blood soaking the white upholstery.

Peter has no weapon, only instinct. His eyes never leave
Michael and Mayu. He lunges, snatching Michael by the arm,
hauling Mayu upright. Gusano's bullets spit past them, smashing
a chandelier into raining crystal.

"Go!" Peter bellows, shoving them out the other side of the room toward the stairs.

They take them two at a time, crashing through the upper level and sprinting down a hall lined with portraits. In the background are gunshots and screams, the building shuddering with each volley. Peter shoulders through a locked door, finding a room with tall windows.

"Move!" He smashes the glass with a chair, cold night air flooding in.

Michael clambers onto the sill, eyes wide as he peers down six stories to the street. A drainpipe runs down the wall, narrow and rusted. He swings onto it, boots scraping the stone, arms trembling as he lowers himself. Behind them, muzzle flashes stutter in the apartment rooms, shouts cutting through the chaos.

Mayu follows. She climbs down fast, breath ragged, the rattle of gunfire getting closer, closer.

Peter glances back. The corridor behind him flares with puffs of dust as rounds chew into the plaster, Gusano making his way through the last of the cartel men.

His shadow stretches across the wall.

Peter grips the pipe, hauling himself out. Metal groans under his weight. Shots crackle above him as a bullet flies from the window. He grits his teeth, climbing down, hearing the fight come to a sudden stop—no more gunfire. Just an eerie silence in its wake.

By the time his boots hit the pavement, Michael and Mayu are crouched behind a line of parked cars, pressed low. Peter pulls them into an alleyway, hearts hammering, lungs burning as they make a run for it.

Behind them is death. Ahead, only shadow.

From the balcony, Gusano watches them vanish into the alley. He steps back inside calmly, reloading as he moves. The carpet is a sea of broken glass and bodies.

One man groans, clutching his stomach, legs twitching.

Gusano doesn't pause. He levels the pistol and puts a round through the man's head. Silence returns.

He takes the elevator back down. Then he's gone, through the shop, out to the street.

His car waits. He slides in, starts it, and pulls away, eyes scanning the alleys.

He's two blocks on when he spots movement. Shadows running—Peter, Michael, Mayu, sprinting across side streets, breathless and desperate.

Gusano presses down, engine roaring as he throws the car down the alley. The car rockets forward, bearing down on them.

Peter sees it coming. He yanks Michael's arm. "Hey, Mikey. Give me a hand."

Together they seize an overfilled wheeled trash bin, shoving it into the center of the alley.

Gusano slams the brakes. Tires scream. The car skids short of the barrier, rocking on its shocks.

Peter's already moving. He pulls a wide sheet of rusted metal from the bin, grips it like a shield, and rounds the side of the car.

But the driver's seat is empty, the door wide open. Gusano isn't there.

Movement—blur fast.

Peter throws up the metal just as shots crack. Bullets spark against steel, ringing in his ears. He heaves the makeshift shield forward—hurling it like a slab. It smashes against Gusano's wrist, sending his pistol disappearing into a pile of spilled trash.

The four of them fan out instinctively, Peter in front, Michael at his shoulder, Mayu just behind.

Gusano stands across from them, calm as ever. He tears open the right leg of his trousers, fingers pulling the cloth apart to reveal a machete strapped against his thigh.

The blade comes free with a hiss, long and wicked, glinting in the light of the full moon.

The alley seems to shrink around them, the walls leaning in. Gusano grips the machete in his good hand. His other arm hangs crooked, fractured, but it doesn't slow him—if anything, it makes him meaner.

Peter squares up with the bent sheet of metal. Michael and Mayu flank him, breath ragged, faces taut. None of them have weapons.

Gusano advances. Calm. Patient.

Then he explodes.

The machete whips down, a blur of silver. Peter shoves the sheet up, steel shrieking against steel, sparks snapping into the air. The impact jars his bones.

Gusano rips back. Mayu is behind him, looking for an angle. He whips the blade around in an arc. She jerks aside just in time, the blade carving a groove through the wall where her head had been.

Michael grabs a length of pipe from the ground, swinging it. Gusano sidesteps, lashes out with a boot—a perfectly timed trip kick. Michael's legs go out from under him, the pipe clattering across the cobbles.

Mayu seizes a bottle from a trash pile and smashes it against the wall, jagged edges glinting. She slashes for Gusano's face. He ducks, twists, and nearly guts her with the return swing. She stumbles as she throws herself back, air hissing from her lungs.

Peter charges, ramming Gusano with the sheet of metal like a shield. They crash into a stack of bins, garbage bursting around them. Gusano rolls away, machete hissing back into a defensive position, eyes cold, body coiled.

He is a machine. Every step measured. Every swing precise.

The fight tears down the alley, boots hammering on cracked pavement. Gusano hacks at anything that moves, blade biting steel and stone alike. Peter blocks with the sheet and parries, shoving him back. Michael and Mayu dart in, striking with fists, bottles, debris—anything they can grab.

A broken bottle rakes Gusano's forearm, blood spraying as he snarls. Mayu smashes a brick against his temple, staggering him for a heartbeat. Michael drives a length of pipe into his ribs, the clang echoing off stone.

Still he comes. Still he drives them.

The alley narrows, then spits them into open daylight—onto the edges of a roaring freeway. Horns blare, tires scream, headlights blinding. Cars whip past, engines snarling.

Gusano barely glances at the traffic. He presses forward, machete gleaming, forcing them across the lanes.

A truck barrels past, horn blaring, wind hammering them sideways. Michael stumbles. Peter yanks him clear as another car screeches by.

The fight scatters them. Peter and Michael are shoved back by a rush of traffic, horns blasting in their faces. They can't close the distance.

Ahead, Gusano and Mayu are driven onto the central shoulder, locked together—predator and prey. His blade arcs down. She dodges, barely, their figures swallowed by the chaos of steel and headlights.

Peter shouts, but the roar of traffic drowns his voice. He and Michael are cut off, powerless to help, watching as Gusano drives Mayu farther down the freeway, the machete glinting with every swing.

Mayu stumbles onto the dirt median, traffic screaming past on both sides. Gusano follows, machete raised, blade catching the headlights. He slashes down, but she twists away, gravel spraying, the edge missing her by inches.

She ducks, jabbing a fist into his ribs, but he absorbs it, unmoved. The machete arcs again, slicing air where her head had been a heartbeat before.

Across the lanes, Peter and Michael make their move. They dash through honking cars. A motorbike screeches past, forcing Michael back to the shoulder. Peter makes it, weaving between bumpers, horns blaring.

He sprints toward the fight.

Michael tries again, but a truck bears down, air horn howling.

He throws himself back, panting. He squares to go once more, but—

Cold steel presses against the back of his head.

Carmichael's voice, soft and venomous, breathes into his ear. "Place your hands behind your back, Michael, or I'll blow your brains into the traffic."

Michael freezes, chest heaving, sweat running down his temple.

On the median, Mayu gasps, stumbling as Gusano looms above her. He raises the blade high for the killing strike.

He doesn't get to make it.

A blur—Peter slams into him from the side, boot hammering Gusano's fractured arm. Pain explodes. The machete wavers, fingers weakening, the killer's snarl breaking into a guttural grunt of pain.

Peter doesn't waste a second. He swings the bent sheet of metal, slamming Gusano back. Mayu dives in, fists flashing. Together they hammer him, forcing him down into the dirt.

The machete slips, clattering. Mayu seizes it, hands slick with sweat and blood.

Gusano lunges—teeth bared, one arm limp, the other clawing for her from the ground. She drives the blade down, planting it deep into his skull with a crack like splitting a coconut.

He jerks, eyes wide, then slumps. The machete handle sticks out of his head as he topples into the dust.

Silence, save for the thunder of traffic.

Peter and Mayu collapse to their knees, chests heaving, sweat streaking their faces. They pant in unison, staring at the body.

Then the realization hits.

"Michael?" Peter spins, eyes sweeping the freeway shoulder. Empty.

Mayu staggers upright, scanning the lanes. Nothing. No sign of him.

Michael is gone.

SEVENTY-FOUR

JUÁREZ POLICE HEADQUARTERS looms like a fortress, ringed with concrete barriers and sandbagged checkpoints. Floodlights glare across razor wire. The air hums with tension—State Police are on their guard. Miguel's Sinaloa men are circling the city like wolves, murdering anyone wearing the uniform of the State Police.

At the gates, Carmichael lowers her tinted window. The guards step out, rifles across their chests, eyes unreadable. She doesn't address them. Instead, she lifts her phone, voice steady, Spanish precise.

"Estoy aquí."

The man on the other end asks her to wait. The line goes quiet with only the faint hiss of static.

Seconds drag. Carmichael sits motionless, fingers poised on the wheel, the weight of the guards' stares pressing in through the glass.

Then the phone crackles. Inside the gatehouse, another call comes through, the landline buzzing sharp against the silence. One of the guards snatches it up, listens, and nods once.

He steps out, signaling the others. The barricade lifts.

Without another word, Carmichael eases the SUV forward.

The gates part, swallowing her into the complex. She follows the curve of the ramp down into the underground lot, the vehicle's headlights glinting off rows of concrete pillars and armored patrol cars.

Officers mill, rifles slung, eyes sharp. The head of the precinct, Gonzalo Jimenez, waits by a steel door.

He smiles when he sees her. "Eres muy valiente viniendo aquí así, vieja amiga."

You are very brave, coming here like this, old friend.

Carmichael steps from the SUV, immaculate in her tailored suit, pearls catching the light. "I need somewhere to stay. And a few men. Not for long."

The commander's smile falters. "You understand your brother is targeting us. In his madness, he has already killed three top state officials—four if you include Guilherme."

Her eyes are cool, voice unshaken. "My brother will not be with us much longer. I can assure you. I merely need a few of your men... and somewhere to keep something."

"Algo?" The commander tilts his head. "Something?"

Carmichael turns and nods at her driver. The trunk pops open.

Inside, hogtied and gagged, Michael Black struggles weakly against the tape. His eyes are wild, muffled sounds strangled in his throat.

Carmichael looks back at Jimenez, her expression unreadable. "I need to keep him here. In one of your cells. Just until I have what I want."

The commander studies her for a long moment, then nods. Men step forward. Michael's muffled cries echo in the concrete chamber as they drag him away.

Carmichael smooths a hand down her jacket, pearls glinting under the fluorescent lights.

She doesn't look back.

SEVENTY-FIVE

THE SAFEHOUSE IS QUIET, its walls still carrying the ghosts of their recent operation: the torture and execution of Guilherme Hermoné. Plastic sheeting still covers the walls of the small room. A rack of empty food containers lines the kitchen corner.

Peter goes straight to the satellite phone. "You said you remembered the number you called her on," he says to Mayu.

"Sure." She recites it from memory, voice steady though her hands tremble.

Peter punches the digits in. The line clicks once, twice.

Carmichael answers immediately. "It's me," Peter says.

"I knew it would be." Her voice is smooth, self-satisfied.

"You have my son."

"And you can get mine back," Carmichael retorts.

Peter exhales slowly. "How do we do this?"

"Get Felix back. Then call me."

He hears the shuffle of movement as she starts to lower the phone. "Put Michael on," Peter barks.

Silence. Then a sigh. Muffled sounds, tape tearing.

Then—

"Hey, Dad." Michael's voice, flat and deflated, comes through.

Peter grips the handset tighter. "How you holding up?"

"Okay for someone hogtied and being held at gunpoint."

A grim smile tugs at Peter's mouth. "That's the spirit. Hold on."

Shuffling again. Carmichael back on the line, sharp and hard. "Get Felix back. You don't have much time. Everything is simple. My son dies, your son dies."

The line goes dead.

Peter lowers the phone. His knuckles are white. The silence in the room is heavy, broken only by Mayu's trembling breathing.

Peter sets the phone back down, jaw clenched. He looks over at Mayu. "Shower. There's fresh clothes in the wardrobe. CIA digs always keep spares. You'll find your size."

She hesitates, then nods. The bathroom door clicks shut, water hissing.

Alone, Peter lifts the satellite phone again and dials a second number. The line pops and crackles before a voice answers.

"This is Charles Rush."

"Charlie, it's Peter."

"Oh, Mr. Black," Rush says, voice rich with amusement. "You have been rather played, I hear."

"Just put Hernandez on."

Another click. "Ah! The fool himself," Hernandez says, almost cheerful.

"Where's Mark?"

"Here. With me."

"Why didn't you explain things?"

"We were in the middle of a firefight with cartel men. Trying to rescue you."

"Not then. Before."

"Because in this game," Hernandez replies, his tone suddenly sharp, "you don't know who to trust."

Peter's voice drops, edged with steel. "Did Olivia know about Carmichael?"

A pause. Then Hernandez sighs. "Yes. She was taking Eduardo to Washington so he could make a statement to the president himself. I told her not to trust DEA. Told her Carmichael had influences that ran deep. But she needed an agency willing to work with her stateside. It was either DEA or Homeland. And with Homeland in deep with ICE, she chose the lesser of two evils. But in the end, it was what got her killed. DEA tipped off Carmichael, and she gave Miguel Sanchez the safehouse. It was Carmichael who sold your girl out. Those agents following you— they were there to slow you down, that was all. Carmichael then had the DEA set you on Acosta and Miguel. The plan was to bring her brother to heel through you."

Peter's grip tightens on the phone. "Why didn't you tell us right away?"

"Because I was waiting to see if I could trust you. You don't go blowing the cover of your life's work to just anybody."

"So that's why you wanted Felix to yourself."

"It is."

"And what are you going to do with Carmichael?"

"Play her," Hernandez says. "Something I could have done if I had her son."

"She has mine."

"So I hear."

"She wants to do a swap."

"And you want help," Hernandez adds, the faintest smile in his voice.

"I can't get that kid back without you."

Hernandez breathes down the line, long and slow. "You know where we are. Now someone wants to speak with you."

The phone changes hands.

"Hello, Peter" comes Deacon's voice, dry and cold.

"You forgiven me yet?" Peter asks.

"You mean for bailing on me," Deacon says. "Yeah, I guess."

"How long was it before Hernandez explained things?"

"Not long after you pulled your disappearing stunt. Told me all about Carmichael. I called him an asshole for not coming clean right away. Now get your ass down here. We better be hauling ass to Sanchez's compound by sundown. I've been watching the satellite feed. They're planning on a big ceremony. Looks like Miguel is gonna let Acosta and his witch do what they want with Felix."

The line goes dead.

The bathroom door opens. Mayu steps out in a robe, hair damp, steam curling out behind her. Her face is set.

"I want to go with you," she says.

"No way."

She comes right up to him, eyes hard. "Yes way."

SEVENTY-SIX

THE GATES GRIND OPEN. Peter and Mayu drive into Rush's compound, headlights sweeping over the scattered remains of the ghost army. Men move like shadows across the yard, rifles slung, eyes hollow. The smell of oil and sweat hangs in the air.

Jonny Hernandez is waiting on the steps of the main house, cigarette glowing. Deacon leans against the wall beside him, arms folded, irritation etched into his face.

"I see you brought a tagalong," Deacon mutters when he sees Mayu step out. "She doesn't belong here."

Mayu bristles, but Hernandez lifts a hand, grinning faintly. "Let her prove herself."

Deacon growls. "This isn't a game, Jonny. She's green."

"She's still standing after everything," Hernandez says, exhaling smoke. "That's proof enough."

Inside the operations room, the table is covered in satellite printouts and grainy drone footage. The compound fills several laptop screens: Miguel's fortress glowing under floodlights, walls crawling with armed men. At the heart, the temple looms, bonfires already lit for the ceremony.

"They're readying for a fight," Deacon says. He points to the images—snipers on rooftops. "And that's just what we can see."

"Inside," Rush adds, his voice tight, "our feed shows movement toward the temple. Looks like ritual prep. They're building to something."

Peter leans over the table, eyes fixed on the grainy image of the courtyard. "Felix?"

"Scheduled for sacrifice by dawn," Deacon replies flatly. "Acosta and La Bruja are already in the ritual chamber."

The room falls silent. Everyone stares at the screens, the enormity of what they face pressing in.

Hernandez spreads his hands. "We've got twenty men left, including all of us. That's it. Twenty against a fortress."

"Outnumbered, outgunned," Deacon mutters. "Suicide."

Peter straightens, his voice cutting through the gloom. "We go anyway."

All eyes turn to him.

He doesn't blink. "We don't wait till dawn. We hit them before the knife falls. We take the fight to Sanchez, cut through, and pull Felix out. No matter what it costs."

A long silence. Then heads nod, one by one. Grim, resigned.

Hernandez crushes his cigarette into the table. "Gear up."

The men move with purpose, opening crates, strapping on body armor, checking magazines. Mayu fits herself into the rhythm, donning a vest, loading a rifle. Deacon watches her, still wary, but he doesn't stop her.

Peter tightens the straps on his harness, checks his sidearm, then runs Olivia's rosary once through his fingers. His jaw sets.

The sound builds—a chorus of bolts sliding, safeties clicking off, boots thudding across concrete.

The slow drum roll before war.

SEVENTY-SEVEN

NIGHT LAYS HEAVILY over Miguel Sanchez's compound. Searchlights sweep across the manicured lawns, slicing beams over the walls. Every corner bristles with armed men —cartel soldiers pacing in pairs, rifles gleaming, radios hissing.

The air vibrates with sound. Low chanting drifts from the temple, carried along the corridors, pulsing like the beat of a heart. Candles gutter in alcoves. Murals of saints and demons flicker in firelight. El Lobo's fortress hums with ritual, with violence.

Miguel stands alone at the edge of the bull ring. His white suit glows under the floodlights, his gold chain catching the gleam. In the pen beside him, the prize bull stamps and snorts, its breath misting in the night air, muscles rippling beneath its black hide. Miguel strokes the animal's flank, eyes shining with fevered devotion.

One of his lieutenants approaches, a hand pressed to his earpiece. He listens, nods once, and leans close. "La ceremonia empieza pronto." *The ceremony will begin soon.*

Miguel's gaze doesn't waver from the bull. His lips curve into a smile.

Inside the temple, Felix shivers as rough hands strip him to the waist. His chest and arms are daubed with streaks of white paint and animal blood, cold against his skin. He tries not to flinch, not to show fear, but his breath trembles in his lungs.

Acosta looms over him, voice a deep rumble as he chants in Yoruba, syllables rolling like thunder. La Bruja circles with rattles in her hands, feathers swaying from her headdress, her painted eyes fixed on Felix as if she can already see his blood spilling into the cauldron.

The nganga bubbles in the corner, smoke curling toward the rafters. Bones crackle in the firelight.

Felix clenches his fists, every detail searing into his mind—the exits, the guards, the blade waiting on the altar. Terror claws at him, but beneath it, calculation stirs.

Outside in the foothills surrounding the compound, the desert air is cool and dry. Miguel Sanchez's home looms ahead, a slab of concrete and firelight against the black sky.

On the northern edge, Peter and Mayu crawl low along a drainage ditch, night-vision green painting the world in eerie hues. Heat signatures glow ahead—two cartel soldiers on patrol, rifles slung, armor tight against their torsos. They're so close Peter can hear the crunch of their boots in gravel. Mayu's breath catches, but she steadies, M4 carbine pressed into her shoulder.

Peter lifts a hand, holding her back. They wait, every heartbeat pounding like a drum in the silence.

Along the eastern perimeter, Deacon moves with six ghosts through a stand of scrub brush, their NVGs glowing faintly. Thermal cams sweep the wall as heat blooms everywhere: guards pacing the parapets, a pair crouched behind a mounted gun, one man smoking, glowing ember bright in the dark.

Deacon raises two fingers, signaling hold. They freeze, lying still as statues as a patrol vehicle rattles past. Dust sprays over them, engines fading. One of the ghosts exhales slowly. They push forward.

At the southern perimeter, Jonny Hernandez leads the rest, crouched in the long shadow of a ruined wall. He studies the feed on a small thermal pad. Dozens of heat signatures flare inside the compound—men pacing the courtyards, rifles cradled, lines of fire overlapping. The place is crawling.

He smirks faintly, like a man stepping onto a familiar stage.

The three teams move closer, inch by inch. Cartel soldiers pass within meters. Radios hiss. Dogs bark in the distance. Sweat drips down Mayu's temple; Deacon's grip tightens on his rifle; Hernandez's men check safeties one last time.

The air itself feels taut, stretched to breaking.

"On my word," Hernandez whispers through their comms.

Back inside the temple, Felix keeps his head bowed, shoulders slack. He lets them strip the rest of his clothing and paint his skin in streaks of white and blood. He breathes shallowly, eyes down, docile as a lamb being led to slaughter.

But inside, his mind works. Every step. Every hand on his arm. Every blind spot.

When one of the Narcosatánicos guards begins fumbling with the rattles laid out on a cloth, Felix sees it—a knife, small and sharp, used to carve ritual markings into flesh. The guard crouches, distracted.

Felix moves like he's scratching his leg, a slow, casual gesture. His fingers close around the hilt. He curls his hand into a fist, knuckles whitening, the small blade hidden within.

No one notices. Acosta chants on, voice rolling like thunder. La Bruja shakes her rattles, feathers swaying, eyes rolling back as if possessed. The guards grin and spit, seeing only a terrified boy.

The witch drifts closer, her silks brushing the stone floor. She bends over Felix, the rattle on her cane hissing inches from his face, feathers trembling with each sharp shake. The sound cuts through the chanting like a snake's warning, meant to hollow him out, to break him. Fear will help guide the spirits to his soul.

Felix keeps his head bowed, hiding the flicker in his eyes. His grip tightens on the knife hidden in his fist.

Acosta joins La Bruja, his painted face looming, voice rising above the drums. The pounding grows faster, harder, a rhythm that claws at the chest. Sweat beads on Felix's skin, the heat of candles and bodies pressing in.

The drums reach their peak, coming to a thunderous stop within the stone walls. And with that, Acosta spreads his arms and declares in Spanish, his voice booming, "Estamos listos."

We are ready.

Two followers step forward at once. They seize Felix by the arms, iron grips clamping down. With the rattle still whispering at his ear, they turn him toward the yawning mouth of the temple proper and march him inside.

The smell hits first. Sweet and rotten.

The chamber opens like a wound in the earth. Torches blaze in iron sconces, smoke choking the air. At its center stands the altar—a pile of rotting flesh and bone, hacked limbs black with decay, strung with strips of skin. Flies swarm in clouds, buzzing in a frenzy.

Beside it squats the nganga, a cauldron oozing thick black liquid, its rim encrusted with dried blood. The stench is suffocating—carrion and rust, corruption given shape.

Felix forces himself not to gag. He clenches the knife tighter in his fist, the blade biting his palm.

They think he's a sacrifice. But he's going to try to prove them wrong.

Outside, Deacon crawls forward through thorn scrub, five ghosts shadowing him. He raises a hand, palm flat. They halt. Ahead, the outer wall looms. Thermal optics flare with shapes—cartel guards pacing, rifles slung, heat blooming from their chests. Deacon marks positions under his breath. His men nod, weapons steady.

On the south perimeter, Hernandez squats against broken stone, the rest of the ghosts arrayed beside him. He peers through a thermal pad, the compound glowing with heat signatures—dozens of soldiers clustered in courtyards, others stationed on rooftops. His lips curl into a tight smile. He speaks softly into comms. "This is certainly going to be a busy night at the office."

North perimeter. Peter and Mayu slink along the shadow of an outbuilding, slipping past two guards, their footfalls masked by the hum of generators. They climb onto a low roof, flat against the tiles. From here, the whole compound spreads before them.

Peter unfolds the bipod on his Remington M24, scope glinting faintly in the moonlight. Mayu lies beside him, spotting scope braced against her shoulder. Her voice is calm, precise. "Left tower—two guards. Rooftop opposite—sniper nest."

Peter exhales, cheek pressed to the stock. Through the crosshairs, he sees the courtyard glow in firelight.

The ritual is beginning.

In the temple, Felix is marched before the altar of rot. Acosta's voice rises into a frenzied chant. La Bruja circles with her rattles, feathers swaying, her painted eyes locked on the boy.

Torches flare, shadows leaping across the walls.

On the roof, Peter adjusts the scope, breath slowing. Deacon's voice comes low across comms. "Eyes on."

"Confirmed," Mayu says, scanning.

Hernandez's tone is velvet, calm as ever. "Wait for my word, Black."

Across three fronts, twenty men hold their breath, the drum roll pounding in their ears as the ceremony begins.

Felix is led onto the altar, bare-chested, painted white and red, his body marked like a sacrificial lamb. He forces himself to go limp, docile, as hands grip his arms and shoulders, pressing him down onto his knees.

Acosta towers over him, chanting in Yoruba, voice low and thunderous, each word like a nail hammered into the air. La Bruja circles, rattles shaking, feathers trembling in rhythm. Her eyes gleam with painted madness, her mouth curling into a rictus smile.

Miguel stands at the edge of the chamber, his white suit luminous under torchlight, gold chain gleaming. He watches with the calm of a man convinced that destiny itself bends to his will.

Felix's heart hammers. In his clenched fist, slick with sweat, the knife gleams faintly. He holds it tightly, hidden, knuckles whitening around it. His one chance.

Hands shove him flat onto the altar—rotting limbs stacked beneath, the stink of carrion smothering him. The nganga bubbles at his side, black liquid hissing, smoke rising like the breath of the dead.

La Bruja looms over him, blade raised high, lips moving in a final chant. Her eyes roll white.

The drums quicken, pounding with the same frantic rhythm as Felix's heart. Chanting rises from the gathered followers—low at first, then surging in a wave, syllables crashing against the walls. Smoke thickens, torches spitting sparks, the whole chamber shuddering as if the stone itself were answering.

Acosta throws his arms wide, his voice booming above the din. He calls on the spirits, on the dead and the damned, his Spanish carrying clear and terrible, "Use this blood to shield us! Cloak our souls from the gaze of his mother! Protect us from her eyes!"

The chant crests, a wall of sound, rattles hissing, drums hammering until the air is alive with frenzy.

They wrench Felix upright, shoving him back onto his knees. A hand fists in his hair, jerking his head back and exposing his throat to the torchlight.

La Bruja glides forward, blade flashing in her hand. Her painted eyes blaze with madness, lips muttering a final prayer as she raises the knife. The rattle in her other hand shivers, feathers trembling like wings.

On the roof, Peter exhales, finger steady on the trigger.

The blade prepares to plunge down—

"Now," Hernandez whispers into comms.

The rifle cracks.

La Bruja's chest bursts red. She staggers back, shock etched into her painted face, the rattle slipping from her hand. It clatters against the stone as the chanting stumbles, falters, the spell of the moment broken.

All hell erupts.

Gunfire tears in from three directions, hammering the temple walls. Cartel guards shout, diving for cover. Bullets chew through pillars and torches tumble, sparks raining down.

Acosta rushes forward, catching La Bruja as she collapses, blood pouring from her chest. He gathers her in his arms, wailing, chanting louder, madness in his eyes.

Felix sees his opportunity. He surges up from the altar.

Acosta turns just as Felix drives the blade into his chest. Once. Twice. Again and again, stabbing with all the fury and terror and rage that's been burning inside him.

Blood spatters across Felix's face. He doesn't stop.

On the roof, Peter cycles the bolt, chambering the next round. He shifts a fraction, crosshairs sliding to the temple steps.

A guard bursts out into the courtyard, AK raised. Peter squeezes, and the man's chest detonates red. Bolt back, brass shell ejects, clattering against the tiles. Another guard takes cover behind a column. Peter punches a round through the stone, and the man drops, screaming.

"Left wall," Mayu calls, voice taut.

Peter pivots, breath shallow, crosshairs tight. One shot, clean —half a skull erased in the torchlight.

The courtyard buckles under the sudden precision. Cartel soldiers scatter, some firing wildly into the dark. Others shout orders frantically, but they don't last long. Peter is steady and ruthless, picking them apart—one at the parapet, one crouched behind a statue, another sprinting for the gatehouse.

"Path's clearing," Deacon rasps through comms. Gunfire crackles on his end. "We're moving in."

Peter doesn't answer. He's already sighted on the next target, breath held, finger flexing.

Below, shadows flood across the wall—Hernandez and his ghosts surging forward, rifles blazing. The ground assault has begun.

And on the roof, Peter keeps firing, each shot another opening cut into the chaos, every kill another step closer to Felix.

The ghost army floods the outer courtyards. Shadows sprint between pillars, rifles cracking. Muzzle flashes strobe the night, painting the compound in bursts of white light.

Miguel Sanchez and most of his men retreat from the temple toward the main house.

Felix staggers free from the altar, drenched in Acosta's blood. His chest heaves, the knife still slick in his hand. For a moment, he just stands there, dazed, staring at Acosta's ruined body.

"Secure the boy!" Hernandez bellows, voice cutting through the chaos.

Deacon barrels in, grabbing Felix by the shoulders. "Move, kid!" He drags him behind a fallen column, shielding him as bullets chip the stone to dust. Felix doesn't resist—he's slack, trembling, eyes wide, almost catatonic.

Peter and Mayu leave the roof and fight their way forward, ducking through the storm of gunfire. Grenades burst, clouds of dust and fire blasting across the paving stones. Cartel soldiers scream, running for cover.

Peter pulls Mayu close, shielding her as shrapnel rains down. They push toward the main house, leaving Felix Carmichael in Deacon's hands.

Ahead, Miguel Sanchez is already moving. Surrounded by his most loyal men, he strides for the mansion doors, his guards closing rank tightly around him.

Hernandez is cool amid the slaughter. He stands tall, voice calm, directing fire like the conductor of an orchestra. His ghosts move with machine precision, sweeping the courtyards, cutting down pockets of resistance.

Deacon shoves Felix behind another barricade, crouching low. The boy trembles, blood streaking his skin, his eyes locked on the knife in his fist. His lips move, but no words come.

"Stay with me, kid," Deacon growls. "Stay awake. You've done enough for one night."

But Felix's stare is distant, hollow, like he's not entirely there anymore.

The ghost army's push stalls at the edge of the main house. A bank of cartel gunmen protect the main residence. They pour fire from balconies and windows, muzzles flashing, rounds hammering the marble steps.

"Down!" Peter shouts, dragging Mayu behind a column. Hernandez dives flat behind a low wall, snapping orders over comms, his ghosts fanning out, returning fire in disciplined bursts. Shards of stone spray across the courtyard as bullets chip the stucco walls.

They're pinned. Progress slowed to a crawl.

Miguel keeps slipping further out of reach.

Inside, he crashes through the mansion halls, his white suit drenched in sweat, chest heaving. The sound of gunfire pounds behind him, echoing through chandeliers and gilded corridors.

He bursts out of the rear entrance, boots slipping on the tiled floor. Beyond the arch of the courtyard lie the stables, thick with the stink of hay, piss, and animal heat.

He stumbles into the small veterinary office. Shelves rattle as he yanks open drawers, glass vials clinking together. His hand shakes as he lifts a tranquilizer gun from its rack, then jams a vial into the chamber.

Not sedatives. Amphetamines.

He stuffs the pockets of his blood-spattered suit with more vials, hands trembling but eyes burning with resolve.

Pushing back into the dark of the stables, he faces the row of heavy doors. Behind them, the bulls shift and snort, hooves scraping against concrete.

Miguel's lips curl into a fevered smile. He has a plan.

Back at the house, bullets slam into the marble façade, ricocheting sparks across the courtyard. The cartel gunmen shout from balconies, muzzles blazing.

Peter signals Mayu to stay low, then pops out, snapping three controlled shots from his M4 carbine. One man topples over a railing; another stumbles back into a window, spraying glass. Hernandez's voice is cool over comms: "Shift right. Suppress."

The ghosts fan out, rifles roaring in measured bursts. Two lob grenades—explosions tear through the lower floor, smoke and fire billowing from the shattered arches.

Deacon's squad swings in from the flank, catching the defenders in a crossfire. Men scream, dropping rifles, scrambling for cover.

"Push!" Hernandez barks.

Peter moves, Mayu tight at his side, advancing from column to column as the ghost army drives the cartel line back into the house. Dust hangs in the air, acrid with cordite. Another balcony clears, then another.

Step by step, room by room, they force their way forward—toward the mansion's interior, the night bursting with gunfire.

On the other side of the house, Miguel moves through the stables, sweat dripping down his temple, breath ragged. The bulls shift restlessly in their pens, snorting in the dark, their massive bodies rippling with contained power. The stink of them fills the air—musky, hot, suffocating.

He grips the tranquilizer gun, jams a vial of amphetamines into the chamber, and fires point-blank into the thick muscle of the first bull's flank. The animal bellows, muscles seizing.

Miguel doesn't stop. He loads another vial, then another, plunging the drug into hide after hide. The bulls stomp, heads thrashing, eyes rolling white. Foam flecks their mouths. They slam against the wooden gates, the walls shuddering with every impact.

"Sí... sí..." Miguel hisses, feverish, shoving more vials into gun. "Furia. Rage. Protect me."

The last vial empties with a sharp hiss. The bulls roar as one, smashing their horns against the barriers, wood splintering, chains snapping loose.

Miguel spins the heavy locks, throwing the gates wide.

The beasts explode into the night, hooves pounding like

thunder. Dust and hay whip into the air as they stampede, snorting, wild-eyed, froth spraying from their mouths.

Miguel stumbles back, chest heaving, watching with manic triumph as the herd tears toward the mansion, straight into the chaos of blood and gunfire.

Peter leads the charge through the mansion doors, Mayu at his shoulder, Hernandez and the ghosts pouring in behind.

Cartel soldiers have dug in, using grand pillars and overturned banquet tables for cover. The ornate halls echo with the hammer of rifles, chandeliers swaying with every concussion.

"Room to room," Hernandez barks.

They push forward, firing and advancing, clearing each gilded corridor with ruthless precision. The mansion becomes a killing ground—paintings shredded, velvet curtains burning, antique vases reduced to shards underfoot, peacock feathers scattering everywhere.

At last, they burst into a vast ballroom, its marble floor gleaming under shattered chandeliers. On the far side, more cartel men are dug in, firing from behind barricades of flipped tables and grand pianos.

Peter drops to a knee, exchanging fire. Then he feels it.

The marble trembles beneath him. A low vibration, growing, rattling the crystal chandeliers that still cling to the ceiling.

"What the hell—?" he mutters.

Then comes the sound—deep, thunderous, like a storm rolling through the earth.

The far doors explode inward.

Bulls. Half a dozen of them, eyes rolling white, foam spraying from their mouths. They charge into the room with impossible fury, horns lowered.

The first cartel men barely have time to scream before they're trampled flat, gored and tossed like rag dolls. A piano is reduced to splinters as a bull smashes through it, horns coated in blood.

Chaos detonates. Gunfire and screams mix with bellowing roars. Tables are overturned, furniture sent flying. A man is lifted on a horn and driven twenty feet through several walls. Another is crushed under hooves, ribs splintering like dry sticks.

"Move!" Peter yells, grabbing Mayu. They dodge between pillars, bulls smashing through walls and staircases around them.

Bullets snap past their heads as cartel men fire wildly, desperate to stop both ghosts and beasts. One bull crashes through a bar, bottles exploding in a spray of glass and liquor. Another slams into a column, marble shattering as dust rains down.

Peter fires as he runs, cutting down a soldier who aims at Mayu. She dives behind a broken table, returning fire with sharp, controlled bursts. The room is a storm of bullets and hooves, impossible to control.

Then a bull smashes through the wall right beside them. The impact is deafening, plaster and wood exploding outward. The beast bellows, thrashing, horns gouging chunks from the floor.

"Go!" Peter shouts.

Mayu dives for the nearest window. Glass bursts around her as she crashes through, tumbling onto the gravel outside. Peter tries to follow, but the bull crashes between them, wild-eyed, blocking the path, swinging its horns from side to side.

"Mayu!" he roars, but the chaos swallows his voice. She's gone, lost to the night outside.

The bull charges again, and Peter hurls himself through a doorway, sprinting down a ruined corridor. Gunfire echoes in every direction. Bulls roar through the halls, tearing men apart.

At last, he escapes the house, bursting across a courtyard and into the stables.

The doors stand wide open, every gate flung back, the pens all empty. Hay is scattered across the floor, trampled into the dirt. Gunfire still rattles behind him, muffled by thick stone, bulls bellowing as they tear through the mansion. Peter moves fast between the empty pens, rifle tight in his grip, boots crunching straw.

Then he sees it. An archway at the far end, half-hidden in

shadow. A stairwell spirals down, narrow stone steps disappearing beneath the compound.

Peter steps onto the stairs and begins his descent. The air grows cooler, thick with dust and the acrid tang of manure. Each step creaks under his weight.

The stairwell empties into a corridor, long and narrow, its walls slick with lime and age. A low rumble shivers through the stone, a sound that makes the hairs on his neck rise. At the far end, a barred metal gate waits.

Peter reaches it, pushes, and it swings open with a groan.

Beyond is a vast round pit, roughly the size of two tennis courts. The earth has been churned into powder by hooves and is littered with bones—rib cages cracked open, skulls shattered, fragments scattered like discarded relics.

Opposite, behind a heavy gate, a bull stamps and bellows, its horns battering the iron with a sound like cannon fire. Each impact rattles the hinges, dust raining from the rafters.

Peter takes a step forward, rifle raised, when behind him, the gate he came through slams shut on automatic hinges, the echo booming like a death knell.

He wheels around, trapped.

Above, laughter—smooth and mocking. Peter looks up.

Miguel Sanchez stands at the rim of the ring, white suit flecked with dirt and blood. In his hand is the tranquilizer gun.

"I gave him the rest," Miguel calls, voice booming in the cavern. He raises the gun, wagging it like a taunt. "Five vials."

The gate creaks open at the far end.

The bull explodes out of it. A monster of black hide and muscle, foam dripping from its mouth, eyes bloodshot, wild with fury.

Peter snaps the M4 Carbine to his shoulder, sights flashing over the beast's head. He squeezes the trigger.

The rifle barks in rapid bursts, muzzle flame strobing under the floodlights. Rounds hammer into the bull's chest and shoulder, jerking it sideways, dust spraying up in sheets.

The animal only bellows, foam spraying from its mouth, hooves gouging deeper into the sand.

Peter shifts and fires again—short, controlled bursts that chew through thick hide, blood misting into the air. Still it comes, thundering straight for him.

He squeezes the trigger again.

Click.

The sound is hollow, brutal. The magazine's dry. There's no time to replace it.

The bull is nearly on him, head lowered, horns catching the glare of the floodlights.

Peter dives, throwing himself flat into the dust as the animal thunders past, its bulk rattling the ground, air splitting with its roar. The horns miss his spine by inches, hooves crushing bones scattered across the pit floor.

He rolls to his knees, jerking the weapon up out of instinct— empty and useless.

The bull wheels in the pit, blood streaking its hide, eyes blazing with pain and fury. Peter hurls the M4 at it. The rifle clatters off its shoulder, meaningless.

It's just him and the bull now.

He dives aside, horns slicing past his ribs by inches. Sand sprays into his face as the beast skids, bellows, and wheels back.

Peter rolls, scrambling to his feet and scanning the ring. Bones litter the ground—skulls and femurs, cracked spines left behind from men who never made it out.

Peter doesn't plan on joining them. Grabbing a jagged piece of rib, he grips it tightly in his hand.

The bull charges again, horns ripping through the air.

At the last instant, Peter pivots, body twisting aside, the bull thundering past so close he feels the wind of its passage. As it flashes by, he lunges in, driving the bone shard upward.

The tip punches into the bull's eye. Blood and fluid spray across his arm as the beast shrieks, rearing, blinded.

It thrashes, charging blind, smashing into the wall. Stone cracks, dust raining down.

Peter doesn't hesitate. He sprints, snatches up another jagged shard of bone, then leaps—landing hard on the bull's back. Muscles bunch and heave beneath him, the beast bucking and twisting, slamming itself against the walls.

Peter clamps on, teeth bared, and drives the bone down into its other eye. Once. Twice. Again and again. Hot blood and fluid spray across his arms as the bull screams, thrashing in agony.

It bucks violently, slamming itself sideways into stone. Dust rains down as Peter is torn loose, flung across the pit. He hits the ground hard, skidding through sand and shards, blood in his mouth.

The bull wheels, blinded, maddened, snorting steam. It charges, horns ripping the earth where Peter had been a heartbeat before.

On his knees, Peter fumbles for another piece of bone, his fingers locking around a femur.

Teeth gritted, he charges the beast, driving the sharp end of the bone into its throat with both hands. Blood sprays, the force jarring all the way through his arm.

The bull staggers, legs giving out. It collapses into the sand, thrashing once, twice—then goes still.

Peter stumbles back, chest heaving, slick with blood and sweat.

Above, Miguel has already left.

Miguel Sanchez bursts out of the stables, lungs heaving, sweat soaking his bloodstained suit. The roar of gunfire fades behind him. Ahead, floodlights blaze across the helipad.

The helicopter waits, rotors already chopping the night air into a frenzy.

Miguel sprints, shoes skidding on the tarmac. He hauls himself up into the cabin, shoving past the doorframe. "¡Vámonos! Get us airborne!" he barks.

The pilot nods, hands flying over the controls. The helicopter lifts, skids scraping free of the ground.

But it doesn't get far.

Bullets rake across the cockpit. Glass shatters, shards spraying Miguel's face. The pilot jerks once, blood fountaining from his chest, then slumps sideways.

With a violent jolt, the machine slams back onto its skids, metal screeching as it tilts and groans.

Smoke curls through the shattered glass.

A figure steps out of the shadows at the edge of the pad. Cigarette glowing, assault rifle held loose, face calm.

Jonny Hernandez.

He strolls forward, casual as a man crossing a quiet street. He climbs into the wreck, boots crunching on glass.

Miguel, pale, teeth bared, scrambles back against the cabin wall.

Hernandez takes a seat next to him and exhales a thin stream of smoke. "You should've taken my deal when you had the chance."

"You wanted me as your puppet," Miguel spits.

Hernandez sighs, almost weary. "Better than a corpse."

He raises his pistol, presses the muzzle to Miguel's temple, and pulls the trigger.

The shot cracks, sharp and final. Blood sprays across the cabin. Miguel slumps, lifeless, head rolling to the side.

El Lobo is dead.

Hernandez brushes ash from his sleeve and steps back out into the night. The cigarette glows, steady in his hand.

Peter emerges from the stables, sweat and blood streaking his face. The night air tastes of smoke and cordite.

Hernandez waits in the courtyard, cigarette burning low, his body armor dusted with ash, his expression unreadable.

Peter's eyes narrow. "Where's Sanchez?"

"Dead." Hernandez exhales smoke and flicks the butt into the dirt. "Now come on. We've got your kid."

Behind them, the compound burns. Flames crawl up the mansion walls, licking at shattered windows. Bulls stagger bleeding through the ruins, horns and hides torn open. Ghost army corpses lie scattered in the dust, their black uniforms shredded, rifles silent.

Felix sits slumped against a toppled column, alive but hollow-eyed, Deacon crouched beside him.

Movement stirs at the far edge of the courtyard. Out of the haze of smoke and dust, a figure staggers into the torchlight. Clothes torn, blood streaking her face, eyes dazed but defiant.

Mayu.

Peter's chest tightens. For a heartbeat, he doesn't believe it—then she drops to one knee, coughing hard, waving off a ghost soldier who rushes to steady her.

Peter strides to her, relief crashing through exhaustion.

The compound burns around them, bulls bellowing their last, gunfire dying into silence.

Hernandez steps closer, smoke curling from the corner of his mouth. He pulls a satellite phone from his vest and presses it into Peter's hand.

"Make the call."

Peter wipes blood from his mouth, thumb jabbing the keypad. The line clicks, connects.

"Okay," he says, voice rough. "I got him."

Senator Carmichael's voice comes cool and level through the static. "And my brother?"

Peter glances at Hernandez, then out at the burning compound. "Dead."

Silence hums down the line. For a moment, only the crackle of fire and the low groan of dying bulls.

Finally: "He should never have followed those freaks. Okay. I'll send you the coordinates of the handover. Don't be late."

The phone goes dead.

SEVENTY-EIGHT

THE DESERT IS A DEAD ZONE, flat and endless beneath the moon. An abandoned airstrip stretches out, cracked tarmac glowing pale under headlights. The only sound is the wind, dry and restless.

Peter steps out of the lead SUV, Deacon and Mayu close behind. Felix is with them, pale and hollow-eyed, wrapped in a borrowed jacket two sizes too big. Hernandez's ghost army fans out, black figures cutting sharp silhouettes against the sand, rifles at the ready.

From the opposite horizon, Carmichael's convoy approaches —armored SUVs, engines rumbling low. They roll to a stop in a line, tinted windows reflecting the moonlight.

Doors open. Men step out in precise formation, weapons slung. Carmichael emerges at their center, immaculate as ever. Behind tinted glass, Peter catches a glimpse of Michael—bound but alive, his face pale in the back seat.

No one speaks. The silence is thick enough to choke on. Tension crackles in the night.

Felix is the first to move. Hernandez signals, and two ghosts walk him forward. He stumbles, pale in the harsh light, Acosta's blood still streaked across his chest and arms. His eyes flick nervously from side to side, but he keeps walking.

From the opposite line, Carmichael steps forward. Her face softens the instant she sees him. She breaks stride, closing the distance herself, and when Felix reaches her, she pulls him into her arms. It's fierce, her polished control cracked by raw relief. She presses her lips to his temple, murmuring something only he can hear.

Across the divide, an SUV door opens. Michael stumbles out, wrists bound, legs stiff from captivity. For a moment, he's all awkwardness, but when his eyes find Peter and Mayu, he straightens. His face hardens, masking fear with bravado.

"Hey," he mutters, as though this were nothing more than another scrape.

Peter closes the distance, gripping his son by the shoulders. For a beat, he just stares at him, as if to make sure he's real. Mayu rushes in, her arms wrapping tightly around Michael.

The families stand reunited, if only for a breath, while engines growl and rifles stay leveled across the dead-zone airstrip.

The exchange is made, but the danger hasn't passed.

The desert holds its breath.

Peter's hand goes to his holster. He steps forward, cutting the distance. The pistol comes up, aimed squarely at Carmichael.

His voice is cold, stripped to steel. "Olivia's blood is on your hands. I said I'd take everyone involved. No loose ends. You're a loose end."

Carmichael freezes. For a moment, her face is stone.

Her guards tense instantly, rifles raising, muzzles swinging toward Peter and his people.

The night teeters on the edge of eruption. Then—
Click.
Cold steel presses against the back of Peter's skull.

A voice comes low, almost regretful. "Don't do it, Black."

Jonny Hernandez.

All around, rifles shift. The ghost army pivots as one—sights no longer on Carmichael's men but on Deacon, Michael, and Mayu. Red laser dots crawl across their chests, breaths catching in the night.

Deacon snarls, eyes wild, "Jonny... what the hell are you doing?"

Hernandez doesn't answer him. He leans close instead, his breath hot against Peter's ear, a whisper meant only for him.

"Just take your son and go."

The words sink like lead.

Peter doesn't move, but the truth slams home: Hernandez has made his choice. He isn't here to fight Carmichael. He's here to bind her. To cut a deal in blood and smoke, to fold the CIA into Daniela Carmichael's new cartel order.

The betrayal tightens around Peter's throat like a noose.

He doesn't turn. The muzzle is still pressed hard against his skull, Hernandez's breath steady in his ear. His voice comes flat, accusing, stripped of anything but ice.

"You're going into partnership with her, aren't you?"

Hernandez's reply is a growl, low and final. "Just take your son."

Across the dead-zone, Carmichael stands silent and victorious. One arm is locked tightly around Felix, holding him close, her chin lifted like a queen in her court.

Peter lowers his weapon, slowly, deliberately, every movement tight with suppressed fury. His rage burns cold now, not fire but ice. He knows he can't win here—not with Michael and Mayu frozen under the sights of Hernandez's ghosts.

The night belongs to Carmichael.

Peter holsters the pistol. His jaw is stone, eyes flat.

Carmichael doesn't speak. She turns, guiding Felix into the armored SUV with a possessive hand at his back. The rest of her convoy follows, engines rumbling, tires grinding over broken asphalt. Dust rises in thick plumes, trailing behind them as the vehicles roll into the night.

Hernandez lingers for a beat. He looks at Peter across the dead strip of tarmac. His expression is unreadable—maybe regret, maybe triumph, maybe both. Then he turns, stepping into the dust, following Carmichael into her new order.

The ghost army remains in place just long enough to make the point. Rifles lowered, eyes blank, they don't even cover Peter and his people anymore. The fight is over. They're irrelevant.

Once everyone is gone, Peter, Deacon, Michael, and Mayu trudge back across the runway toward their battered SUV. No victory, no relief—just silence and the sound of engines fading into the distance.

Dawn breaks over the desert, washing the horizon in pale gold. The airstrip lies behind them, empty now, only tire tracks and boot prints left in the dust.

They walk in silence.

Deacon mutters at last, voice low and rough, "Played like fools."

Mayu says nothing. Blood is still streaked beneath her fingernails, dried and black, a stain Gusano left behind.

Michael stays close to his father, step for step, not speaking—just keeping pace, his silence louder than words.

Peter squeezes Olivia's rosary in his fist, the beads digging into his palm, eyes fixed on the pale horizon.

The war is over. But not the right one.

EPILOGUE

EVENING LIGHT WASHES the cemetery in pale gold. Wind moves softly through the cypress trees, stirring the silence.

Fresh earth is mounded under a simple headstone.

OLIVIA WREN

1985–2025

Peter and Deacon stand side by side in plain suits. No uniforms, no medals, no flags. Just two men in borrowed black, shadows long across the grass.

Deacon's voice is low and rough. "I can't believe they made us sign those phony reports. Threatened us with treason charges if we ever even whispered the truth. It's like she never existed."

Peter's jaw tightens. "She was one of us."

They stand in silence, looking down at the name cut into stone.

After a while, Deacon asks, "They told you where you're going?"

"Reassigned to Asia." Peter nods. "They'll keep me busy and far from here." His voice dips. "For now."

He kneels, touching the fresh soil with his hand. In his fist is the rosary—its beads dulled, blood still woven into its history.

Deacon shakes his head. "We bled for nothing, brother. Used like dogs. And now the kennel's locked up tight."

The wind stirs again. Peter doesn't answer. He doesn't have to. The rosary clinks softly in his hand. The unspoken promise hangs heavily between them: They'll remember, even if no one else does.

———

BRIGHT STUDIO LIGHTS flare against polished glass and white-toothed smiles. The *Good Morning America* set gleams, every surface engineered for comfort.

Senator Carmichael sits flawless in cream silk, pearls at her throat. Beside her is Felix in a dark suit that hangs a little loose on his shoulders, hair combed neatly. He looks younger than his years, though the cameras don't see it.

The anchor beams. "Senator Carmichael, Felix—thank you for being here. A miracle escape from cartel captivity! The nation is celebrating with you this morning."

Carmichael dips her head with practiced humility, voice warm and modulated. "We are grateful beyond words. My son's survival is nothing short of providence. I want to thank every agency, every brave soul who made his return possible."

Applause ripples from the studio audience.

The anchor turns to Felix. "Felix, you've been through so much. How are you feeling? What's next for you?"

Felix clears his throat, his posture stiff. "I want to follow my mother's path—public service."

The audience applauds again, louder. The camera closes in on his smile. But for a heartbeat, his eyes flicker—a shadow crossing them, haunted. The flash of blood on his hands, La Bruja collapsing under Peter's rifle. Acosta's gurgling scream.

Then it's gone. He smooths it over with a boyish grin.

An hour later, Carmichael and Felix are sitting in the leather interior of a black SUV, the studio lights fading in the rearview.

Carmichael turns to her son, pressing a kiss to his forehead. "Perfect," she murmurs. "Absolutely perfect."

Felix says nothing. He looks out the window, jaw tight, silence pressing against the glass.

Carmichael's phone buzzes. She answers, listens for a few seconds, then replies, her voice clipped and low, "Yes. That's right. No loose ends."

She ends the call, sets the phone aside, and leans back. The tinted glass catches her reflection—poised, immaculate, regal. Ascendant.

———

NIGHT. The bullring pit blazes under floodlamps, light bleaching the sand to bone.

Two men stumble into the dust, shackles clanking, burlap sacks over their heads. Guards shove them forward, rough hands on their backs.

The sacks are yanked free.

MacCready blinks against the light, his face streaked with sweat, eyes wide with fear. Gary Stanton spits sand from his mouth, his jaw tight, panic just beneath the surface.

Above them, leaning against the barrier, Jonny Hernandez lounges like a man at ease. Cigarette glowing, tie loose, jacket unbuttoned, he watches with the calm detachment of a king surveying peasants.

"Well, boys." His voice carries easily across the ring. "You fucked up. You were seen. Can't have that."

MacCready breaks first. "Please—we did what we were told, we—"

"This is bullshit!" Stanton snaps, voice cracking.

Hernandez doesn't even look at them. He exhales a long stream of smoke, watching it curl into the floodlight glare. "You know," he says, almost conversational, "back in Miguel Sanchez's day he would've put on a real show. Let the bulls have a little fun."

He glances toward the iron pens at the far end of the ring—dark, empty. "But the bulls are all gone these days. So I guess it'll have to be firing squad instead."

He nods.

From the shadows along the barrier, a line of gunmen steps forward—silhouettes hard against the lights, rifles already shouldered.

MacCready and Stanton freeze, looking up.

"Look—"

The rest dies under the sound of automatic fire. Muzzle flashes strobe the pit. The air fills with dust and thunder as bullets tear through flesh and sand alike.

When it's over, both men lie still, the floodlights painting their bodies stark white against the red-streaked ground.

Jonny watches a moment longer, the echo fading into the desert night. He straightens his jacket, brushes sand from his cuff.

"No loose ends," he murmurs, flicking his cigarette into the dust and walking away.

———

A SMALL HOUSE sits on the edge of a dusty US border town, the road outside stretching empty into the evening light.

Inside, a little girl in a faded school dress perches at the window, chin resting on the sill. She watches the road with solemn eyes, the glass glowing gold around her.

"Where is he, mamá?" she whispers. "He said he'd come to my play. He never misses."

Her mother kneels beside her, brushing tangled hair back from the girl's face. Her tired eyes soften with sorrow. "I told you. He's missing. Nobody knows where he is."

The girl shakes her head, voice cracking, stubborn through the confusion. "But abuelito always comes when he says he will."

The mother's hand lingers on her cheek. "Come away from the window, sweetie."

Reluctantly, the girl slides down from the sill. She glances back one last time, over her shoulder.

The window glows with the last light of day. Beyond it, the road runs empty, stretching forever into the horizon.

Her reflection hovers faintly in the glass—a small face searching, waiting.

A child's grief for a monster she'll never know as one.

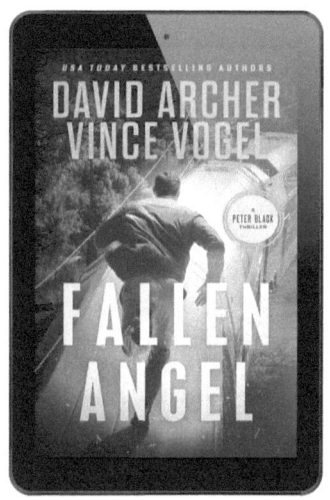

WANT MORE FROM THIS WORLD?

Right House readers get access to **exclusive origin stories**—full-length prequels written only for this list and unavailable anywhere else.

Start with the Peter Black origin story, *FALLEN ANGEL*, by visiting:

vip.righthouse.com/peter-black

Or scan the QR code to get instant access.

(Easy to unsubscribe. No spam. Ever.)

ALSO BY DAVID ARCHER

Up to date books can be found at:
www.righthouse.com/david-archer

MAYA FROST FBI THRILLERS
What the Dead Confess (Book 1)
When the Wicked Prosper (Book 2)

ROGUE THRILLERS
Gates of Hell (Book 1)
Hell's Fury (Book 2)
Ice Burn (Book 3)
Judgement by Fire (Book 4)

BEN CARTER LEGAL THRILLERS
Dead Man's Jury (Book 1)
Trail by Murder (Book 2)
The Hitman's Lawyer (Book 3)
Final Defense (Book 4)
The Hour of Guilt (Book 5)
The Guilty Juror (Book 6)

JACOB HUNTER THRILLERS
The Kyiv File (Book 1)
The Bogota File (Book 2)
The Havana File (Book 3)
The Amsterdam File (Book 4)
The Saint Petersburg File (Book 5)

PETER BLACK THRILLERS
Burden of the Assassin (Book 1)

The Man Without A Face (Book 2)
Unpunished Deeds (Book 3)
Hunter Killer (Book 4)
Silent Shadows (Book 5)
The Last Run (Book 6)
Dark Corners (Book 7)
Ghost Operative (Book 8)
A Fire Burning (Book 9)
Dawnlight (Book 10)
Dead Ice (Book 11)
No Loose Ends (Book 12)

ALEX MASON THRILLERS
Odin (Book 1)
Ice Cold Spy (Book 2)
Mason's Law (Book 3)
Assets and Liabilities (Book 4)
Russian Roulette (Book 5)
Executive Order (Book 6)
Dead Man Talking (Book 7)
All The King's Men (Book 8)
Flashpoint (Book 9)
Brotherhood of the Goat (Book 10)
Dead Hot (Book 11)
Blood on Megiddo (Book 12)
Son of Hell (Book 13)
Merchant of Death (Book 14)
Extinction C-14 (Book 15)
A Vengeful God (Book 16)

NOAH WOLF THRILLERS
Code Name Camelot (Book 1)
Lone Wolf (Book 2)
In Sheep's Clothing (Book 3)
Hit for Hire (Book 4)

The Wolf's Bite (Book 5)
Black Sheep (Book 6)
Balance of Power (Book 7)
Time to Hunt (Book 8)
Red Square (Book 9)
Highest Order (Book 10)
Edge of Anarchy (Book 11)
Unknown Evil (Book 12)
Black Harvest (Book 13)
World Order (Book 14)
Caged Animal (Book 15)
Deep Allegiance (Book 16)
Pack Leader (Book 17)
High Treason (Book 18)
A Wolf Among Men (Book 19)
Rogue Intelligence (Book 20)
Alpha (Book 21)
Rogue Wolf (Book 22)
Shadows of Allegiance (Book 23)
In the Grip of Darkness (Book 24)
Wolves in the Dark (Book 25)
Olympus Must Fall (Book 26)
Children of the Empire (Book 27)

SAM PRICHARD MYSTERIES

The Grave Man (Book 1)
Death Sung Softly (Book 2)
Love and War (Book 3)
Framed (Book 4)
The Kill List (Book 5)
Drifter: Part One (Book 6)
Drifter: Part Two (Book 7)
Drifter: Part Three (Book 8)
The Last Song (Book 9)
Ghost (Book 10)

Hidden Agenda (Book 11)

SAM AND INDIE MYSTERIES
Aces and Eights (Book 1)
Fact or Fiction (Book 2)
Close to Home (Book 3)
Brave New World (Book 4)
Innocent Conspiracy (Book 5)
Unfinished Business (Book 6)
Live Bait (Book 7)
Alter Ego (Book 8)
More Than It Seems (Book 9)
Moving On (Book 10)
Worst Nightmare (Book 11)
Chasing Ghosts (Book 12)
Serial Superstition (Book 13)

CHANCE REDDICK THRILLERS
Innocent Injustice (Book 1)
Angel of Justice (Book 2)
High Stakes Hunting (Book 3)
Personal Asset (Book 4)

CASSIE MCGRAW MYSTERIES
What Lies Beneath (Book 1)
Can't Fight Fate (Book 2)
One Last Game (Book 3)
Never Really Gone (Book 4)

ALSO BY VINCE VOGEL

Up to date books can be found at:
www.righthouse.com/vince-vogel

PETER BLACK THRILLERS

Burden of the Assassin (Book 1)

The Man Without A Face (Book 2)

Unpunished Deeds (Book 3)

Hunter Killer (Book 4)

Silent Shadows (Book 5)

The Last Run (Book 6)

Dark Corners (Book 7)

Ghost Operative (Book 8)

A Fire Burning (Book 9)

Dawnlight (Book 10)

Dead Ice (Book 11)

No Loose Ends (Book 12)

JACK SHERIDAN MYSTERIES

A Cross to Bear (Book 1)

The Clay House (Book 2)

Into The Woods (Book 3)

The End is Nigh (Book 4)

A Step Into The Dark (Book 5)

Holier Than Thou (Book 6)

Streetlight City (Book 7)

An Offering for Sin (Book 8)

ABOUT US

Right House is an independent publisher created by authors for readers. We specialize in Action, Thriller, Mystery, and Crime novels.

If you enjoyed this novel, then there is a good chance you will like what else we have to offer! Please stay up to date by using any of the links below.

Join our mailing lists to stay up to date -->
righthouse.com/email
Visit our website --> righthouse.com
Contact us --> contact@righthouse.com

facebook.com/righthousebooks
x.com/righthousebooks
instagram.com/righthousebooks